COVETED

COVETED

SHAWNTELLE MADISON

BALLANTINE BOOKS • NEW YORK

Coveted is a work of fiction. Names, places, and incidents either are products of the author's imagination or are used fictitiously.

A Ballantine Mass Market Original

Published in the United States by Ballantine Books, an imprint of The Random House Publishing Group, a division of Random House, Inc., New York.

This book contains an excerpt from the forthcoming book *Kept* by Shawntelle Madison. This excerpt has been set for this edition only and may not reflect the final content of the forthcoming edition.

ISBN 978-0-345-52918-3
eBook ISBN 978-0-345-53229-9

Printed in the United States of America

www.delreybooks.com

Cover illustration: © Gene Mollica
Cover design: Drew Pennington-McNeil

9 8 7 6 5 4 3 2 1

Ballantine mass market edition: May 2012

Thanks, Mom!
All those childhood years of imaginary play
and talking to myself have finally paid off.

ACKNOWLEDGMENTS

First of all, I have to thank my partner in crime, who helped whip me into shape as we embarked on this publishing journey together. You are the best Grammar Chick ever, Sarah Bromley, and I hope to be as awesome as you someday. I also have to thank Cole Gibsen, Amanda S. Berry, Jeannie Lin, Kristi Lea, and Dawn Blankenship for reading my book and offering fabulous feedback. You ladies rock! Another round of thanks goes to the writers of Missouri Romance Writers of America (MO RWA), who taught me how to critique as well as take criticism from others.

I also have to give my heartfelt thanks to my literary agent, Jim McCarthy. You push me to be a better writer, and I feel very grateful to have you in my corner.

Thank you, Tricia Pasternak, my wonderful editor, who made my dream of publication come true.

To Vera Aginsky, my Russian Studies professor when I was at ISU, you introduced me to the beautiful world of Russian culture and left an impression on me that I'll never forget. I'd also like to thank my friend Julia Richardson, who helped me whenever I had questions.

I have to thank Dyanne Davis, who has supported me with words of encouragement. An even bigger thanks and biker-witch high five goes to Angie Fox. I've leaned on her for many things and she's not only a wonderful author, but also a wonderful friend.

And finally, thanks to my husband, Segun. If you want to have our wedding renewal vows done Ming the Merciless style, I'm ready.

Prologue

Five Years Ago

Lying naked, with his hands intertwined in mine, Thorn Grantham made me promises. A promise for us to try to make our long-distance relationship work. A promise for him to move closer to New York City to be with me. And finally a promise to remove these handcuffs once he's had his way with me.

With mischievous hazel eyes, Thorn pulled a bottle of chocolate syrup out of his suitcase.

"You wouldn't dare," I whispered. My gaze darted from my perfectly pressed sheets to my pristine bedroom. It would take hours to clean up the evidence of our love-making.

His eyes darkened. "You gonna stop me?"

In a flash, he popped off the top and jumped on my bed. I jerked against the cuffs holding me hostage, but it didn't do any good. Thorn knew all too well that I wouldn't so much as scratch let alone break my antique Victorian headboard to escape. Especially after he squeezed a line of warm chocolate from my neck down to my inner thighs. My heart skittered from the heat in Thorn's eyes. From the sweet scent of the chocolate in the air.

Thorn's gaze never left mine as the tip of his tongue

traced a path along the chocolate. Swirl after swirl of his tongue heated my flesh.

Shouldn't I be worried about the mess? *What* mess? The mess of having my toes curl in waves of ecstasy?

Thorn's head descended, proving to me again and again how he could unravel me like a tightly bound corset.

Making love to Thorn wasn't a casual affair—it was an Olympic event that taxed both the mind and body. When we'd decided to hook up at my place a few days ago, I hadn't expected him to use such things in my bedroom. Nor did I expect that in a million years I'd allow food in my bedroom. And have it smeared on my bed . . .

After he'd indulged in every inch of my body until we were both satisfied, I wanted to sleep. But that sure as hell wouldn't stop me from keeping my room clean. With a chuckle, Thorn obediently helped me wash the bedding. When we'd wrapped up cleaning and had a bite to eat, he bid me farewell.

Kissing the top of my head, he whispered, "See you in a few weeks."

"You promise?"

"Of course. It'll take the apocalypse to keep me from you."

"A zombie one or the Mayan kind?"

He thought for a moment with that smile of his. "Both."

With me assured, he left the bedroom. As I sat alone in my apartment, I had no idea that this would be the last time I'd make love with Thorn. And that there were some promises that couldn't be kept.

Chapter 1

W*erewolves* in no shape or form should own a fast food restaurant. No pancakes, no frozen custard, and for goodness sake, my people needed to stop peddling pizza. In my opinion, any establishment where my food could potentially grow microscopic wildlife wasn't my kind of place to eat. That pretty much left fire-grilled food on the menu, and the only good thing any werewolf grilled well these days was a well-done burger. And Archie's sold the best double-stacked burger on this side of the Toms River. If the animal walked and men speared it, then Archie burned it the best.

"Hey, Natalya, you're here early," said Jake, the cashier.

I averted my eyes after I placed my order. As usual, I was the lowest-ranking werewolf in the whole joint. "We're really busy now that the weather's cooling off."

Jake offered a friendly smile. "How's Bill?"

"He's fine. Still the grumpiest boss ever."

I ended the conversation and hid out in my usual booth while my food cooked. As much as I loved Archie's burgers, I preferred to keep to myself while I ate.

As I waited, travelers coming off the Garden State Parkway came by for chow. They weren't like those tourists who walk around with fanny packs and cameras. Instead, they smelled of money—the cash they were about to spend on other people's old junk at one of the many flea markets that lined the Parkway.

Ten minutes later, Jake's younger sister, Misty, brought out my food on a tray. My mouth watered at the sight of the double cheeseburger and fries. But that snotty were-wolf didn't even bother to acknowledge my presence. She simply dumped the food in front of me and strolled off. A single bright-red gob of burger sauce landed on my pristine blouse.

My eyes wide, I gaped at the stain as my chest tightened with alarm. And I thought *I* was crazy. The way she flung food on my table each week, it was clear that she had no idea how every spill, glob, and splatter drastically increased my stress level. With a shaking hand, I frantically wiped the spot with a stain pen.

And all this after I'd spent a half hour this morning meticulously pressing my clothes. With my light chestnut-colored hair brushed to perfection and my low-heeled shoes shined, I'd felt like I could survive the day in relative peace.

Well, as peacefully as a werewolf who obsessed over everything could. I didn't advertise my condition, but if you saw a chick scrubbing her clothes with an industrial-strength stain pen, you might assume she's a bit of a clean freak. With an obsessive-compulsive disorder, I took clean freak to the next level. But even with my condition, I lived what could be called a normal life.

Archie's had been my lunch spot for the past few years. And no matter how bad the service was, or the conditions, I refused to eat lunch anywhere else.

My food was cold before I had a chance to take a bite. But it didn't matter. I savored the burger anyway—that is, until two familiar faces entered the restaurant.

Everyone in South Toms River knew Erica Holden and Becky Knoll. They didn't work. Well, they worked at being rich, I guess. After college in New York, they came back into town to spend Erica's rich daddy's money.

"Jake!" Erica gushed. "You have the order ready?"

Jake's hungry eyes took in Erica's perfect blonde hair and cotton candy–pink sweater. The garment stretched across her boobs and hung on for dear life.

"It's coming up right now. Took us awhile to grill that many deluxe burgers." He leaned forward. "Are you having a few guests over?"

Becky laughed and flipped her chocolate-brown curls behind her ear. "Erica's picking up Thorn's favorite burgers. She's so sweet."

"Nice to hear the prodigal son's returned home."

They were ten feet away, but even from that distance I could sense the excitement sliding down Erica's back. The name gave me the same honeyed feeling.

Thorn Grantham.

My heartbeat quickened and the burger nearly caught in my throat. I flared my nostrils and focused on Erica. Through the scent of fancy perfume and chemical-strength deodorant, an underlying scent was there. Thorn was back. And Erica had likely tried to run her manicured fingernails all over him. Probably made a valiant attempt to rub herself against him too. Over the years, her stints at becoming Thorn's groupie weren't anything new to me.

I averted my eyes and finished my food. I had just seven minutes left in my lunch hour—and no time to waste sitting there staring at Erica.

By the time I left for work, she was long gone. As I stalked out of Archie's, I caught the scent of Misty's satisfaction as she cleared my table. Even though she always mistreated me and never cleaned up after her customers, I'd still left her a full tip.

I worked at the Bend of the River Flea Market, or The Bends as the locals called it, which was three blocks away from Archie's. I didn't mind walking over every day. The fresh air was good for my soul.

And maybe I would even see Thorn on the way to work. I had a feeling, though, that he would be back at the Granthams' log cabin off in the woods—meeting with his father, the town's abominable pack leader.

On the way back, a local organic farmer in overalls waved at me. "Have a good afternoon, Nat."

"Same to you, Stanley."

Every day after lunch he waved at me, and then, after I passed by, stared at my legs. I didn't have any interest in sixty-year-old men—especially ones with pencil-skirt fetishes. But like the majority of humans in the world, he didn't know that he was ogling a werewolf every day.

And perhaps he'd be even less inclined to act so friendly if he knew that werewolves weren't the only strange thing lurking around here.

Eventually, I reached The Bends, a large, old building nestled between a parking lot and another flea market. But The Bends wasn't just another flea market.

The Bends offered the best deals among the flea markets along the eastern seaboard. Bill was a great employer and all, but I was the brains of this operation. With a computerized inventory system and online store for our more expensive stock, we offered a level of service most flea markets—supernatural or otherwise—just couldn't match.

Growing up as a natural-born werewolf, I'd been exposed to the supernatural world from the crib onward. It ranged from witches visiting for grade school sleepovers to band practice with the fairy folk. After selling all the strange things we had in the store, I suspected that even stranger things than crooked witch wands and haunted capes lurked around New Jersey to buy. If you checked the right places and had the enchanted eyesight to find them you had a chance. Of course, that left humans out of the mix.

I entered through the back, an outdoor area covered with a long, steel awning. During warmer weather, we sold more of our wares on the rows of tables out here. I headed inside the shop and dropped off my purse in the business office. The office was closed off from the shopping floor by a large set of wooden doors. Two minutes later, I was back in the mix—in the crowded main room, with a roomful of Saturday shoppers browsing the long aisles.

My boss approached me from the loading dock. "Hey, Nat, about time you got back. The harpy who bought that Victorian vase on Thursday is back. She said the merchandise had flaws."

To regular folks, Bill looked like a tall, thin man with wire-framed glasses. To my eyes he resembled the cartoon character Dilbert—but to my nose he reeked of magic with a bitter tang of iron.

He was a goblin, entrenched in a glamour—an invisibility spell that hid his true appearance.

"Flaws? You're kidding, right?"

He pushed his glasses up his nose. "She said something about scratches on the bottom." He tilted his head to glance at the customer. "She's upsetting the other patrons."

Normally, I would have taken over for the other cashier so she could have lunch, but now that would have to wait. "I'll handle it." *Like I always do.*

As I walked over to the harpy, I first noticed another scent overpowering the haze of magic. The woman had doused herself in cheap vanilla perfume. Her flashy ensemble matched garish bright pink sandals with a beaded denim shirt and capri pants. Her platinum-blonde hair was stark against her penciled eyebrows. I stifled a laugh as I wondered what wildlife dwelled within her teased mane.

My irate customer wasn't an ordinary woman. Under the guise of a heavily makeup-covered dame she lived day to day as a ghastly birdlike creature with sharp claws. She hid from human eyes using her magic. This whole encounter didn't surprise me, though. Along with the unfortunate circumstance of having a human head on a bird's body, the poor thing's name derived from the Greek word for "snatching stuff."

"Can I help you?" I asked.

"I bought this original 1889 Moser glass vase on Thursday." She pushed the fragile vase into my hands. "I unwrapped it this morning to find my purchase scratched on the bottom. I paid a lot of money for that damn thing."

"Scratched? That's impossible. I wrapped this particular package before you picked it up."

"Well, you don't know how to handle expensive antiques, then." She shifted and put her hands on her hips. I could almost imagine black feathers rustling.

With a huff, she searched for Bill. "I asked to talk to the manager."

I leaned forward. "I'm more than qualified. First of all, you bought an 1885 vase. I had our specialist catalogue it. And second, I don't mishandle the merchandise." I checked, and sure enough the bottom was marred with scratches.

"Well, your staff is incompetent."

"Incompetent? I handled and prepared your purchase—" I was just about to really begin my rant when the door swung open and Thorn Grantham entered the store. For half a second, I paused. The mere thought of him being in the store knocked me off-kilter.

At over six feet tall, he towered over the rest of our customers. His messy wheat-colored hair appeared windblown. The man was as attractive as I remembered him. He didn't look in my direction, but before he turned his back to me, I caught the glint of his amber-colored irises. How many times had those eyes hypnotized me? My belly quivered slightly. From the back of the room at one of the computers, I continued to explain to the harpy how the staff, or should I say, how *I* meticulously catalogued everything on the computer.

"As you can see by these photographs and the time stamps on the front, your merchandise didn't have scratches on it. Matter of fact," I glanced briefly at Thorn's back, "these scratch marks are rather tiny and resemble claw marks."

Thorn finally turned in my direction—and winked at me. Damn, he'd seen me. Pleasure poured down my back, but still I continued my tirade against the cheapskate harpy who hoped to con my boss out of two hundred dollars.

The harpy hissed, "Are you trying to imply that I made those marks?" A swirl of dark magic floated around her and tickled my nose like black pepper.

I stifled a laugh. From across the room, I heard Thorn talking to Bill.

"I never thought I'd be taking over as alpha of the pack so soon," Thorn said. "And I'd almost made a *life* for myself in San Diego. But with the Long Island pack closing in to take over the township and the forest, I'm afraid this whole area is in danger."

The news was quite unexpected. I clamped down on my emotions, hiding them from both Thorn and the harpy. I couldn't allow this crazy lady to rile up the wolf straining under my skin. "Would you like to look at the video cameras that record the packaging room? Perhaps we could show you the video of the packaging process?"

If the harpy were a teapot, steam would've shot out of

her spout. She ignored the computer and continued to stare me down.

I hadn't hunted in a long, long time. My skin burned at the possibility of a full-out fight. But my control was solid, unmoving. Like a caged animal, the hungry wolf inside whined as I whispered, "Either way, Mrs. Kite, there's no evidence for a claim that The Bends is at fault. If you'd like to take this problem up with my manager, I'd be more than happy to call Bill over."

Mrs. Kite smoothed her shirt and then gripped the denim with her claws. Claws that nearly ripped the thick material. "Like I said before, *Wolf*, I want to see the goblin. My problem is with him."

The word "wolf" slithered off her tongue like a black warning. Still, I figured I was safe for now, even though I'd never tangled with a harpy before. In the middle of a store, with all these humans around, there's no way she'd go all out—and risk ruining her bedazzled outfit.

"I'll go fetch Bill. Just a moment, Mrs. Kite."

I walked over to Bill, who was still chatting with Thorn. As I approached, my heels clicked on the linoleum floor. At first they kept pace with the rhythm of my heartbeat. But as I closed in on the two men, I could smell Thorn—he smelled of a warm summer breeze—and my heart sped up and my palms grew damp.

He said to Bill, "The Long Island pack's getting squeezed for space by the Brooklyn pack, so you need to watch out." He shrugged. "I'm sure you would've heard about the threat of an attack sooner or later. But you're a friend of my family, so I thought I'd bring the information to you directly."

Bill glanced at me briefly. "Yeah. Just another reason for me to pack up and leave this place. You werewolves always need to piss in someone else's backyard." Bill noticed the harpy in the back with her hands on her hips.

"I see our customer wasn't satisfied with the anal filing system you developed." He cursed under his breath. "I'll catch you later, Thorn. I have to go stuff crazy into a can."

Bill stalked away, leaving Thorn and me to stare at each other.

My breath caught in my throat when he said, "Hey, you."

"Hey, you." We used to greet each other that way five years ago. I thought I'd know what to say to him, but my brain locked up. All of a sudden everything in the room that needed my attention called out to me. The furniture against the west wall wasn't lined up correctly. The vases on the fourth table were in a precarious position. Three kids with their preoccupied mother ran around a table full of lamps. I tried to ignore the loud thumps of my heart.

He took a step toward me. "You look good."

Welcome back to Earth, Natalya.

"Nothing much has changed."

"Oh, I can see it has. When I left, you were on your way to becoming a hotshot New York content editor if I remember right?"

"That kind of fell apart."

The job was perfect for someone like me. Content editors were the thorough souls who read over books and check to make sure everything was true. With my keen eye, and my neurotic tendency to remember everything, I ascended quickly up the business ladder. But after Thorn left, I just couldn't cope with anything anymore, and receded into my own little world. And that was the end of my dream job.

His eyes bore into mine. "I'm sorry about that."

I wanted to glance away in submission, but he held on to my gaze steadily, as he always did. Not in a battle for dominance, but in a dance of sorts, where he read my mind and caressed my soul. If I were a cat, I would've rolled on to my back and purred.

But then the door opened, and in came three werewolves to shit on my parade. Rex, accompanied by his two younger brothers, strolled over to Thorn and me.

"We got the supplies. You ready to head out?" he asked. As the eldest, Rex spoke for the other two as if they were mutes. I thought of it as a sign of their lack of intelligence. One of his brothers fingered the antiques while the other one stood with his hands in his pockets.

"Yeah, just a moment. Go wait for me."

With his dark eyes and attractive coal-black hair, Rex was Thorn's dark mirror image in every way. Except for the need to dominate. For Thorn authority came naturally. Rex just tried it on like an oversized coat.

Rex turned to leave, but his eyes flitted in my direction. I averted mine immediately, but not in time. "You got a problem?" he asked.

"No," I mumbled.

"Rex, go wait in the car." Thorn's growl rumbled in his chest as a warning.

When a wave of anger floated off Thorn, Rex backed away. My feet locked into place as my heart skipped a beat. Longtime rivals, the two men had always vied for dominance when we were growing up, but Thorn always emerged as the stronger one.

"It's good to see you, Nat." He touched my hand briefly and headed for the door.

As the men left, Rex barked, "We got fifteen minutes to get to the mill. What are you doing talking to her anyway? She's not pack anymore."

His words bit into my neck and slumped my shoulders. I'd heard them before, but it was worse knowing that Thorn had heard them. Now he knew I was living in South Toms River as a rogue werewolf.

For a brief second, for the first time in a long time, I had hope for something new and positive in my life.

But with the impeding attack from the Long Island werewolves, I knew things in South Toms River would go downhill—and I'd come tumbling after.

Chapter 2

I *didn't* bother turning on the radio for my drive home. Instead, I rolled down the window and listened to the sounds of the twilight. The forest's symphony lulled me as I followed the twists and turns to my cottage on the southern edge of town.

The woods surrounded my home, offering a wall of protection from the outside world. As I drove down the long driveway, I spotted my serene two-story cottage. With its bright red shutters and whitewashed wood, the house stood out beautifully against the foliage surrounding it. It was an escape for me.

But isolation had its drawbacks too. It was only because I was so far away from the rows of homes in the subdivisions that I hadn't won any awards for my curb appeal. I'd spent hours meticulously lining up golden sunflowers and fragrant chrysanthemums—and hardly anyone ever saw them.

Just another sad example of a life without friends and family hounding you for attention.

I parked my Nissan Altima in the garage and entered the unlit home. With my keen eyesight, I didn't need the fading lights of the setting sun to see the shameful thing within my own home.

My hidden shame.

But I looked away from it and headed for the kitchen, then pulled a glass from the cupboard. The perfect rows of wine glasses gazed back at me, beckoning me to check their alignment. I resisted the urge and fetched some water from the fridge door's dispenser instead.

Silence permeated the house as I entered the living room. To get in, I had to pick my way through a narrow path between the white boxes that crowded the room. But in just five minutes, I was perfectly cozy: I had a fire burning in my grand fireplace, and with my Costco-sized bags of marshmallows, chocolate bars, and graham crackers, I made four generous s'mores.

As I did every Saturday night, I sat there alone. Instead of spending a night in the city with friends, I watched the light of the flames dance against the walls. The only sounds were the snap and crackle from the fire echoing along the stacks of boxes.

Nevertheless, the neat lines of boxes offered a strange sort of comfort. They didn't make snippy comments about my behavior. The enticing scents of nutmeg and cinnamon floated over them. And inside every box were smaller boxes.

With a baby wipe I cleaned off my hands and picked out a large maroon-colored box from inside one of the white boxes. I felt a rush building inside my belly, and a sprinkle of goose bumps on my arms. From inside the maroon box I carefully pulled out a Christmas nut-cracker.

The wooden figure gave me such joy. The jewels on his hat cast giant green and red lights into the corners of the room. To keep him safe, I used a plastic bag to protect his hand-sewn clothes. So he appeared pristine every time I took him out, even his tufts of white hair and black dots for eyes.

Everything about him promised a perfect holiday filled with a Christmas tree and family. Everything I owned made me the same promises. All I had to do was buy it, stack it neatly in boxes, and then take it out to feel comfort.

How I longed for someone to comfort me.

"You look so handsome. I bet you'd take out a hazelnut without a second thought, buddy."

When silence answered me, I peeked at my phone. Maybe my mother would call like she had last week. She'd joked that it was purely by accident—that she'd meant to call Pizza Hut or something. But I knew she worried about me once in a while.

And, well, my mother thought fast food like pizza violated the sanctity of her kitchen. So I knew she had to have been thinking of me.

Reluctantly, I wrapped up the nutcracker and put him back into his box. What would Thorn think if he ever saw me like this? Trapped in a house alone with hundreds— no, keep it straight—I was trapped here with exactly 423 Christmas, Hanukkah, and even Kwanzaa holiday decorations.

I even went out of town on special trips to buy them. I remembered the nice elderly black woman at the Africa Emporium in Middlesex staring at me as if thinking, *What's this crazy lady doing stroking all the Kwanzaa candles?*

I bit my lip and sucked in a deep breath. Seeing Thorn had released an ache in my soul. I wasn't the same woman he knew when he left suddenly five years ago. I wasn't like this back then. The ache spread deep into my stomach as a tear trailed down my cheek.

His scent lingered in my nostrils. I imagined his golden eyes. The memory of those eyes gazing at me from the middle of the forest filled me with a happiness I thought I'd forgotten. Those beautiful nights of running free without the chains of order and organization pulling me down—

But am I destined to live like this for the rest of my life? Alone in a house with ornaments in boxes to oc-cupy my time?

Why do I dwell on things like this? I cleaned up my food and went upstairs. Might as well head to bed and concentrate on surviving tomorrow.

But after tomorrow? The months to come would in-clude the possibility of seeing Thorn, yet not being able to be with him. In the meantime, I'd continue to live here with my friends. Yeah, my "friends." I snorted.

Pretty sad that a nutcracker couldn't warm a lonely bed.

Around three a.m., the sounds of footsteps outside my house forced my eyes open. I froze. Heavy footsteps stomped on my flowers near the front bay windows. I angled my head to catch any scents but, from my down-wind position, all I could smell through my upstairs bedroom window were the fall-blooming flowers in my garden.

The subtle sounds of fingers gripping the living room windowsill doused me in fear. Of all the houses in this town, I bet the Long Island werewolves had picked the house without a decent weapon. (And I most certainly couldn't use my reindeer cake-cutting knife. I refused to soil my cutlery, and even butter knifes were sharper.) And what if they broke into the house? Tore through my things to search for me? They might step on one of my boxes or knock a figurine off the fireplace mantel.

Did I have anything deadly to use other than my claws or bare hands? I could see the local paper now: *Crazed Woman Brings Down Burglar with Hordes of Holiday Cheer.*

Without a sound, I crept from the bed and opened my door. Of course, it squeaked. I winced and mentally added a can of WD-40 to the grocery list.

Since my sneak-attack plan was squashed, I thundered

down the stairs and swung open the door. Instead, my attack would come on strong. After all, I had boxes of ornaments to protect.

The stone porch chilled my feet as I plodded down the steps. To my keen eyes, the front yard was alive with late-night activity. A single fox scurried toward the far grove, while a cottontail chased after another. But I detected nothing large moving—until something stirred in the dark shadows among the ivy that clung to the side of the house.

Light blue eyes peeked from around a corner. A scent drifted to my nose—one that I'd never forget, since it brought memories of a more pleasant past.

Cheetos.

"Come on out, Aggie. I can smell the Cheetos crumbs on your jeans from a mile away."

A groan from the distance. "Hey, Nat. I didn't want to wake you up."

"With that racket, you'll wake up half the Jersey shore."

Agatha McClure walked up to the porch with a small bag in her hand. Eyes the color of shiny sapphires peered back at me and I quickly remembered her from my teenage years. Aggie was tall, rich, and outspoken, but from our past experiences together, I knew something more swam underneath that shiny veneer.

I took a step forward as she advanced toward the house. "What are you doing here? I thought you moved back to New York." I hadn't seen her in over five years. All this time I would've expected her to be married and socializing in the Hamptons, not standing here with a single suitcase. How time had changed for everyone.

"I did. I couldn't take the negative vibes up there anymore." She pushed her red hair behind her ear. A streak of blonde highlights framed her face. "I'm moving out west to Vegas."

I nodded with a wry smile. "The city of opportunity."
She wanted to come inside, but I didn't plan to invite
her in.

"My Greyhound bus stopped here and I need a few
days to build up my reserves to buy another ticket."

"Well, I can drive you to the Motel 6 down the road.
They have comfortable rooms."

She took another step toward the porch. My heartbeat accelerated.

"Nat, I don't have a place to go. If I had the money, I
would've gone there."

I rolled my eyes. Oh, why didn't she have some well-
to-do relative up north in Englewood who could offer
her a place to stay? My home was my sanctuary, the one
place where no one judged me.

She smirked. "You act as if you're hiding dead bodies
in there."

If she only knew the truth.

Aggie tilted her head and gave me a knowing smile.
"What's wrong, Nat? You're acting funny." She'd known
me so well once—during the darker days and the lighter
ones.

I released a long sigh. After all, this was Aggie—not
some stranger who'd judge me. "Come on in."

Aggie bounded for the steps and let out a soft squeal.
"We're going to have so much fun. It's been so long
since we've seen each other."

She continued to ramble as we entered the house. On
any other day, I would've wished I'd had time to shift
the boxes in the foyer to make more room for visitors,
but this time I didn't.

"Did I catch you at a bad time? You moving?" She
peered at the boxes.

"No." I left it at that. She'd figure it out soon enough.
A fog of silence fell over us and I led her to the kitchen
and turned on the light. As a hostess who was also hop-

ing to distract her visitor, I knew I had to offer her something to eat. I opened the fridge and pulled out some deli
meat. "You want a roast beef sandwich?"

I didn't glance at her face after I asked the question.
From her body language, I perceived her concern. The
tilted head and the thin line of her rouged lips spoke
volumes. She didn't need an explanation. Most homes
didn't look like mine.

"I'm not too hungry."

I tried to find my voice so I could scramble out of this
awkward situation. "If I remember correctly, you were
never one to turn down a roast beef sandwich with all
the fixings."

"Nat . . ." She approached me. Her shoes scraped
against the shiny floor. I didn't dare check to see if she'd
trailed in mud.

"I even have fresh dill pickles from Barney's."

If she'd had ears on the top of her head, they would've
gone up. "Barney's still sells those things?"

"Yep, and if I remember right, other than Cheetos,
you ate those things every time you visited me."

I pulled out the items I needed to make the sandwiches.
With the subject of my home temporarily tabled, Aggie
set her bag on the floor. I abandoned the food to put it
someplace other than the middle of the kitchen.

She frowned. "I can take it to my room."

I picked up the bag and headed for the guest room off
the living room. "No need. I keep an efficient house." I
shook my head after I said it. Oh, the irony.

She followed me but stopped cold when she reached
the guest room. "Where do I get to sleep?"

I placed her bag on a box on top of the bed—a bed
covered with ornament boxes, plastic-covered doodads,
and other holiday stuff like gaudy sweaters and lawn
ornaments. The only thing missing from the scene was
"Jingle Bells" playing in the background.

"You can sleep here. While you eat I can clear this little bit of stuff out. I have room . . . in the garage." This was my overflow room. Oh, shit.

"Nat, where did all these things come from?"

I squeezed past her to return to the kitchen. "You know, lots of places. The Home Shopping Network, flea markets, brief trips to New York." I waved my hand as I spoke. I offered her that, "Oh, everyone does this kind of thing" look.

She leaned against the counter and frowned. I briefly inspected the floor and was relieved to find it free from mud.

"Nat, I thought you'd improved. It's gotten worse, hasn't it?"

I turned on the radio to the local jazz station to calm my nerves. I knew this would happen. "The last couple of years have been a bit hard, but I've managed okay."

With a flourish, I added condiments to her sandwich and placed it on a perfect plate with a dill pickle on the side. The meal was almost good enough for a professional photo in a magazine. She took the offered food and sat down to eat. On the surface, I knew she wanted to press further. But Aggie rarely turned down food, and I used her own vice against her.

We'd met each other years ago at a camp for "troubled" werewolves. At the time, my parents had told me the place would help me focus on important things. I didn't do well among the others until I met Aggie.

Her rich parents couldn't find a regular therapist to help their daughter with her overeating problem, so they sent her to Camp Harold for the summer. I had fond memories of the ten whacked-out werewolves who'd sat in a circle around the campfire talking about their problems.

Aggie tore into the sandwich, grinning widely between bites. If someone *had* to show up at my door, the best person in the world was her.

With Aggie settled, I left the kitchen to figure out where I could move the ornaments I was storing in the guest bedroom. I couldn't use the bathroom. (No way in hell.) The attic was out. (Filled to the hilt.) And so the last possibility left was the tiny shack I'd bought a year ago.

While Aggie slept into the early morning, I lumbered about outside. I'd originally bought the tall tin shed at the local home-improvement store as a place for my stuff. But then a few years ago, a flood drove me to bring my precious ornaments into the house.

One hour later, as the sun peeked over the horizon, I assessed my work. I'd have to suck in my stomach to enter the tiny space, but I'd done my job and created a box-free space for my guest.

But what bothered me the most was the certain knowledge that, by tomorrow, I'd be sneaking some of the boxes back into the house.

Chapter 3

M_{ost} people slept in on weekends. But since I worked in retail, I woke up early in the morning like clockwork to perform my duties at The Bends. So it was quite unfortunate that I'd spent the past three hours moving boxes around. Now I had only thirty minutes to rest before work.

As the alarm clock droned, I stared at the flashing digits with disdain. I could've hit the snooze button, but such a move was completely against my nature. I had never arrived late to work. *Never.* Even if I'd participated in a triathlon before work, I would still show up on time.

After a brief shower, I dressed in my usual outfit—a champagne-colored blouse and black pencil skirt. The way I saw it, why spend time deciding between clothes?

The guest-room door was shut when I left my room. Only the sounds of the humming refrigerator filled the room while I prepared a perfect cup of coffee. *Anyone* could start the day off right—all it took was two tablespoons of coffee to six ounces of water.

As my hands moved, I went over my last-minute details before work. I left Aggie a note that I'd stop by with lunch from Archie's. Before I departed, I said a few Hail Marys, praying the house would remain in the same state until I returned.

Reluctantly, I entered the garage. But I paused three times before opening the car door. *Leave the house.* It wasn't as if Aggie would burn the place down. *Don't think about stuff like that!* She didn't smell like smoke last night, so I convinced myself to climb into my car so I wouldn't be late.

Most flea markets opened later in the day on Sundays. But Bill, the clever and greedy goblin that he was, opened his establishment at nine a.m. on the dot. I arrived promptly at eight-forty-nine to see three cars waiting in the lot.

As I left my car, I waved at one of our die-hard customers, Mrs. Weiss. The eighty-year-old witch showed up every three days in a suffocating wave of lavender perfume–laden clothes. As a fellow supernatural creature, she ought to have known about my keen sense of smell—and how offensive her lavender perfume would be to a werewolf. But it's not as if proper conduct around werewolves is advertised on cable television. Like most of The Bends' other supernatural shoppers, we hid our true nature in the shadows.

Other than Mrs. Weiss, all our supernatural customers had a good reason to shop early. Every Saturday night, Bill received a shipment of magical items, which he put out first thing Sunday morning. I entered the showroom to find him grumbling over those very same boxes.

"Bill, we're opening in ten minutes. Couldn't you have opened these things in the back office?"

Not only had he strewn brown wrapping paper all over the cleared pathway, but he'd also left bits of white packing peanuts all over the floor. What made matters worse was Bill's lack of organization.

"Did you catalogue any of these—wait, why do I bother asking?"

Bill grunted a reply while he placed a set of wands in the display case. With a bit of goblin magic, he cast a spell to spread glamour over them. By the time he finished, the wands would look uninteresting to regular folk like humans.

In the meantime, I watched him carelessly cram the merchandise inside. My anxiety rose with every careless move he made. What if he damaged a wand? Hell, how could the clerks figure out how much anything *cost* if he didn't label them properly? Before I started hyperventilating, I shoved him out of the way.

"Go open the registers!" I hissed.

From behind his glasses, the goblin's eyes twinkled. He snickered and strolled away to the back office. Did I hear that mischievous man whistle a lively tune while he loaded the cash into the registers?

I had five minutes to pick out three or four wands for Mrs. Weiss. Unfortunately, I didn't have time to photograph and catalogue the multitude of bristly twigs. But I did have one thing on my side: The elderly witch bought her wands as gifts, and picked them solely by appearance. The darn thing could've shit magical bricks, but if the twig sparkled in the noonday sun, she'd buy it.

By the time Bill opened the door, I'd managed to photograph three of the wands and add them to the computer system. Seven customers filed into the showroom, with Mrs. Weiss bringing up the rear. With seconds to spare, I placed three wands with price tags in the display case just as she lumbered toward it.

"Got any new pretties this week?" Her voice rattled in her tiny five-foot frame.

"We have several new fire-witch wands. But I took the time to personalize this selection just for you." I offered a pleasant smile and used my soft-spoken saleswoman voice. I saved my "Are you crazy lady?" voice for irate customers who tried to hustle the store.

To be honest, I told every valued customer that I'd personalized the selection for them. I've worked at The Bends for several years and learned a few things about magic outside the werewolf realm. Of course, all this on-the-job training wouldn't teach me what werewolves couldn't do. Cast spells to figure out what kind of magic the wand performed. But based on the type of wood (mahogany, cherry, etc.), I could recommend the right type of wand—whether it would match with a water, earth, or fire witch.

Mrs. Weiss squinted at the wares and touched the glass. From behind her I heard Bill yell, "Your mom is on line three, Nat. She told me she'd hold."

I nodded and continued to smile at Mrs. Weiss. She'd be good for another twenty minutes while she sized up the merchandise. "I have a call. I'm assuming you need time to decide."

The elderly witch waved me away with a twirl of her fingers. It was a relief. A break from the cloud of lavender perfume would do me some good.

I picked up the phone in the back office. "Hi, Mom. This is unexpected. Is everything all right with Grandma?"

"Your grandmother is fine. She's knitting another sweater for Sasha." The television was blaring in the background. As an old, hard-of-hearing werewolf, my maternal grandmother liked to have the TV on full blast while she knitted sweaters for my brother Alex, or Sasha, as he was lovingly called. I fully expected Grandma Lasovskaya to head toward baby socks someday to encourage Alex to snag a good Russian woman and knock her up.

"Could you head into the kitchen? If I can hear the TV, you're too close." The sound lowered.

"Anyway, I called your house to invite you here for dinner. I wanted to leave you a message, but someone else answered."

I played with the phone cord to calm my nerves. Not a good day. Who else had Aggie answered the phone for? "Oh, that's Aggie. You remember her, right?"

"Oh, yes, the sweet girl from that camp." My mother went silent for a moment. We didn't discuss the past much. The past five years involved events that I didn't want to rehash.

My mother continued. "Aggie told me she'd love to come over with you to eat dinner tonight. Did she always used to invite herself over?"

"If the event involves food, Aggie has no shame. Either way, I think I'd enjoy having someone on my side for once." As the words left my mouth, I wished I could snatch them back. I never spoke to my mother like that.

"Natalya, is something wrong?"

After a deep breath, I noticed that I was gripping the phone tightly and that my other hand was a fist. This outspoken version of Natalya had come out of nowhere. But I had business to attend to today. So I'd grace my family with my presence at this rare dinner and then just head home like I always did.

"Nothing's wrong, Mom. I've just had some irate customers to deal with today."

"Oh, you'll be fine. Your grandma always told me every storm is followed by sunshine."

I nodded even though Mom couldn't see me. She'd invited me to dinner. Maybe my resentment was without cause. Maybe the wounds of the past didn't run as deep as I thought.

Several hours later, my workday ended. I arrived home and breathed a sigh of relief as I entered the foyer: My house was just as I'd left it. That was, until I entered my kitchen to find "Julia Child" baking her heart out in my once-clean kitchen.

"Hey, Nat! Check out the goods. You're gonna love what I made for dinner tonight."

I gaped as my blood boiled in my veins. *Remain calm. Don't look at the flour all over the floor.* But then the spilled pineapple on the counters drew my attention. *Ignore that too.* I tried to close my eyes against the evidence, but I couldn't: the soiled spoons, filthy bowls, and broken eggs left *in* the carton.

Her eyes widened when she saw my face. "Don't worry about the mess. I'll clean it up before we leave." Aggie showed off one of her masterpieces, which she'd stored in my plastic cake container. Most likely a moist pineapple upside-down cake from the smell. I tried to convert the straight line of my lips into a smile, I really did.

"If you had a gun right now, you'd shoot me." She tried to laugh, but it came out as a croak.

"Clean. Now." I whispered the words, but even though I'd tried to speak gently, my friend scrambled to pick up the mess.

"Nat, I'm so sorry. I thought I had enough time to clean up before you came home."

I simply nodded in response. How I wished I could close my eyes. Ignore the nagging panic attack that threatened to steal my breath. After a few deep breaths, I managed to help her clean the kitchen like it was a nuclear-waste site.

Fifteen minutes later, we left the house with two desserts in tow.

My parents live in one of the comfortable subdivisions of the South Toms River township. Most folks would never guess that 10 percent of their neighbors howl at the moon once a month. This subdivision in particular has a large population of supernatural creatures.

As I pulled up to park on the street, I saw my brother, Alex, leaning against his Dodge truck. I could faintly hear him talking on his cell phone to one of his many girlfriends. Hopefully, she'd get more attention than the ten other dames he had on speed dial. As the golden boy of the Stravinsky family, my blond-haired, blue-eyed brother was the epitome of a truck-driving, womanizing, hot-blooded werewolf male who tried to get into the pants of any woman. And he didn't mind if she had an extra pair of magical arms or legs either.

Aggie hauled one of her goodies while I carried the other. Alex waved in our direction before we entered the split-level Colonial. The house was brimming with family members and the scents of a wonderful dinner. Uncle Boris, Aunt Olga, and Aunt Vera sat in the living room with Grandma, watching a Russian-dubbed soap opera. Whether it was from a tape or satellite TV I didn't know. They argued among each other in Russian over the actions of a heavily rouged heroine as she held some man close to her bosom.

While we stood to the side watching them watch TV, three more uncles sat at a card table playing gin. Every now and then, one of them would express his concern over the Long Island werewolves.

"We don't have enough strong hands to protect the whole territory," one said.

"Yeah, too many young pups and old men," another whispered.

The final one added a card to the table. "I think with Thorn on our side we have a chance."

The South Toms River pack's territory was a lot to manage for a small pack. Our land bordered on great running grounds, like Double Trouble State Park. With its miles of forest, creeks, and cranberry bogs, our territory was actually a perfect target for other packs who were hoping to grow—like the Long Island pack.

In total, our pack had about fifty square miles. The land between us and the neighboring packs, the Burlington and Trenton ones, blended a little, but we had enough space to keep everyone somewhat happy. Evidently the Long Island pack had noticed how optimal our place was and wanted to break up the happy family.

Grandma Lasovskaya interrupted my thoughts to beckon me over. The long centuries had treated her well. Her light brown eyes had seen the world before skyscrapers and cars—even before the construction of Moscow's Saint Basil's Cathedral in the late 1500s. I leaned in to kiss the soft skin of her wrinkled cheek. She sat in her usual spot, wearing her floral dress with brown stockings. Every time I saw her, she exuded warmth and comfort. "Hey, Grandma."

"You look good." Then she added with a sad smile, "I wish you'd come over more."

"I wish I could too," I replied as she patted my hand fondly.

I turned around to introduce Aggie to everyone. Most of my relatives ignored me, but Uncle Boris acknowledged me by asking her, "You're not one of Sasha's girlfriends, are you?"

Aunt Vera huffed. "Sasha doesn't date women taller than him."

With perfect timing, Alex entered the house. My younger cousins thundered into the living room and nearly knocked him over. My mother poked her head out of the kitchen, her sharp blue eyes on the kids. The short woman yelled in Russian, "You kids stop running all over the place. Like a pack of wild animals." She glanced at Aggie and me and spoke in English. "You brought food. Come into the kitchen."

I knew Aggie felt out of place. She stood there smiling, though, while everyone around her chattered like squawking hens. From what I remembered, she lived in New York with her father. She'd never told me about large family dinners. Large, loud, Russian family dinners anyway.

Aggie placed the desserts on the crowded counter. "I brought pineapple upside-down cake and a pecan pie."

"They smell good." My mother stood over a golden, crispy turkey that sat next to two other prepared turkeys. As I assessed the cornucopia of food available, I had to admit that I'd missed the dinners. My mother always cooked enough food to feed a wedding party. She somehow managed to accomplish all this without dirtying her day-to-day clothes: some business-casual slacks and a dressy blouse. My mom worked during the day as a schoolteacher. When she left work, she gave in to her strange addiction to her stove and cooking utensils. After my parents had moved into this house years ago, their first major project had been a complete overhaul of the most important space—the kitchen.

My mouth watered and my wolf's stomach growled. Right beside one of the turkeys lay a generous bowl of *olivie*. I could taste the delicious potato salad with my mother's homemade sour cream. On the stove soup bubbled in a kettle with the lid firmly placed on top. My nose told me that Mom had fulfilled my father's desire for slow-cooked borscht.

I had fond memories of my mother offering me salami with Russian bread and cheese in this room. But even with the food, this kitchen felt slightly foreign, like it was a place where I didn't belong. I turned away from the *myasnoe assorti*. I didn't feel like checking out the fancy lunch-meat plate.

Aggie took in the scene with a vibrant glow. To her, my mother was the patron saint of food preparation. "All this food smells so good. I'll have to ask for recipes."

She'd said the right thing. "Why, thank you," my mother said. "My sisters might've been able to catch the food, but I could always baste and bake it." She turned to me. "Did you say hello to your grandmother? She always asks about you."

I nodded and tried to forget about the lack of a warm reception. After all, my grandmother, at least, had always given me cards and knitted keepsakes. Then two of my cousins approached me from behind, interrupting my thoughts.

The younger one, Peter, frowned in my direction. "What are you doing here?"

The older one pulled him away and snickered, "My dad said to ignore her." I stood there as a wave of embarrassment hit. My shame turned into anger. If he wasn't ten years old, I would've slapped the taste of his foul words out of his mouth.

Aggie's mouth dropped open. She took a step forward to reprimand the boy, but I blocked her.

I turned to my mother, who'd appeared ready to intervene as well, and stammered, "D-do you need help setting the table?"

Aggie tried to tug my arm. I ignored her stern face as she leaned toward me. "Are you going to let that kid talk to you like that?"

"It's fine. I can handle it."

"Handle it? Let's see how well he handles my foot up his ass. Pups shouldn't talk that way to adults."

If Aggie only knew how much his comment hurt. To those kids I ranked even lower than the house cats that slinked around the place.

"Everything's fine, Aggie. Drop it."

My mother continued to cook and at first I thought she'd remain silent. But then she surprised me by saying, "I hope his mother won't expect any favors from me anytime soon. Especially with such disrespectful children. In my day, I would've had a sore cheek for a smart mouth."

I agreed with a halfhearted nod, but the question remained: How had things gone so wrong with my family? I looked to Aggie as her gaze took in my relatives. The Stravinsky brood came from the old country, and my family held tightly their werewolf ideals. The Code, as we formally called it, included customs such as arranged marriages to achieve a higher ranking within the pack. It also taught us that weak werewolves created vulnerable points. Such things implied that even as an able-bodied woman, I represented a hole in the line of defense among my family. To them, this just wasn't acceptable. Right now aspects of the Code meant nothing but frustration to me.

I yanked Aggie into the dining room to help me add plates and silverware to the tables. She fumed as she placed spoons and forks. "I can't believe your family treats you like an outsider. When did this happen?"

Why wouldn't she let it go? "I said drop it, Agatha McClure."

Aggie knew that tone. I rarely called her by her full name. She had a higher rank than the majority of the werewolves in this house, but she knew when she'd pushed too many of my buttons.

During dinner, things seemed to settle down. Aggie relished the food with gusto as serving after serving of turkey was placed on her plate. She even inhaled the *seledka pod shuboy*—a layered dish of sliced herring, cubed potatoes, and various other veggies. Most of my American friends couldn't stand the stuff. Meanwhile, one of my eager aunts shoved Alex into a seat next to her.

"Why don't you want to sit next to a pretty girl?" gushed my aunt Vera. Aggie most certainly wasn't Russian, but like any zealous relative, my aunt could spy a high-ranking she wolf from a football field away.

Alex offered his boyish grin and jabbed at Aggie. "I've known her so long she's practically my adopted sister by now."

Aggie rolled her eyes and took another bite of turkey. She knew she wasn't his type since she'd never take his shit—the man was known for hopping from woman to woman like a flea on a werewolf's back.

Aunt Vera turned her attention to our guest. "So what did you do before you moved here?"

Aggie paused in the middle of a bite. I hadn't asked such a question. I assumed she'd talk about her previous life when she was ready. "My father has business dealings in New York. I worked for him for a little while." She placed another large portion in her mouth. An easy way to deter most people. Not my aunt, though.

"You went to college with Nat, didn't you?"

Aggie shook her head.

I leaned forward to save her. "She went to NYU. I was at the University of Pittsburgh at the time."

Clad in pearls and a black dress that fit a bit too tightly, Aunt Vera swarmed her prey like a hungry barracuda. "How many siblings do you have? Any other brothers or sisters in the area?"

Good God, I guess if Aggie didn't work out, why not hit up one of her single, affluent sisters? Thank goodness she didn't have any.

Aggie choked a bit on her food. "I'm an only child."

"How nice. Your parents must've spoiled you rotten."

Aggie took a generous gulp of her wine. "Yes, they did."

Then she turned to me. "Nat, did you know the praying mantis female eats the male after they mate?" She picked up her knife and cut into her meat with enough force to bend the fork. "She starts by biting off his head."

Way to go deep with that football pass, Aggie.

My aunt took the hint and shifted away to butter her bread. From past experiences, I suspected Aggie had won a reprieve from her questioning—for the next twenty minutes anyway.

I tried to pay attention to Aggie's small talk, but I

couldn't help overhear two cousins around my age. They sat across the table from me, their voices chirping with gossip. "Did you hear that Thorn is back in town?"

The other sighed. "I didn't expect him to come back. I'd drop my boyfriend in Boston for a few hours in a barn with him."

My cousin Sofia laughed. "With Erica around, I wouldn't try that." She played with her fingernails. "I heard she put another woman in her place for gawking at Thorn not too long ago."

The food in my mouth turned to wood. Even with my mother's succulent turkey and gravy, I couldn't stop the despair from hitting me. I glanced briefly at Aggie and saw her staring at me with concern. I didn't want her pity.

I couldn't escape Thorn's presence. No matter where I went. During high school we hadn't crossed paths that much, but we'd attended the same college and through a serendipitous set of events our relationship had blossomed.

Dwelling on the past only made me feel bitter. Spiteful to the point of hoping one of my little jerk cousins, who was stuck at the kiddie table, would spill milk or something on his handheld game console. That would serve the little twerp right!

My empty wine glass urged me to take another drink to dull the pain. After an evening like this one, I deserved another helping. With resolve, I filled the glass to the brim with merlot and toasted everyone who'd pissed me off today.

There were plenty who'd happily do it again tomorrow. So I silently thanked my parents, who bought the stuff in large quantities.

Chapter 4

As I sat cataloguing another set of flea market items on Monday, I realized I had survived having Aggie stay over at the house so far. At first, the woman had made things quite stressful, but I found that if I concentrated and told myself that *everything* could be cleaned, I didn't need to have my fists clenched, ready to knock her into next week with my hairy paws.

The customers today went in and out, but I was distracted by the merchandise more than usual. I tried to remind myself that I didn't need more holiday decorations. I was perfectly fine with what I had. I didn't need the beautiful St. Nicholas ornament with Santa skating on shiny plastic ice with a mistletoe and—oh, look at his nose, it glowed like Rudolph's!

I mentally slapped my hand and focused on the screen. These types of distractions had increased ever since Aggie had showed up. Usually, I worked in my own little world without the distractions of family, marauding werewolves on a takeover spree, or hot ex-boyfriends who came back out of the blue looking hotter than ever.

A ring from the customer-service desk outside the office drew my attention. Bill didn't answer it—most of the time, he chose to ignore the damn thing. I had once thought he just couldn't hear things sometimes—but then I learned that goblin hearing was just as good as werewolves'.

But when I was in the middle of a task I hated to stop before completing it. The ringing continued as I finished printing the tag for a carnival-glass candy dish.

The incessant noise increased to the point of unnerving aggravation. I glanced through the office window to see Bill standing not more than ten feet away.

I bit my lower lip and tried to think of how many ways I could torment that goblin.

Maybe by hitting him where he'd feel it the most. His pocketbook.

I stormed out of the office and greeted the customer. It was one whom I didn't expect to encounter: Rex's youngest brother.

"What are you doing here, Melvin?" My voice lowered of its own accord. Even though Melvin was part of the pack and three years younger than me, he still outranked me.

His gaze darted to the door. A few strands of his ill-kept black hair fell into his face. His dark hair was his only point of resemblance with his brooding brother. "Rex would kill me if he knew I did this . . . but Thorn asked me to talk to you."

After hearing Thorn's name, I leaned on the counter and nodded.

"You need to be careful. You know that rogue wolf who made it into the pack last year?"

I nodded again. "Wendell?"

"Yeah, he's in charge of watching the perimeter of our territory off Highway 3. He's gone missing. Nothing but an empty house with busted-in windows."

I didn't understand why they let Wendell watch the northern boundary. He had a keen eye and all, but every once in a while he walked around town having a chitchat with himself. A chit-chat that at times bordered on a raging debate.

"Any traces of a struggle? Blood or a scent?"

He shrugged. "He didn't give me a lot of details. He only said that we should be on the lookout for danger since our territory has been breached." He kept his gaze attached to mine as if he wanted to convince me that he'd given me all the information. When his nostrils flared twice, I dug deeper.

"Anything else?"

He paused before he whispered, "His girlfriend's missing too. Thorn and Rex found her blood in the forest. There'd been signs of a struggle."

My stomach churned uncomfortably. He had a girlfriend? Maybe she was the one who'd driven him to talk to himself. Either way, our territory had been breached and now I lay exposed. I had no pack.

The door to the store opened and the breeze that flowed through the room chilled my arms.

"Thanks for telling me this, Melvin."

Melvin stuffed his hands into the front pocket of his sweatshirt before he walked out of the store.

Customers continued to mill about around me, but I couldn't move. Other than Aggie in my home, I didn't have anyone else. What if the Long Island werewolves turned up, searching for others to kidnap? Would they do to me what they'd done to Wendell's girlfriend? My heart raced and all I could do was clench the glass counter. I worried about things far too much, and today was only making things worse.

Finally, I willed my legs to move so I could help a customer. I had a decision to make. And if I didn't make a move soon, I might be the next casualty.

As I drove toward the Grantham cabin that evening after work, hundreds of reasons popped into my head to turn around. What if Aggie was trashing my house? Perhaps I had an important call on my answering machine. And those flowers she stomped on when she tried to break in—didn't they need my care?

I resisted change with all my being. Hell, Aggie's visit was painful enough, but to drive up to the Grantham home and approach the pack leader—this was too much. But I had to do it if I wanted to be safe.

Nestled within the forest and surrounded by tall pine trees, the Grantham cabin had an imposing presence. The setting sun cast a haunting glow on the windows and the dark wooden columns in the front. With the two second-floor windows as eyes, the two-story structure almost looked like a fire-breathing monster that waited for me to approach. No wonder it had been years since I'd visited this place. I pulled up to see Thorn's younger brother, Will, mowing the lawn. The second-in-command in the pack, Will was a younger version of Thorn with buzz-cut hair. He'd recently graduated from high school and now attended the local community college.

Will addressed me as I left the car. "Hey, Nat. This is unexpected."

I glanced once at his face before looking at the ground. "I came here to see your father on pack business."

"Is everything okay? You seen any strangers roaming around?" He took a step forward and brought the scent of fresh grass to my nose. He didn't smell like Thorn, but my nose knew they were related.

"Nothing suspicious. Thorn's kept Bill updated so far."

"My dad's in the house. You'll find him in the living room watching TV."

I turned to leave, but then remembered Aggie. "So that I don't cause any trouble, I need to tell you that Agatha McClure is staying at my house."

Most werewolf packs tracked strangers in their territory. As the daughter of a high-ranking outsider, Aggie ruffled the feathers of the other females in the area.

"I already knew. Your father called the cabin yesterday and told us she's at your place. Someone from the pack already stopped by to check on her at your cottage."

As I walked to the house, I wondered why Aggie had never told me that someone had stopped by. Not that it was important. Folks avoided my place as if an obsessive-compulsive disorder was a cold you could catch.

I'd never seen the inside of the cabin before. As a child, I'd visited this courtyard with my parents on important occasions, but the invitations had ended when my illness had overwhelmed me.

I knocked and waited for permission to enter. My stomach soured, and I hoped Thorn was out patrolling the territory. This move was hard enough. I'd already wiped my wet palms on my skirt a few times in anticipation of what was to come. The rapid beat of my heart thundered in my chest. I could always save face and turn around.

With a reluctant heart, I prepared to head back to the car, but Will came up behind me and opened the door. "No need to knock. Dad never answers while his favorite show is on."

I'd learned long ago that Farley Grantham didn't act like other pack leaders. What made him different from others was that he was an asshole. A miserable old asshole.

I entered the foyer and peered into the great room. At the far end, Farley sat in a La-Z-Boy chair with his feet propped up. Two other men sat in corners guarding him. They were as still as stone until I approached. Their piercing yellow eyes followed me as the rifle shots and hoofbeats of a Western played on a big-screen television.

John Wayne droned on about justice as I stepped forward. Will shut the door behind me and I jumped.

Farley's blue eyes went to slits while he examined me from the other side of the room. How had a man who had once stood tall over many turned into such a gaunt, bitter person? His blond hair darkened over his ears, where gray hairs grew. I could see faint traces of Thorn in him—the strong chin and broad shoulders—but I knew Thorn more closely resembled his mother, who had passed away when we were kids.

"What do you want, girl? Hurry up. My show is on." He clicked a button on his remote. Silence suddenly permeated the space, which didn't help my anxiety. Hearing John Wayne in the background would've been better.

The open window behind him offered a beautiful view of twilight in the woods. I tried to find strength in the forest.

I hurried to his side, trying to ignore the stacks of weathered newspapers and empty potato chip bags. The venerable patriarch lounged in the chair and continued to rest his knee injury. Two years ago, a rival pack leader had challenged the miserable coot to become alpha over the pack and nearly won. Farley's knee injury hadn't healed well, and after that old age and a vicious chest cold had caught up with him.

His eyes went from my face down to my toes. Fear crept up my spine. He glared at me like an adult chastising a child.

A cough shook his body before he sputtered, "I know your mouth works, so use it, girl."

Even though I sensed a presence moving upstairs, I didn't falter. My back stiffened and words flooded out. "I've come today to petition you for reentry into the pack."

He huffed. "You picked the worst time. With the Long

Island werewolves breathing down my back, you think I'd allow a weak link on the front lines?"

"I could help. If you give me a chance."

His dark blue eyes flashed yellow. "I've seen your place. And I've seen you around town. You would be a liability."

His words bit into me and I cowered self-consciously. I had to make a choice. I could nod and move on, or I could make a final stand. "If you'll have me, I want to reenter the pack, sir."

"Didn't you hear me the first time? The Long Island werewolves are a real threat. And the weak will fall first. Don't you value your life?" He leaned forward in his chair and shook his fist in my direction. "I need the strong to stand by my side. They'll aim for the weakest link first, and you'd be it."

I tried to find the words. I'd already begged. "So the answer is no?"

"You're lucky I tolerate your presence in the area. Your grandmother was a close friend of my father, and I honor their bond by allowing you to stay." He resumed the film and dismissed me with a wave of his hand. "Be sure to close the door as you go. It jams once the weather gets a bit cold."

For a second, in my fog of disappointment, I didn't move. But then one of the werewolves in the corners shifted, so I scrambled back.

With a heavy heart, I left the house. I staggered into the car and sat. The sounds of a flock of blackbirds filtered inside and mimicked the pounding of an impending headache. My mind tried to wrap around starting the car, but I couldn't move.

Why the hell did I do this to myself? Since the pack was under attack, I honestly thought I had a chance to help out. A new beginning. But after speaking with Farley Grantham, I felt two feet tall. Unworthy. Defective.

A bunch of self-defacing words that echoed through my skull.

Anger bled into my vision, and the wolf inside wanted to smash its fist into the steering wheel. She wanted to tear into the soft fabric of the seats and rip apart the clean material I tried so hard to maintain.

Instead, I opened the door and walked toward the woods beyond the house. I discarded my heeled shoes and headed into the darkness. This was the one place where I didn't care to wander. Too dirty and too wild, the woods were anything but serene. But in my stressed-out state, I plodded through the brush without caring that it snagged my panty hose and skirt. Tears streamed down my cheeks, but I continued walking and listened to the sounds of the wind whistling through the trees. A gentle breeze brushed against my face and caressed my cheek like a fervent lover.

But my time alone ended when strange sounds alerted me to danger. My nose told me nothing stirred in the forest, just ground squirrels and rabbits. I crouched low and backed toward a clutch of trees. The tall ferns hid my body, but as a lone female I wouldn't stand a chance if more than one wolf attacked me. How long had it been since I'd defended myself? Or even cared to do so?

Or could the situation be even worse? Had Farley sent a wolf from the cabin to take me out? My fingers dug into the earth. The scent of pungent moss filled my nose. I stooped low and hoped I wouldn't be found. The cracks of footsteps against branches on the forest floor thundered close. My eyes squeezed tightly shut and I waited for the first blow.

Would my parents come looking for me if I disappeared? They knew that in human form I hated the filthiness of the woods. That was one of the many reasons I didn't run with the pack anymore.

Suddenly, the birds went silent. I held my breath. Oh, shit. Even the animals in the grove knew I was screwed. Could the attacker hear my heartbeat? Did I sound like a wounded animal baring its neck for slaughter?

Out of the brush, a creature leapt at me and landed a few inches from my face. My mouth gaped, and Thorn's scent enveloped my senses. Even in human form, with the wolf stirring within his blood, he was a menacing presence.

Golden eyes stared me down. I averted my eyes and grabbed my chest. I'd never expected that it was *him* sneaking up on me. Was he the noise I'd heard upstairs in the cabin, lurking while I pled my case?

I opened my mouth to greet him, but he snarled and closed in behind me. But I didn't need words. He smelled my fear.

I resembled stone, perfectly unmoving as his nose tickled the back of my neck. Then he lowered and swiveled around to face me. His hot breath blew against my thin shirt. The breath I tried to hold escaped and I leaned forward. Thorn growled deep, and I stiffened immediately. *Don't move!* He always won this game. Pounce and then retreat. Claim and run.

With one swift movement, he advanced again. His rough hands grasped my upper arms and bit into my skin. My heart thundered in my chest, and I couldn't resist wetting my dry lips. He pushed his nose against my cheek. The pain from his grasp was nothing compared to the passion melting within me. It had been so long since someone had touched me like this.

The cool air brushed against the line of sweat that formed on my back. Waves of heat from his body assaulted me. My blood boiled as his breathing became ragged. Sharp nails pierced the skin of my arms.

"So tightly—wound." He descended and nipped at my breasts. I inhaled sharply when he grazed the nipples that poked out from the flimsy material. The urge to initiate the change grew from my belly and slid up my back.

He leaned in closer and I turned my head to the side. "Lose the clothes," he growled.

I complied. Part of me didn't want to do this here. After Thorn had left, the comfort of my home and the grounds around it had allowed me to run free—alone.

But when an alpha male like Thorn spoke, I had to obey. My body contorted and the change enveloped me. I fell over the precipice and surrendered to the wolf chained within. The process of changing into a werewolf isn't the most beautiful thing. Only the older wolves like my parents and grandmother could meld into the wolf like warm mercury in a vial.

My mother told me the pain of change for a pup is similar to the pain of childbirth. She'd told me that our transformation wasn't shape-shifting into a new form, but into the body we were meant to be within. Thus the pain from the broken, shifting bones—the contorting limbs—was the punishment for the human to bear. I guess the older wolves had paid their dues. Thankfully, I've found that as I've grown older, the change has been less painful. But once in a while I still groan when my femur snaps in half like fragile spaghetti.

In my new form, the forest unfolded into millions of scents and sounds. From the rhythmic notes of the blackbirds to the urgent croaks of the frogs. I rolled onto my back and savored the music. After my transformation, I was free from my bonds. The wolf didn't care about the damp darkness around me. Only the closest interesting smell. Out here there was no such thing as organization, only impulse and carnal cravings. No drug compared to feeling this free.

Thorn circled my body twice before he bit at my heels. Time to move. He set off with a brisk pace away from the coast—and deeper into the forest. His gray-and-black form darted ahead through the brush.

After a mile he caught the scent of a cottontail. In seconds, we went from a relaxing trot to a full run. My senses were now so sharp I could even hear the rabbit's heartbeat echoing against my skull. As I gave chase, a trail of clues revealed the animal's path—from a disturbed branch to tiny footprints left in the soil. All the little details I clung to during the day—the wolf cared nothing for them.

Thorn bounded over a rotten oak and drove another cottontail from its hiding place. I left his side to chase *my* prey. For three minutes, I pursued the rabbit. But I had no desire to end its life tonight—the wolf was more than happy to simply run and hunt.

Of course, that didn't stop Thorn from returning to my side with his cottontail in his mouth. He deposited the lifeless animal at my feet and circled to lie beside me. Dinner? I hadn't eaten wild game—or should I say, recently dead game—in years.

The warmth of his body next to mine brought a comfort I didn't want to let go. For just that moment, hope floated from our private grove into the night sky.

I woke up a few hours later. In the time that I'd slept, Thorn had left my clothes in a haphazard pile beside me. My nakedness didn't bother me. What did bother me was the bereft feeling of waking alone. I missed those moments in the past when we'd gone out into the woods and run free before making out like horn dogs into the morning. But that was more than five years ago. Baggage sucked.

I was in the middle of throwing on my bra and skirt when Thorn emerged from the trees dressed in his jeans.

"I didn't expect you to come by the house earlier," he said.

So he knew what had happened at his father's house.

I took a deep breath and wiped the dew from my legs.

"With Wendell's disappearance and the Long Island werewolves coming in and all, I thought it would be a good idea to align myself with the pack. The safest thing to do." I avoided his eyes, but I knew he was assessing me.

I glanced at him briefly, only to catch him staring at my breasts. He hadn't changed a bit.

"You know as well as I do that I would protect you."

"I'm an outsider. I don't see that happening."

"You know that's not true." He took a step forward and placed his hands in the pockets of his jeans. "I thought I'd have more time to prepare . . ."

I licked my dry lips. "What did you find out at Wendell's place?"

"Nothing you need to worry about."

"Don't give me that bullshit, Thorn. What happened to his girlfriend?"

A lone muscle in his neck twitched. He gave no other sign that the worst news was yet to come. "We found a trail not far from the house as well as four sets of footprints. They dragged two people out of the house and their trail ended at the edge of the forest."

I opened my mouth to press him further, but he spoke before I could. "We found her blood on the ground along with a piece of her shirt. Other than that, we don't know if they're dead or alive."

"Who's the tracker?" I wondered if one of the Stravinskys had been asked.

"Rex's on it now."

The forest around us was quiet, a little too quiet for my current mood. Thorn sat down beside me. He scooted close enough for heat to rise between our bodies—yet far enough away that we didn't touch. Those lips beckoned me to kiss them. And the wolf in me begged for release.

"I asked my father in your stead to allow you entry," Thorn said.

I laughed. "I'm sure he told you no as well."

"That he did."

I swallowed deeply. "It doesn't matter anyway."

"It does to me. I told him that I'd refuse to become alpha if he didn't let you in."

"You did what?" I prepared to stand, but his arm snaked out and held me down beside him. He released me, but his hand paused as if he wanted to touch me again.

"Somehow, someway, you will become part of the pack again, Natalya."

"He evidently doesn't think I'm fit to be a part of it."

"Well, I do." He sighed. "I escape this place to start a new life, only to come back to a falling house of cards. But the one thing I didn't expect to find here was you."

He didn't speak for a few minutes. "When I left San Diego, I returned home and found mountains of responsibility. Much more than one person should bear." He shook his head. "Seeing your future laid out in front of you gets old."

Curious now that he'd finally opened up, I asked, "What did you do?"

"I used my business degree to work as a manager in a tech company." He shrugged. "Shirt-and-tie kind of thing while rotting away in a cubicle."

"Must've been nice since you wanted to leave here so bad." And leave me behind.

"Sunshine and oceanfront property is nice and all, but there's nothing like the northeast." He gazed out into the trees. "Do you remember our first time together out in the forest?"

"Yes." I thought of it every time I hunted with him.

He laughed at the memory and leaned in to brush his

fingers against my knee. "I have no idea how you survived that first semester without hunting."

"Well, sightings of large wolves roaming the campus wouldn't have exactly helped with student and faculty recruitment."

"True, but you're not a human. You're a werewolf."

The memories of enjoying my freedom with him filled my senses. Thorn had taken a fellow South Toms River gal and whisked her away into a state park north of Pittsburgh. During spring break, while other college kids enjoyed the beaches, we hunted, we slept, and—for the first time—I made love with someone. Not just sex, but all-consuming, back-bending, good-God-where-did-that-fifth-orgasm-come-from sex. I sucked in a deep breath at the thought. How easily he triggered the hungry wolf within me.

"We had a few good years," I said. "But college is about transitioning into adulthood. A job. A new place to live." I hoped my words had strength behind them.

"I still shouldn't have left. I chickened out. Not only did I leave behind all those things my dad wanted for me, but I left you behind as well."

In the weeks after he'd left, I'd wondered what my answer would've been if he'd asked me to go with him. Would I have willingly left my family? The life I'd made in New York City?

He continued. "Now I have to protect the pack. And we both know Will isn't ready to assume leadership. Not only do I have to worry about everyone, but my father is making long-term plans for the Granthams to join with the Holdens. A power merger with a marriage." He rubbed his eyes as if the burdens of the pack weighed him down.

So that was it. He'd made a deal. Someday he might mate with Erica and I'd be left alone again. How did I get myself into such a mess? Did he even know I still wanted him?

His fingers twitched near my thigh—so close, yet so far away. "Don't worry. We'll think of something. This isn't over yet."

Every word Farley had said echoed through my head, but Thorn's lingered too.

I had a chance. And I refused to go down without a fight. Broken or not, I had the drive to succeed—and soon enough I would rejoin the pack.

Chapter 5

$D_{on't}$ you have a Greyhound bus you need to catch to head west?" I asked Aggie. For the third time, I sorted through a box of Hanukkah items. Not the average after-work activity.

"I can't leave my good friend with the threat of an attack looming." Aggie used a poker to stir the fire before she made another s'more.

I huffed. "An attack isn't coming yet. Thorn told me he reinforced the patrols in the area. And anyway, we both know you wouldn't stay here to hang out while a pack of angry werewolves breaks into my house."

"Well, by that point I'll have the bus ticket, and I can go wait at the bus station while they burn your cottage down. I may even be nice and help you haul out your boxes."

My mouth gaped and then I laughed. "You'd better not run away from them. Come here. I need backup to protect my little friends."

"Your little friends? Do you have an ornament vibrator in there? Now that would give me a merry Christmas and a happy New Year."

I threw a graham cracker at her head. "I'm not that kind of girl."

She snorted. "I sure am." Somehow she stuffed an entire s'more into her mouth.

"That's your third one. Aren't you full?"

For a moment, a guilty look flashed over her face. "Not really. Did you want one?"

How did she maintain her figure? It had to be her werewolf genes. "No, thanks. But we do need to make a trip to the store."

"You're storing enough food here for the next apocalypse. The deep freezer downstairs could hold a dead body."

"Maybe I should take your measurements for it." I stood and placed the ornaments back in their box. "I want to pick up a few cleaning supplies."

Aggie rolled her eyes. "Oh, I forgot. I spread disease."

I wanted to deny her statement, but I couldn't come up with a truthful statement. Instead, I continued with, "I also need to look at clothes."

She started to put the s'more ingredients away. "Why do you need more clothes? You dress nice all the time. In the same outfit, if I may add without hurting your feelings."

"Well, I've decided to try to improve myself. And that means stirring the pot, so to speak."

She paused as she kindly placed the food exactly where she'd found it. "What's wrong with how you are now? Other than hoarding holiday stuff—"

"It's been five years since you've seen me, and I don't have much to show for it. I have a house, a job. But other than that I don't have much else." The boxes almost swallowed the hallway. Most of the time they looked so imposing. "I want something more. A relationship, maybe. And the only way to jump on that horse is to buy some clothes for a date."

"With Thorn?"

"Not yet. He's sort of not available."

"Are you ready to ask a guy out?"

"It's already happened."

Her forehead wrinkled. "You mean you asked a guy out while you were at work today?"

I cringed as I remembered the encounter. Of all the men to take the plunge with, I'd asked the last person in town I'd actually want to date.

I recounted to her how, while I was pondering my next move, I spotted Quinton, the janitor for The Bends, wiping off the counters. The guy had the goth thing going for him, with his slicked-back raven-colored hair and midnight eyes. He towered over everyone in the place, and slinked around casting spells. Creepiness followed our resident necromancer like an army of brain-gobbling zombies.

And yet somehow, after I'd chanted to myself, "Starting fresh. Starting fresh," I'd walked up to Quinton and asked him what his plans for the upcoming weekend were.

No one had ever asked him such a question before, so he stammered for a moment. "N-nothing really. Just another weekend working in my herb garden, I guess."

Before I lost my nerve (and since I'd already jumped off the deep end) I had asked him if he wanted to go to Roger's Place for some Italian with me. I more or less expected him to say no and end my embarrassing test-drive. To my horror, though, he replied, "An evening out sounds like fun. I've never been there before. But I heard their cannoli is divine."

After asking Quinton out, I realized that it had been our longest conversation ever since I'd started working at The Bends. Most of the time, I didn't need a drawn-out speech to talk to him about the overflowing garbage or the two pending orders for a furniture pickup at the dock. Bill had told me that during Quinton's spare time he used herbs from his garden to stuff the recently deceased like Thanksgiving turkeys and bring them back to life. I told myself that with all the crazy men out there I could've done a lot worse.

And that was how I'd managed to snag a date on Friday with a necromancer.

Aggie laughed as she picked up her purse to leave the house. "You are *not* going out with that guy. I'll ask out the first sane man I see at the grocery store for you before I let you go out with *him*. Even my dad has more French fries in his Happy Meal than a janitor who spends his free time practicing necromancy."

As we drove into the shopping center's parking lot, I said, "I can't do that to him. He's a nice guy."

"A nice, creepy necromancer. Do you know what those guys do? Do I need to spell out necrophilia?"

I frowned and selected a parking spot. "Not every necromancer is having a personal party with the dead bodies they conjure."

"How do you know?"

Once we got to the store, I knew her silence meant I'd won—for now. But I wouldn't be surprised if Aggie showed up with the local insurance guy for a lunch date. We patrolled the aisles for my cleaning items. Aggie of course balked when we passed the chips aisle.

"Why can't I buy Cheetos?"

"You get orange dust all over everything. I thought *I* had issues. You practically carry an open bag every time I turn around."

Agatha pursed her lips and paused long enough to grab a bag of barbecued chips. She thought I didn't see, but I thought I'd give her until the checkout lane to give them up.

With my cleaning supplies in my basket, we waited at the only available checkout line. Aggie, ever impatient, glanced ahead to grumble about people who never remember to bring a debit card and force others to suffer while they write checks with the calligraphic handwriting meant for signing the Declaration of Independence.

Once we reached the front, of course, we were the only ones in line, with no one behind us. Go figure.

The clerk at the register wasn't hard to miss. With her round belly and snapping gum, she looked like a college student who'd accidentally gotten knocked up. But she smelled *different* somehow—I detected an aroma that made me think of the forest. One that invited me to run free. The sweet scent of magic. Aggie tilted her head and leaned forward. I stomped on her foot. This wasn't the time to be rude and smell someone else's butt to figure out what breed they were.

I had a feeling we'd just encountered a nymph. This ancient Greek protector of nature had pale skin that glistened, like morning dew dripped from her arms. I didn't detect any glamour on her, but she smelled ethereal.

And right then, my brother Alex picked exactly the wrong time to make a purchase.

"Hey, Nat." He casually tossed a box of condoms on the conveyor belt.

The nymph, whose name tag read *Karey,* peered at him with emerald-green eyes. "About time you showed up."

A den of snakes could have popped out of her head as she glared at him.

His smile faded as he saw her belly from around the corner. Their eyes went back and forth and my first thought was, *Alex, you've been a naughty boy.*

She somehow completed my transaction without looking away from Alex for a second. One hand scanned my items and flew on the register while the other gestured at my brother.

"You think you can just have a week or two with me and then ignore my phone calls?"

Alex's hands went up in surrender. "Look, Karey, it's not what you think."

I wanted to whisper to Karey that it actually *was* what she thought, but Alex was in enough trouble at the moment.

She was even able to carry on an argument *and* box groceries at the same time. "I've been searching for you for weeks. You never come to this store anymore, and your parents tell me they haven't seen you."

I glanced at the conveyor belt. Somehow two candy bars had replaced the box of condoms. My brother wasn't *that* dumb.

"My parents said nothing about you being pregnant. I mean, are you sure I'm the father?"

My transaction was done, but for some reason I stood there and watched the train wreck in progress. Aggie chuckled from beside me. Should I save my brother by taping his mouth shut?

"Maybe this is all because I'm not the nice werewolf girl your parents expected to show up at the doorstep. I want your cell phone number right now." She placed her hands on her hips. "You're not skirting your duties as a father here, pal."

"If that's my baby, I plan to do the right thing."

I could almost see my mother now. This would make the best Sunday dinner—ever. Even if my family wasn't willing to tolerate my presence, I'd still pay money to see how *this* situation went down.

My brother bought the two candy bars and scribbled his cell phone number (the real one) on the receipt. With a serious face, he followed Aggie and me into the parking lot.

I tried to think of something serious to say, but Aggie opened her mouth first.

"Alex, you should be more careful. How do you know she doesn't have a venereal disease or something?" She turned to me with a frown. "Can nymphs get crabs or something?"

"I wish I could tell you." I raised my voice and leaned into my brother as we approached our cars. "Since I can keep my legs closed, I'll never have to worry about that."

Alex harrumphed. "I made a mistake. I never thought nymphs could get knocked up!"

I laughed. "Do you ever read Greek myths?"

Aggie couldn't contain her laughter as she joined in the fun. "Yeah, I remember reading something about Zeus jumping into the sack with anything that had a vag."

"If you could keep this quiet for a while, I'd appreciate it." His face turned serious and his eyes darkened. Maybe Alex *was* the father.

I grabbed his arm. "Is it yours?"

"I'm not sure, but Karey's not the type to sleep around." He ran his fingers through his blond hair. I envied the glossy color he'd inherited from our mother.

"Well, give me a call later if you want to talk about it."

He nodded and headed over to his truck. I more or less had expected my parents to match him up with a nice Russian werewolf girl from the big city. My brother was wild, but I'd never predicted an unplanned pregnancy with a tree nymph in his future.

Chapter 6

After two days of watching my back, I didn't want to venture out at night. Not the best way to start dating. But no matter what my problems were, I had to take a positive step toward feeling normal. And normal people went on dates.

"Are you sure you want to do this?" Aggie asked. "I can hook you up with the pharmacy technician at Walgreens."

I frowned as I stared at my clothes on my bed. That poor human would never know what hit him. "Are you my date pimp now?"

"I'm your common sense trying to knock you over the head."

The dark purple blouse and jean skirt that Aggie had helped me select left me wary. My hands began to sweat, and I paced in front of my bed. Before I'd set it down, I'd pressed the blouse against my cheek. No matter how nice these clothes were, to my nose they smelled brand-new and artificial. In contrast, my usual clothes had a familiar feeling that would bring comfort—but they wouldn't help me reenter the pack.

Aggie sat on the floor with a bowl of barbecued potato chips in her lap. "You okay?"

I took a deep breath. "No, I'm not."

"I can call this guy and tell him you're not coming."

"It's not him. It's the clothes."

Aggie's eyebrows lowered. "All you need to do is put them on."

With clenched fists, I tried to suppress a rising panic. The rapid staccato of my heart echoed in my ears like the thunderous hooves of Clydesdales. "I know that." I squeezed my eyes shut as I tried to imagine myself wearing the clothes. I tried to visualize myself in them with a smile. A strained smile, but an attempt nonetheless.

I reminded myself: *This is what normal people do.*

Stifling heat filled my face, but I picked up the purple blouse.

Aggie touched my hair in concern. "Do you take medicine for your panic attacks?"

"I used to. But, well, the side effects didn't agree with the wolf."

"Yeah, I was lucky I didn't need medication for my problem. My parents simply locked the fridge door." She touched the jean skirt. "Maybe you could take a pill tonight to help you through the worst of it," she suggested.

I faintly remembered the last time I took the drugs— shaking wildly as the wolf tried to escape the calm the pills forced on my body. Maybe the side effects wouldn't be so bad. It'd been several years since I'd taken the happy capsules.

I handed Aggie the blouse while I went into the bathroom to take half a pill. As I downed it, I thought with dread, *Bottoms up.*

Aggie waited patiently while I took the next twenty minutes to put on the blouse and skirt. She commented briefly that she was glad I'd given myself two hours to prepare. "Is he picking you up?"

"No, I'm meeting him there."

"That's good. I felt uncomfortable about him taking you home in his hearse."

"He doesn't have a hearse. It's a black station wagon."

She rolled her eyes and popped a chip into her mouth. "I spotted it in the parking lot at The Bends the other day. You might as well call it the Death Mobile."

Even with Agatha's snippy quips about Quinton, I still found myself headed to Roger's Place to meet him. Diners were heading inside, with a few casually waving in my direction.

For once, I almost felt normal. But as the local hermit-in-training, my appearance at the local Italian place still attracted plenty of interest.

"Nice to see you out and about," said the owner of the flower shop down the street from The Bends.

I kept glancing at my watch, wondering if Quinton was running late. He still had four minutes, but I like punctuality.

Through the long window in the doors, I spotted a tall shadow and my heart leapt. Part of me wanted Thorn to appear and take Quinton's place. Instead, the necromancer made his appearance holding a bouquet of red roses. He lumbered toward me wearing a suit jacket, and a nice pair of slacks.

I couldn't suppress the smile that broke out on my face. I hadn't expected him to be, well, not that bad-looking. Dark circles lined his eyes, but his irises were a fairly attractive midnight blue. Under his cologne, I caught the faint scent of sawdust and salt. (What the hell did he do with those zombies?)

I scratched my hand faintly as he offered the flowers.

"For you," he grumbled in his deep voice.

"Thanks. You ready to eat?"

"Yeah."

As we took our seats, I hoped our conversation would progress beyond three- to four-word sentences.

The waiter brought our menus and we read them in silence. "I highly recommend the lasagna tonight."

Our waiter, a high school kid named Matt, did such a

good job selling the lasagna, we placed two orders and Quinton added a bottle of wine. And then we sat there staring at each other.

He broke the silence with, "You look nice tonight."

I touched the collar of my blouse self-consciously. It had been a while since someone had noticed my attire, but I guess if one wears the same thing every day it doesn't make much of an impression.

"Thanks." I peered at him as he blinked blankly in my direction.

"Have you ever eaten here before?" I asked.

"I work all day at the flea market and then do a night shift elsewhere. I don't make time for candlelight dinners."

And I thought *I* was a loner.

Matt returned and brought us the bottle of wine. Quinton offered to pour me some, but I declined.

"I had some meds this evening and it wouldn't go well with it." Speaking of meds, I actually felt less anxious for once, which was strange, since by now I should've gone into a full-blown panic attack over the prospects of something outside my usual routine. No TV dinner while I watched my regularly scheduled programming.

My metabolism was so quick, drugs usually hit me fast, so I'd expected the worst. But other than a strong urge to line up my silverware, I felt like I'd made positive progress this evening.

"Your invitation to dinner surprised me."

I glanced up to see him take a sip of his wine. Time to make conversation. "As coworkers, we don't get a chance to talk much at work. Either I'm helping the customers at the register or you're doing the beast-of-burden thing in the back."

I cringed inwardly after I said "beast of burden." I was definitely out of practice on this dating thing. Perhaps my next stab at small talk should involve speculating on the weird ingredients whose scent emanated from his car? I knew he wasn't running a meth lab, but the guy carried around enough embalming fluid to mummify half the township.

"I don't get out much." He leaned forward and tried to smile. His toothy grin had a rather maniacal appearance. "From the way you're always working behind the counter it seems like you needed the dinner too."

"Do I look that busy?"

"Unfortunately, you do. You're always on time to work, and when Bill needs you to stay late you never argue. Well, if you argue I never see it."

I nodded at the appropriate times while he talked about his life in South Toms River. He'd moved here a few years ago from Iowa to settle down closer to the sea. He'd hoped to refine his craft before starting a family to continue his legacy. It didn't take long for me to realize I wasn't attracted to him.

I tried to steer the conversation away from fornication and families with the first thing that came to mind. "Did you know Bill's so old he tanned leather during the Dark Ages?"

He was about to answer when we had unexpected company. Now, most folks expect their waiter to show up to check on them, but I noticed something different about the guy carrying our food. Not only did he have hanging flesh and caved-in eyes, he also had the distinct scent of the undead.

Quinton turned to see what I'd frowned about. "Oh, shit."

I hadn't expected to hear him curse. But who wouldn't when one of the undead you'd conjured showed up to serve you dinner—in your waiter's uniform.

"Where is the boy?" Quinton's face turned sour. His voice took on a musical nuance and flowed through my body from my toes to my fingertips.

"I am yours and serve only you, Master. Your waiter was unworthy."

Now I knew why I didn't date. If Aggie were here right now, I believe "I told you so" would be her eloquent words.

I squirmed uncomfortably in the seat as a worm dropped out of the zombie's sleeve. I planned to leave the *former* waiter a large tip. If he had a pulse, that is.

"Leave the food on the table. Once I have excused you, you'll return the uniform to the original owner. You have disobeyed me and henceforth will suffer the consequences."

When the food was placed in front of me, I knew I wouldn't touch it no matter how much the hungry wolf wanted to eat. I'd been served by a guy whose rotting limbs were bound together by duct tape and magic. Who knows what germ-laden microscopic body parts had fallen into my lasagna?

"I think I should call it a night," I murmured.

"Don't worry about Neil. It was an honest mistake." Quinton waved his hand as if everyone had a zombie show up with their dinner once in a while.

"I thought I was hungry, but, well, the smell kind of killed my appetite."

"What smell? I use only natural ingredients when I conjure the dead. He should smell of rosemary and myrrh."

Rosemary and myrrh, my ass. He smelled like my brother's shoes on a bad day. To my werewolf nose, it was no different than if I'd jammed my nose into a funky armpit.

I placed my napkin next to the plate of bubbling lasagna. The aroma drifted to my nose, but I couldn't think as I watched Neil stand there obediently before his master. With these kinds of incidents going on, how the hell did necromancers ever hook up?

I imagined two necromancers trying to get it on, with

their undead minions standing by with a condom. I shoved the intruding thought away and said, "I've lost my appetite and I think I should head home."

"Look, you really don't need to go."

Neil left his post to block my way. "Master is speaking and has asked you to stay in your seat."

I rolled my eyes and tried to ignore the uncomfortable churning in my stomach. "Tell your—friend to move, please." With twitching hands, I fished a few bills from my purse.

With a single nod from Quinton, Neil moved out of the way.

The stench from the walking corpse filled my nose as I passed it to leave the table. For some reason, even though the evening had been a disaster, I felt like I couldn't just leave Quinton.

"I'll see you tomorrow at work. I hope you—find the waiter's body." As I headed out the door, I flinched from my words. *Find the waiter's body?* If there was a top-ten list of bad date lines, mine had to be in the top five.

To avoid any zombies who might've been displeased with my dinner performance, I hurried to my car. I placed the key in the lock, but it was too late. I smelled the presence of strangers surrounding me.

Chapter 7

They smelled of sand and salt from the shore. Three members of the Long Island pack swept in around me. Their dark eyes went from black to glaring yellow.

I froze in place. With no allies around me, I was screwed.

"We caught a pretty one lurking around at night alone," said the one closest to me. He wore a black leather coat and jeans, and his dirty blond hair flowed to his shoulders.

"I would think so, Clive," whispered another voice. From the corner of my eye, I spied a man leaning against an Oldsmobile. He cocked his head in my direction.

Clive came closer and I closed my eyes as fear surged through my body. My mind wanted to flee, but somehow my body shut down and my legs turned to jelly. Why did the wolf choose to remain still now?

My attacker's breath smelled of pizza and beer. Such things shouldn't have frightened me, but the way he drew in a deep breath and examined me for a few seconds made me shake. He'd know soon enough.

"She's not of the pack. But I smell the alpha on her for some reason."

I feared my legs wouldn't hold me up. I continued to grip the key lodged within the lock and glanced at my wide-eyed reflection in the car window. *Move it! Don't just stand there!*

The two others moved closer to me. Clive grabbed my hand and yanked the keys away.

"You seem meek enough," Clive purred as his fingers clutched a wad of my hair. "Can I keep her, Derek?"

Derek's hand flew up to deny the request. He moved like a leopard approaching its prey. He looked about as good as a hungry viper would to a mouse. His face was marred by a long scratch that went from his forehead down to his chin. He grinned to reveal enlarged canines. The third man smiled too, revealing gold teeth that gleamed under the parking lot lights.

My hand quaked within Clive's grip.

"There's something different about you." His nostrils flared before he ran his nose against the back of my skull.

I mewled and tried to move forward, but Clive's grip on my hair locked me in place. My pulse thundered in my ears, making it difficult for me to plan an escape.

"Inferior stock," Derek mumbled.

"But I want her," growled Clive.

"That doesn't matter. No wonder she's not part of the pack. Kill her."

My eyes widened as spots appeared in my vision. Tears stumbled down my cheeks. This wasn't my time. Not like this—

"You left your coat." All of us turned at the same time to see the zombie named Neil holding out my light jacket. Of all the times to have the undead show up.

How come no one smelled this guy approaching?

"What the hell is that?" asked the third attacker.

An ominous voice reached us from the building. "Is there a problem, gentlemen?"

In the distance, Quinton stepped into the light. Hope

flooded my body, then reality hit. I wished Thorn stood in his place.

Derek barked, "Fuck off! And take your decomposing pet with you."

"The lady is under my protection tonight. You should leave her alone."

Even though I'd brushed the janitor off, he hadn't taken it to heart.

Derek and Clive guffawed. Then Derek took a step forward and ripped one of Neil's arms from its socket. The zombie's limb flew through the air and plopped down in front of Quinton. Bits of gray flesh fell on his shiny black shoes. A finger landed on his shoulder and Quinton removed it.

Derek turned to his cohorts. "Rip him apart. I don't need any adversaries in Luther's way when he gets to town." The two others advanced on Quinton.

But the guy just stood there as two deadly werewolves closed in on him. I tried to scream out for him to run, but my mouth refused to move. I closed my eyes while Derek sneered, "Since you stood up to us like a man, we'll end your life quickly, necromancer."

A series of footsteps, and then the overwhelming smell of moss and earth hit my nose.

"I'm not worried about that."

The heavy footsteps paused and I opened my eyes to see that we'd been surrounded—by an army of the undead. Quinton had conjured hundreds of zombies with a silent siren call.

The two men took several steps forward, but Derek halted their progress.

Gold Tooth sneered, "We can take them."

Between clenched teeth, Derek said, "Shut up, Ty!" He cursed under his breath. "I don't like these odds. No matter how hungry you are for a fight."

I blinked again and again at the circle of the undead. Men and women stood shoulder to shoulder with their empty eyes focused on us. A mysterious, opaque fog had drifted in and covered their legs.

Derek frowned. "This isn't over. You shouldn't have interfered in our business. If you value your life, you'll leave the area."

One of Quinton's eyebrows rose and a grin spread across his pale face. The man may have round-trip tickets to Creepyville, but he also has the balls of an African elephant. "I'll take that under advisement."

Derek backed away and headed for his car. Clive released me and shoved me to the ground before following him. My hands scraped against the sidewalk to catch my fall. Thanks to swift werewolf healing, the burn lasted only a few seconds before my body began to heal the opened skin.

In the distance, the army retreated into the shadows while Quinton walked toward me. He offered a hand to help me up, but I refused. (He'd just pulled a zombie's finger off his shoulder. A *decomposing* finger.)

Quinton waited while I dusted myself off. I had to say something—he had rescued me.

"Thanks. I appreciate what you've done for me."

"Not a problem." He gazed at my mouth and licked his lips. "Do you want me to give you a ride home?"

I was grateful, but I'd also been creeped out enough for the evening. "I'll be fine. I have someone staying at my house, so I won't be alone."

I turned away to look for my keys on the ground.

He offered them to me and said, "This may seem awkward, but even with what's happened tonight I did have a good time." I offered a small smile as he cocked a wide grin. His pale skin contrasted starkly with the deep color of his eyes.

"Yeah, before the dead waiter showed up we had some pleasant conversation."

He blurted, "Don't worry about our first waiter." He made a gesture toward the restaurant. "I made sure the boy's in good health."

I breathed a sigh of relief. Quinton might drive a Death Mobile and reanimate the dead, but he did have gentlemanly tendencies. "That's good news. 'Cause, boy, did he deserve the tip I left him."

"That he did."

Our conversation died away so I took a step back. "Thanks for an interesting evening, Quinton."

As he walked away he whispered, "It was my pleasure, lady. See you at work tomorrow."

I jumped in my car and gunned the vehicle out of the parking lot. The screech of my tires offered minimal comfort as I sped home.

The ever-optimistic Aggie saw my wild eyes as I entered the house. "Are you all right?"

I pulled off my shoes and mumbled, "I don't even know where to begin." The heat in the house didn't prevent the chill running over my skin. The familiar stacks of boxes didn't offer me their usual comfort. Such trinkets couldn't fire guns.

"Did he try to cop a feel or something? I told you— necrophilia."

"Actually, he was plenty interested in my flesh-and-blood body. But he wasn't the worst thing I had to endure." I sat down on my couch and rested my face in my hands. "I got big problems, Aggie."

She plopped down beside me, but her presence didn't push away the feeling of Clive's hands on my body. I whispered, "The Long Island werewolves are here. And they've marked me for extermination."

*   *   *

With the threat of death hanging over my head, I wasn't surprised when Thorn called me a few hours later.

"I heard something happened. Are you all right?"

By this point, I was calm, but Aggie relieved my fears by standing guard in my living room.

"Yeah, you didn't need to call." Yes, I did need to hear his voice, but I wouldn't admit such things.

"I need to finish another sweep of the area, but I'll stop by your place later to check on you."

I sat up in my bed. "I'll be fine, Thorn. Aggie's keeping me company."

"I'll still check anyway. This kind of attack was unexpected. I need to figure out why they'd come for you."

Based on what Clive had said, maybe they wanted to clear out the weaker wolves first. Cull the herd. Oh, God. Would my grandmother be in danger next?

"I'll see you in a while." I heard the dial tone.

I thought I'd lie there and wait for him, but I drifted to sleep.

Dreams blended into reality as I woke up with a pillow pressed against my face. My breaths came out in gurgled gasps. Close to my ear I heard Rex's deep voice purr, "About time the exterminator came by to take out the trash." I thrashed and struggled until I woke up again covered in sweat.

His words continued to reverberate through my mind. He'd called me out as a rogue wolf a week ago. It's a damn shame he held just as firmly to the events of the past as I did.

A quick glance at the clock told me I'd slept for a few hours. Damn nightmares plagued me to no end when I was stressed. And when my stress increased, my insomnia did too. After an hour or two I became an advertiser's dream. Up late and itching to buy, I usually whipped out my credit card to forget my troubles. Instead of getting up to watch TV, I adjusted the pillows and curled into a ball. After a night like tonight I needed sleep.

But the sounds of fingers scraping my window open alerted me to danger. I was turned away from my window and I couldn't stop myself from shutting my eyes and whispering, "Please go away."

Where was the brave wolf who'd raced out of her house to face Aggie while she trampled her flowers? That wolf had had her life threatened by the Long Island werewolves, thank you very much.

My breath quickened. They'd come for me in the late night to finish what they'd started. I bet Aggie had fallen asleep with the bag of Cheetos she thought she'd hidden from me.

Hands touched my shoulders as someone crawled into my bed. I tensed for the first strike. Somehow, the warm hands suppressed my jump. They circled my torso as Thorn whispered, "It's me. You'll be all right."

He held me close and then turned me around to envelop me in his arms. "Go to sleep, Nat."

"You shouldn't sneak up on me like that."

"I thought you were fast asleep until I saw you move when I came in."

I rolled my eyes. "After the evening I've had, you think I wouldn't be on edge?"

"I'm sorry about that. I thought the pack had more time."

"Evidently not." I remembered Clive's hand gripping my arm and shivered. The wolf in me wanted to rip him to shreds. Instead, the frightened human spoke. "I don't know if this place is safe anymore."

He placed his hand on my cheek. "I won't leave until I know you're safe and asleep. Lie still and rest."

With him beside me like this, did he expect me to sleep? I squirmed.

Against the crown of my head, he chuckled. "I am a man, and I do get turned on. I'd appreciate it if you'd go to sleep and not move like that."

I suppressed a grin as sleep drifted back into my body. When he relaxed, my fingers slowly moved down his arms.

He breathed in deeply and whispered, "Don't do this to me. You know I'm meant for another." His voice was ragged and thick with desire, but I felt like I'd been doused in cold seawater.

Bitter and rejected, I swallowed and wanted to push him away. So close, yet so far away. Another reminder that he would belong to Erica one day. Then why was he in my bed right now? Holding me close to the point that I knew our heartbeats matched.

No one from my family called asking what had happened. South Toms River wasn't a megametropolis, though. The information would leak out and everyone would be told before dawn. Even worse, Erica would know Thorn had come to my bed.

Yet I'd only heard the phone ring twice. And none of the callers had asked to talk to me. Who had Aggie spoken with?

Silence prevailed as my bottom lip trembled. I wouldn't cry. Not with him beside me. Did he know how much he tormented me?

Eventually, I fell asleep. When I woke up the next morning to the incessant chirps of my alarm clock, an empty spot remained where Thorn had lain. I curled up in my covers and couldn't suppress the stream of tears. A pain churned within my stomach, searing and sharp, when I glanced at the indentation in the bed. The space was warm, and the bereft feeling in my heart speared my senses. I rubbed my nose against the pillow, where his scent lingered.

His shampoo and subtle cologne flowed through my nostrils. It wasn't fair. I was making an effort. Would all my work be in vain?

Work that morning was a chore for once. After Aggie dropped me off, with stern instructions to not leave for lunch, I began cataloging new arrivals. Saturday mornings, after the initial rush for the best products, tended to be quiet and tranquil, with just a few out-of-town visitors passing through.

But nothing could have prepared me for the storm that was Erica Holden. A wave of expensive-smelling perfume followed her into the market. A few of the male patrons followed her with their eyes. As a powerful female, she walked with a strut. When she strolled across the room, she moved with a purpose. From the way Bill watched her ass, her purpose today was most likely being eye candy.

She made a beeline for the customer-service desk— just in front of the business office where I worked. Instead of marching straight in, she waited by the desk. Her manicured fingernails clicked again and again on the display case glass. She knew I worked on the other side of the closed doors. She also knew I'd understand that she wasn't here to sample shiny wands. Under normal circumstances, a woman like Erica wouldn't be caught dead in a place where one bought "used" stuff.

"Natalya, I need to speak with you." Ever the lady, she called me out without ringing the bell for service.

I left the office without conscious thought. Damn higher-ranking females.

Her aquamarine eyes followed me as I walked behind the service counter. I met her eyes once and immediately averted them. I knew my place.

"I heard about what happened to you last night." She

paused for a moment as if she expected me to say something. But why should I? Erica wasn't stupid.

"With the Long Island werewolves coming in to take over our territory, it's important that Thorn focus on the good of the pack. Distractions, such as the one that involved you, are unfortunate, but shouldn't occur. Your family has been part of *my* pack since before I was born. It would be a shame for them to get hurt due to your actions."

If smugness were a fragrance, Erica would reek of it. She didn't offer a smile. But if one could call her facial expression something, I'd call it a smirk.

"This is your one and only warning. Stay away from Thorn. He won't always be there when you call."

I wanted to bite back that I hadn't called Thorn. But such words to someone like her were quite imprudent. Instead I said, "And what if Thorn comes to see me?"

"He won't. We'll come to an agreement regarding people like you."

People like me? My fingernails cut into my palms. Where the hell was the woman who'd stood up to the harpy? *That woman has the sense to know that there's a big difference between a pushy harpy and a werewolf who'd take me behind the store to rip my throat out.*

"Do we understand each other?"

I nodded faintly and continued to avoid her eyes.

"I expect you to speak when spoken to. Is that clear?"

Now she poured it on and went from uptight bitch to a word that even I won't repeat for fear of a virtual smack from my grandmother. "Loud and clear," I mumbled.

Erica prepared to leave, but then paused and smiled. "Thorn belongs to me. Don't cross me." Her sneer merged into a smile that could've been covered in cotton candy. With a quick dab of lip gloss, she left the place as if all she'd done was share secrets with a girlfriend.

One shopper waved in her direction and greeted her warmly.

"Damn bitch," I muttered—after she was a safe distance away.

Part of me wanted to sulk and hammer the idea into my head that I should just forget about Thorn. The wolf within, though, didn't want to go down without a fight. It hungered to claim him as its own.

But how could I ever compete with a woman like Erica?

Chapter 8

Are you sure you're ready for therapy? That's a big step."

Aggie's concern touched my heart, but after the fiasco with Quinton and the attack from the Long Island werewolves, I needed to take a positive step toward sorting out my life.

I had to come to terms with the fact that hoarding had negative side effects. Buying ornament after ornament wasn't normal behavior, but somehow part of me felt that it was right. As I gave the Home Shopping Network my credit card number, I reveled in the delicious shiver within my belly when I knew my holiday cheer was on its way.

Aggie finished preparing the Monday morning coffee. "Do you want me to go with you tomorrow afternoon? It's not safe around here."

"I'll be careful. I've made several trips to Dr. Frank in the past. Another trip won't hurt."

She shrugged and headed into the kitchen to work on a pot roast. My mother had invited her over for dinner. At first, Aggie had refused since I wasn't invited. But my mother told her point-blank that the dinner was meant for matchmaking—with Alex. I guessed he hadn't told my parents that he'd possibly impregnated a tree nymph.

Before I left for work, the phone rang. I ignored it

since I was on schedule—that was why the answering machine was invented.

But as I placed the key in the ignition I noticed that Aggie didn't answer it either. Perhaps she saw a telemarketer on the caller ID and decided not to answer. Curiosity compelled me to wait for the answering machine.

I strained to listen and heard a man's gruff voice say, "Miss Stravinsky, I'm calling in regards to Miss McClure. My employer, Mr. McClure, is searching for his daughter." Then some mumbling that I couldn't make out, and then a new voice interrupted the previous one. "Aggie, if you're there, pick up the phone. It's Dad. Look, I know you're angry with me. We can work it out. Just give me a call." Then the line went dead. Aggie didn't pick up the phone, and I had a feeling she never would.

There would be plenty of time for me to ask Aggie what was up between her and her father. But, as of right now, I had work and my own issues to tackle.

As the day became evening it proceeded well. Since I hadn't been invited, I told Aggie I'd stay at home, but with a rough tug she pulled rank and told me I'd have to come with her.

"You are not staying alone in this house." She growled, "That's a direct order."

My eyes widened, and I marched to my room to freshen up. Aggie hadn't pulled rank in years. From my bedroom, I cried sarcastically, "Friends don't let friends pull alpha rank on them."

"Too bad. Request denied."

Thirty minutes later, we pulled up to my parents' house.

"Aggie, do you really want to date Alex?"

She shook her head. "He's not my type in the least. Especially since he may have knocked up a tree-frolicking nymph." With a grin, she pushed the pot roast into my hands. I saw the evil glint in her eyes and smelled ulterior motives.

"What plans are you brewing?"

We left the car. Before I turned the doorknob, she said, "If you want to change your life, then you need to re-unite with your family. This is part one."

I huffed. "Good luck with that one."

We entered the house to find everyone settled at the long dinner table, with a single empty space next to Alex. My mother saw me enter holding the pot roast. None of her body language indicated malice—only curiosity. Her gaze then went to the matchmaking victim.

"Glad you could join us, Agatha." She touched Dad's shoulder. "Could you fetch another seat for Natalya?"

My father nodded in my direction. At least my parents could be civil even though I hadn't been invited.

I placed the pot roast on the table and leaned over to my grandmother to kiss her cheek. With both hands, she grasped my face and returned kisses on each cheek.

"Looking good, Nat," said Alex before he took a gulp of his wine. He'd dressed in business casual, as if to impress my parents, but we all knew he'd just discard the tie later to gallivant off to the local bar and scope out girls.

After placing a napkin in my lap, I peered across the table to see Aggie ogling the smorgasbord. Her meager pot roast was dwarfed by the roasted pig my mother had skewered. The braised skin was so shiny I could see Aggie's wide eyes reflected in it. I couldn't resist a chuckle. A few more dinners, and Aggie might want to marry into the family solely for the food.

Everyone passed around their bowls so my mother could scoop thick vegetable soup into them. Pleasantries about the day's events turned into slurps and smacks. (For werewolves, food etiquette only goes so far.)

As everyone ate, I hoped I wouldn't have to contribute to the conversation. What could I say?

In his deep, booming voice, my father opened with, "Looks like the poor economy has hit PharmTech."

I shifted my gaze to my dark-haired father, by far one of the largest werewolves I'd ever seen. For the past few years, he worked as a prized machinist at one of the local factories. As usual, he sat quietly eating his wife's food and scratching the shiny bald spot on his head.

"I thought that was a rumor," Alex said.

"I wish I could say that, my boy, but I've heard layoffs are coming. Our educated brothers will lose their jobs and leave rogue werewolves roaming about for food."

This wasn't the first time the area had been affected by a downturn. I remembered when my father lost his job in the eighties. My mother still refused to discuss what my father had done for the organized crime groups in Atlantic City—the nights when he came home with the stench of death ground under his claws. I wondered from time to time if his turbulent past was a distant memory.

Alex wiped his mouth with his napkin and raised his eyebrows at Aggie. (As if she cared.) "Things will bounce back. Five years ago it was the mill. Before that we lost the shopping center."

Aggie's head swiveled like a lug nut on a rusty screw. "What do you think, Nat?"

Of course she picked the perfect time to drop-kick me into the fray. With four bites of ham in my mouth I managed, "There are jobs out there. People just need to be willing to work outside their comfort zone for a while."

The click of utensils and eating filled the silence before my father replied, "That's true. But it's hard for a father of four pups to support a hungry family on a cashier's wage."

Alex pushed the food around on his plate. "I'm sorry about all this matchmaking, Aggie. My family is a bit pushy."

"No need. I came here for the food."

I about choked on my ice water.

He turned to our mother. "Why not hook Aggie up with cousin Yuri? Doesn't he call here every fifteen minutes?"

I finished my drink and poured another. "There's no one with a pulse who'd want to deal with him." Well, there was that harpy. Maybe she'd con people less if she had less free time to ogle antiques.

My mother tilted her head. "What's that noise?" I dropped my fork and then heard it. The dull crash of glass breaking outside.

Alarmed, Aggie and Alex jumped out of their seats to race toward the front door My parents and Grandma scrambled to follow them. Alex reached it first and thundered outside. I peered over Aggie's shoulder to see Karey next to Alex's Dodge truck with a crowbar carving into the side. I scrunched my face as she screeched, "I hope you enjoyed your dinner with your little whore!"

With her task finished, she jumped into a car with another nymph behind the wheel and peeled away. A fuming Alex stalked over to his ruined truck while we surveyed the damage from the curb.

In her thick Russian accent, I heard Grandma read the words carved into the side. *"Eat shit and die, you cake-sucker."*

No one bothered to correct her error. Thank God.

My mother placed her hands on her small hips and spoke sternly in Russian. "Alexander Fyodorovich Stravinsky. What the hell just happened here?"

"Mom, call the police, please," he pleaded.

With a stern face, my father returned inside, I hope to find a phone. But since the cops were humans, what could we tell them? Especially when the report should include how my brother's truck had been keyed by a pregnant tree nymph with a crowbar.

*   *   *

I squirmed in my leather seat while Dr. Frank, a white wizard psychiatrist, assessed me the next afternoon. "After our talk yesterday I think you would do well with CBT as well as my group therapy sessions each week. You responded well to it the last time we worked together."

I remembered all too well what CBT, or Cognitive Behavioral Therapy, included. I'd have to confront my obsessions head-on and learn to avoid my compulsions. Then through group therapy, I'd have to talk about it. From past experiences with Dr. Frank, I knew the therapy worked. After going through three months of aggressive therapy and a regimen of medicines, I'd found myself with a new job in New York City as a content editor. I would've stayed there too if I hadn't broken down after Thorn disappeared. On days like these, I couldn't believe I'd regressed just because of a man. But at the time, Thorn and Aggie were the only people who'd believed in me.

"I don't think group therapy is necessary right now," I said.

The white-bearded wizard leaned back in his chair. His light gray eyes stared me down as if he could see every crack he had to fix. Over the years, Dr. Frank and this office hadn't changed. I'd sat in this same chair back when I was a teen. Before my little collecting habit began, I used to wash my hands—a lot. A clean thirteen-year-old with a mother who preferred clean hands in her kitchen was one thing. But my repeated tasks were enough to make any parent wary. Especially the ones where a werewolf teen couldn't manage to leave the house without sanitizing every surface. So my parents took me to Dr. Frank. Since werewolves have such a souped-up immune system, we rarely needed physicians. In my case, though, I had a problem that couldn't be fixed easily. With nowhere else to turn, my parents tried magic, a source my mother despised. Thank goodness, Dr. Frank was a great psychiatrist and wizard. He had an arsenal of options that didn't require magic to outright alter his patients' behavior. In the end, he'd recommended that I spend the summer with other werewolf teens at Camp Harold.

Dr. Frank broke the silence. "You have problems with relationships. I think that's due to your obsessive-compulsive behavior. Didn't you tell me your family still doesn't interact with you?"

I shouldn't have told him about that. I found a minuscule crack on the wall and focused on it. "Yes, I did. But last night was a—first step toward some kind of healing process." A first step—on Jupiter, perhaps. Its citizens were full of hot gases.

I looked for another distraction, and my gaze moved to the rows of leather-bound books behind him. I smiled when I realized that every one of them was in alphabetical order, without a single trace of dust. Did Dr. Frank have a diligent secretary, a great sorting spell, or some obsessive behaviors of his own?

"I have a great group of individuals, and they offer each other support, which can be hard to find in the supernatural community. Fortunately for you, we have a meeting tonight. Why don't you find a place to have a bite to eat and come back for the meeting?"

I nodded reluctantly. Dr. Frank knew best.

He interrupted me as I stood. "And Natalya?"

"Yes?"

"I'd like you to come back without any shopping bags this time."

Damn, he was good.

I arrived in Dr. Frank's conference room a few hours later—without any bags. Of course, during my trip out into the mecca of trinkets that was Manhattan, I'd managed to avoid most of the shops that had once been my favorites.

That old wizard sure knew how to torture a woman.

Eight seats formed a circle, with the large mahogany table moved to the side. A lovely setting of fresh coffee and doughnuts sat on a small end table. Two people stood next to it sipping coffee. I took a seat, but peeked briefly at them. Both smelled of magic, in particular the woman with the soft chestnut-colored hair. Her voice came out as a whisper. The man who stood behind her towered over everyone, at over six feet-plus, but his shoulders hunched as if he were trying to occupy less space.

A few others entered the room and sat down as Dr. Frank filed in behind them.

"Good afternoon, everyone. Nick told me he's running late, so let's sit down and get started with introductions since we have a new member."

Of course, everyone's eyes moved in my direction. I gripped my purse and recrossed my legs. If they kept this up, I'd start tapping my heel against the wooden floor.

It wasn't as if I'd never been here before. I recognized at least two faces from the group. Quite unfortunate to see them here. Raj, a minor Indian deity with multiple arms, had a lesser form of OCD. I couldn't see his true form through his glamour, but from the gloves on two of his hands, I knew the poor man continued to wash them at every possible opportunity. Another familiar face was Heidi, the mermaid with thalassophobia. She hadn't lived in the ocean since the age of twelve. Her six-pack of Evian water rested in the pocket of her backpack. I guess you gotta do what you gotta do.

The new faces, though, made me wary.

Dr. Frank took one of the free seats and placed his hands on his knees. The shininess of his leather shoes distracted me before he spoke.

"I can sense high anxiety in the room, so let's relax for a bit before we go through introductions."

The door suddenly opened and a man joined us. Another wizard, my nose told me. Not a powerful one with great magic—just your average white magic–casting wizard. He murmured a brief "Sorry" before he plopped down in a seat. His black trench coat matched his shiny black shoes. He definitely had the lack-of-color thing going, with midnight-colored eyes and hair. A goth wizard? Had I missed a trend circulating the Northeast?

Our gazes locked briefly before Dr. Frank worked his magic. A wave of calming energy flowed from the psychiatrist through the room. I thought he would've made a great snake charmer. The wolf within me folded into soft jelly. Smiles formed on everyone's faces.

A moment of embarrassment hit when the goth wizard and I exchanged a glance. Not the best way to meet someone new—with a blissful, cheesy grin on your face. Especially when their grin was attractive.

"Good. That didn't take long. We have someone new among us today." He smiled in my direction. "Natalya, could you introduce yourself to everyone?"

On a temporary high from Dr. Frank's magic, I told everyone my name, and then everyone else followed suit. The tall man I'd seen earlier was Tyler. He lived as one of the rarely seen supernaturals, the earth-dwelling dwarves. Due to their normally short stature, they tended to keep to themselves, so I didn't see his people very often. Either way, I didn't need a psychology degree to see the potential problems with that guy.

A Muse named Abby sat quietly on the other side of Dr. Frank. She didn't look at anyone and simply mumbled her name. The poor thing appeared withdrawn and tormented.

Last came Lilith, a succubus who for some sad reason didn't come off as a man-eater to me, and finally the latecomer, the wizard who introduced himself as Nick. I couldn't figure out his problem, but it would show itself soon enough.

Dr. Frank began our therapy with an open conversation. "Last week, we talked about urges and how we suppress them to prevent anxiety. Does anyone have any success stories to talk about or incidents they want to get off their back?"

Heidi the mermaid leaned forward. "Friday didn't go too well."

Dr. Frank nodded to offer encouragement.

"I had an offer for a date with a really nice guy I'd met at the fish market. But after I learned he was a fisherman, I dropped him like bad bait off a crooked hook."

The succubus smirked. "At least *someone* asked you out." She'd applied so much foundation I wondered if the circus had come to town.

"I'm not in the mood for your negativity today, Lil," Heidi snapped.

Lilith stared at the ceiling while Heidi continued to discuss how her fear of the ocean had led to relationship issues. "I haven't seen my family in decades, and the medication isn't working. I'm wondering if I need to consult a water witch for suggestive hypnosis."

"How have the exercises gone?" Dr. Frank asked.

Heidi frowned. "Poorly. I think I need a partner for the next one."

"I don't mind helping you out," Raj said.

"Good job supporting each other. Natalya, how was your week?" Dr. Frank looked in my direction.

Where should I begin? "My life isn't going as planned." Others nodded around me. "My problems have complicated my relationship with my family." I paused, trying to collect my thoughts. It was weird for me—usually my mouth kept going on its own. "I wish I had more dates too. Not that I'd invite someone over anyway to see all the boxes I have stored there."

Raj coughed, then wiped his gloves off with a an anti-bacterial wipe. He used an off-brand that tore too easily. I should recommend a better one to him after the meeting.

Dr. Frank addressed me. "Anxiety disorders do have an effect on the family members of the sufferers. But with an open mind and dialogue, you can make progress toward resolving your issues."

I smiled and nodded at his words.

"So you're a hoarder?" Lilith asked. Before she spoke, she winked at Tyler. He quickly glanced away as I grimaced. Again that word "hoarder." People these days used it like a curse to sling mud at people like me.

"I *collect* certain things." After I said it, I realized I hadn't even convinced myself.

Between lips smeared with garishly red lipstick, she said, "If you're up to your armpits in trash, then you're a hoarder."

Nick snorted. "Like you have room to talk, Lilith. You can take your hand off my knee, by the way."

From her seat beside him, the succubus sighed and removed her hand. The she-demon desperately needed a fill-in on her manicured mess.

I finished with, "Like everyone here, I have problems I need to face."

Dr. Frank took a sip of coffee and pointed to Lilith. "You seem to have a bit of animosity today. Did you complete your exercises this week?"

"Yes, I did. And they all failed. Not a single guy wanted to go out with me."

I had to bite the soft tissue of my cheek to prevent my potty mouth from informing her of the obvious. If that woman was using magic to catch men, she was as defective as a backward doorknob.

"We talked about this. You need to adapt to your new circumstances," Dr. Frank said.

I wanted to add that perhaps she should stop trying to hunt men to drink the essence of their soul. But that wouldn't add to the cohesive, supportive environment that Dr. Frank wanted to build.

"She can't help herself." Tyler stared at the floor. "Just like I can't help it that I'll never find a dwarf woman to appreciate who I am."

Now, Tyler was an unfortunate sight. The guy could easily have been one of those underwear models plastered on huge billboards in Times Square. But somehow, the cosmic soup of genetics had created a man with the body of Brad Pitt. Who'd have thought?

Heidi laughed, her voice melodic. "Tyler, with a body like that, you need to widen your horizons."

I piped in with, "I second that motion."

For the next twenty minutes, Dr. Frank went over exercises for everyone in the circle. Knowing that some of the assignments might be difficult for some of us, he paired us up with buddies.

He told Heidi that she'd have to make another trip to the beach, even if only to feed the seagulls bread. Her partner, Tyler, had to touch base with other dwarves in a public setting. When Dr. Frank turned my way he said, "Natalya, I think I'll have you work with Nick this week."

My gaze shifted to the wizard across from me. For some reason, I focused on a single fleck of silver in his right iris. It flickered like a blinking star.

Nick blurted, "But I thought I always worked with Zac."

Dr. Frank sighed. "Zac had a setback this week."

"But he made great strides last week."

"I thought so as well, Nick. But a warlock who casts

spells every time he sneezes can get himself into a bit of trouble." Dr. Frank tapped his empty coffee cup and it vanished. "And the binding spell therapy doesn't work well during the high pollen seasons."

Nick nodded. "I'll give him a call, nonetheless, to check on him."

Among all the misfits in the room, Nick really stood out—he just didn't seem like one of us. He sat up straight and his gaze bore directly into you. If he had anxieties, they didn't show on the outside. And most of the folks in the room had quirks related to anxiety disorders. My curiosity got the best of me and he caught me staring. I glanced away, but not before he offered me a small smile.

"I'd like you two to take a weekend day to exchange an item of value with each other. You will return it to the other person at the next meeting. The key is for you to part with your personal property and then really think about whether it was necessary for your day-to-day survival."

What kind of exercise was that? Didn't matter. I was sure I could find something in my home I could pawn off on the wizard.

"Thanks. That should be it, everyone. I'll see you during your private session with me during the week. Hopefully, the next time we talk as a group everyone will have made forward progress."

Everyone stood so I did too. From across the room, I heard Dr. Frank say, "Oh, Mr. Fenton?"

Nick paused at the door. "Yes, sir?"

"Make sure Ms. Stravinsky gives you something holiday-oriented. And in a box."

As I walked out of the room, I gave Dr. Frank the evil eye. Damn, that old wizard knew me too well.

Nick waited for me outside the office. The white wizard

leaned against the hallway wall. "Do you have a phone number or e-mail address I can use to contact you?"

As I approached him, I detected a scent I'd never smelled before. It tickled my nostrils like cinnamon. "We don't really have to exchange stuff this week. We could try it next week if you like."

From the face he gave me, I knew Nick wouldn't let me wiggle past the assignment. Teaming me up with him was yet another smart decision on Dr. Frank's part.

I fished in my purse and pulled out my card from The Bends. "Here's my contact information at work. I live in Jersey."

He nodded and placed the card in his coat. "I'll be in touch this weekend." With a brief flash of light, he shimmered out of existence.

The drive out of town allowed me to drift away on a cloud. The endless towns passed by, and I used the time to think about the positive aspects of my life. I had a home and a job. Okay, this should be where I come up with a vast list and go through a *Christmas Carol* moment where I learn that things are going my way. But I couldn't.

Thoughts of a job and a home only went so far when you had a pack of killers on your heels—and the man whom you thought was the love of your life belonged to someone else.

Chapter 9

For the first time in years, I almost didn't make it to work on time.

The culprit wasn't an attack from the Long Island were-wolves or my plan to hide all my ornaments from Nick. On my way to work I passed a garage sale. And those heartless people had put all their Christmas stuff out for sale. Their loss was my gain.

Eager to initiate the hunt, I pulled over to the side of the road and joined the other early-morning shoppers.

The house was a rickety one off the side of the road, with dirty old shingles dangling off the roof, warped siding, and a porch large enough to host a Stravinsky family reunion. They lived not far off the highway and had plenty of parking spots on their run-down lawn. Of course, the condition of their home didn't deter me from stalking their goods. I gingerly walked across their muddy lawn, undeterred in my goal to reach the house.

At first I tried to walk in the street, but for the sake of not turning into roadkill I'd spotted on the side of the road, I braved the curb to reach the wares.

Part of me pleaded with myself to get back in the car to reach work on time. The urge to check my watch nagged at me like one of my little cousins. But when I spotted a whole table full of holiday cheer, a pleasant feeling swept over me. A stirring in my senses, just like when one enters a bakery full of cakes and candies. Your mouth waters in anticipation of holding a warm treat in your hand.

I felt that way when I reached the table. Eager. Excited. Elated. For a second, I was worried that an elderly lady was going to beat me there, but her destination turned out to be a rack of ugly hats. I would *never* buy a hat owned by someone else. For all you know, the previous owner might've been carrying the black plague in their mullet. Especially with hats labeled *"I got me a virgin fer Christmas!"* Right next to a dirty, holey hat that read, in large letters, *"Jersey Bred and Jersey Truckin'."*

Before I even touched anything, I assessed the cornucopia on the table. I had a limited amount of time, and there was plenty to keep me occupied. I had the eye of an antiquarian, but the restless hands of a five-year-old at a candy store. Without conscious thought I snatched a Christmas print Crock-Pot cover, two Frosty the Snowman oven mitts, and a set of broken Christmas lights. (They were labeled as "broken," but if I find the time I'll get them fixed—someday.)

The woman collecting the money grinned when she saw me coming with my hands full. She sat behind a card table with her money box ready to accept my cash.

"Is that it?" she asked.

"Oh, no." I set my items on a free spot next to her. "This is my pile. I'll be back." I glanced at my watch. Shit. I needed to move much faster.

With time running out, I ran into the same battle I always encountered. The urge to buy everything versus the fact that I had no room at home. Why did I buy broken things, assuming that I'd fix them later? Then of course I'd remind myself that I only bought stuff I could actually *fix,* like Christmas lights. And I didn't discard stuff in a haphazard pile in my house. Every new ornament got a box and a thorough cleaning. So why not add a few more?

Every new shopper who passed the table stirred my blood. Two ladies brushed by the table with one picking up a Christmas tea set. The minute she put it down—hard enough to crack the delicate porcelain—I snatched it up. I had to take the four cups' teapot and their respective saucers home before some other garage sale shopper wannabe without scruples broke them.

I hauled my final box to the checkout. The gushes of happiness overrode the nagging feeling to see how much I'd taken. And then I remembered that I was in therapy to combat this very problem.

Before I could change my mind, I placed the box on the card table with a heavy thump.

"Did you find everything you wanted?" She made me feel ashamed. A little anyway. I'd bought enough to empty my wallet.

I kept my voice even. "Yes, a few things."

She tried to move the box to go through it. It didn't budge an inch. "Wow, you're strong," she said. She came around to the other side of the table to fish out the ornaments.

I stole a glance at my watch and gasped. I had eight minutes to pack up and get to work. "Is there any way you could move faster?"

I pulled out my pocketbook. Time to wheel and deal. The woman wanted to wrap every damn dish in newspaper. "How about thirty for everything?"

Her mouth formed an "O." I'd made her a generous offer in my opinion. I tried to look indifferent, keeping a straight face so I didn't look like a shopaholic pining for my next fix.

"How about forty? That tea set is collectible."

I couldn't help smiling. "If it's so collectible, why are you selling it at a garage sale?" I didn't see a collector's label on the bottom of the saucers. I also didn't have time to go into such details.

"Thirty's fine." She shrugged. "Just clearing out a few things." She motioned to a man sitting in a lawn chair, enjoying a morning beer.

"Hon, could you help this nice lady carry her things to her car?"

For a second, I was disappointed that she didn't want to haggle. But as I helped the man carry my Christmas cheer to my car, I didn't care. I couldn't wait to clean my new ornaments. To find places for them in my home. I'd make them beautiful again. Make them shine in ways their previous owner, that woman, never had. By the time I was done, those ornaments would feel *loved*.

I reached The Bends in record time. I must've built up a few karma points, since I managed to avoid every cop on the Garden State Parkway. When I pulled into the parking space, next to other shoppers waiting to get inside, I expected the day to progress well. With several boxes of goodies in the backseat, the only thing that could bring me down today would be if Bill managed to mess up the SKU numbers in the store's catalogue system again.

I opened the door and turned to see someone leaning against my car. How Thorn managed to sneak up on me every single time was a mystery I needed to figure out.

My gaze darted to the boxes in the backseat as he strolled over to me. "You're up early."

"Night shift." His voice sounded far away. He paid no mind to the boxes filled with red and green in my car.

I tried to keep my eyes on my final destination, my work, but Thorn had approached me with his arms crossed. "How are you feeling?" he asked.

"As good as I can under the circumstances. Did you find Wendell and his girlfriend?"

"No leads. Rex said their trail went cold after they passed through Double Trouble State Park."

I figured as much. If I had to choose a tracker, Rex would've been last on my list. That asshole couldn't track a carousel horse's path. But Rex's lack of tracking skills wasn't what kept me standing here, especially with the need to get to work. I had something else lingering on my tongue.

"Why do you keep checking on me? Erica doesn't seem to approve." There, I'd said it.

"Damn it, Nat. You let me worry about Erica. What I'm doing here with you right now has nothing to do with her."

"Well, she sees me as a threat."

His eyes narrowed. "What did she say to you?"

I couldn't lie to him. He knew when I lied or withheld information. "In no uncertain terms am I to come in contact with you." I paused for a moment and ran my fingers along the wrinkles in my shirt. "Why are you checking up on me?"

"You're my friend. I refuse to give that up for her."

I wanted to ask him what other feelings brewed within him, but a seal formed over my mouth. Once he'd told me that I was his moon. At this moment, I felt like I was as far away as the Dog Star, Sirius, is from Earth.

I started to take a step toward my job, but he laughed and leaned back against the car.

"I just remembered the last time we hunted together." He offered his golden smile. "Before I left."

I laughed and moved next to him. He turned his head toward mine. The sunrise appeared behind him and cast an angelic glow around his head.

"I distinctly remember the time you led me toward the swamp."

"Hey, it's not my fault you're gullible."

"As a pack leader, it's your job not to lead your flock astray."

He pushed my shoulder affectionately. "You should follow your nose instead of the person ahead of you." His tone turned serious. "Sometimes you have to depend on your own abilities and not those of your alpha."

I nodded.

"You have a keen eye, Natalya. I still don't understand why everyone doesn't give you credit for Deirdre."

Deirdre. My mood immediately darkened. Five months before Thorn had left, one of the local girls had gone missing while her Girl Scout troop camped in the forest. The police had formed search parties, while the werewolves had organized themselves. A few rogue wolves had been roaming in the area and we were afraid they might find her first.

No one asked me to join their search party, so I'd headed out alone into the darkness. From the Girl Scout camp, I'd tracked Deirdre's position. I squeezed my eyes shut, recalling how I'd found her. How the unhinged anger and hatred had emerged from me, like a consuming fire—

I found my voice. "Yeah. Good thing I joined in the search that night."

He wrapped one arm around my shoulders and gave a squeeze for support. His hand lingered on my arm, adding heat to my skin. The pure torture quickened my pulse.

An awkward moment passed. Then our eyes locked for a moment and a hot sliver of passion passed between us. But I didn't need eyes to sense his desire. His scent changed from calm to excited within seconds. He broke the stare and took a few steps to the side. We couldn't keep doing this to each other. The invisible line that connected our bodies drew taut like a rope.

"I can't keep you out here forever. You better get inside."

I wanted to ask a thousand questions. Did he think about me after he left? Did he date anyone else while he was away?

As I walked away from him, I didn't need to turn around to know his eyes were on my back.

If not for the full moon, I never would have met Thorn.

Back at the University of Pittsburgh, I'd somehow survived my first semester as an English major. But my second one didn't seem likely to go as well.

Like every English major, I had to take English composition for my degree. It was a damn shame the professor didn't know the value of deodorant. From the grumbles of other students who'd survived his class, I suspected that he'd gone au naturel for a long time.

I waltzed into the classroom, only to march right back out. Under most circumstances I could endure the smell, but the moon stirred the wolf under my skin. My senses flared and receded with uncomfortable frequency. On any other day of the month, I would've sat in the back of the class, but on that first day, I just couldn't take it. I'd smelled worse, but geez, if you could smell that from ten paces away, would you want to hang out there?

So I marched across campus through the snow to the registrar's office and prepared to stand in a long line to get a new class.

Before online registration arrived a year later, I heard the upperclassmen refer to this line as Purgatory. The name fit. Heaven if you made it to the end, and hell if you gave up to return another day. While I waited I tried to occupy myself with a book, but my nose kept urging me to turn around. I caught the scent of a wolf behind me—a male who reminded me of home.

Two girls joined their friend ahead of us. "Oh, c'mon," the man behind me groaned.

He leaned toward me and whispered, "I bet if we growled we could scare them away." His voice resonated with me, drawing me to turn around and face him. I'd seen him many times back home, but I'd never stood this close to Thorn Grantham before.

"You look familiar," he said.

"We're from the same town."

His eyebrows lowered. "Yes, we are." The line shuffled forward. "Well, then, I'm glad I get another chance to get to know you since I missed out on the last one."

I wanted to roll my eyes, but it's hard to mock an attractive man. Even the girls ahead of us turned in our direction, hoping to catch his eye. The trio included two blondes and one who wished her dye job could get her classified as one. They tried to spark up a conversation, and even when Thorn kept focusing on me, they didn't stop trying.

"You're taking a freshman course? You don't look like any freshman I've ever seen," said the tallest one.

He offered a lazy grin. "I guess I look mature for my age."

I stifled a laugh. Male werewolves during the full moon smell like canned sex. If I hadn't had home training from my parents, I would've rubbed my face all over his chest. It was a nice chest too.

"So what are you doing after you escape from the line?" the bold fake blonde asked him. Even though she was wearing a heavy coat, one couldn't miss the healthy helping of breasts straining beneath it. Most men couldn't resist those things. I assumed my short conversation with Thorn was coming to an end.

"Natalya and I plan to head down to the coffee shop for some studying," Thorn said. "We're taking English composition together and need to scope out a better study spot."

I opened my mouth to speak, but his smirk stopped me. A blush tickled my cheeks. That tricky little devil. How did he know my name?

The woman nodded and turned back to her friends.

"How'd you know what class I need to take?" I asked.

He gestured to my backpack. "Your schedule is in the see-through pocket in the front."

I tried to hide my smile. "How observant of you."

He crossed his arms. "I could say the same about you." He had a way of saying words that turned my insides into a buttery mess. I'd known him for twenty minutes and I already wanted to hand him my take-my-virginity-please card.

We strolled through the line for a bit. I wished I had something eloquent to say. Unfortunately, all I came up with was, "We don't have to meet for coffee later." The words stumbled out and I wished I could've snatched them from the air. Especially since most normal women didn't try to retract an opening for a date. But I guess I didn't exactly qualify as "normal."

"You can't back out now. Especially since you need to tell me your plans for the full moon."

For the past few months, the full moon had just meant that I paced the rooms in my tiny apartment alone. I also never interacted with the meager number of wolves on campus. "I don't have any plans."

His golden eyes twinkled as he rested a warm palm on my shoulder.

"You do now."

It's amazing how time has changed the world around me. And yet while I worked at The Bends that morning, I felt as if I were standing still the whole time. My fingers lingered on the Haunted Heather collector's set of porcelain figurines. For the third time, I'd pushed the moaning pieces of porcelain around into different arrangements. Damn enchanted antiques. Every time I touched one, it groaned right on cue. To quell the desire to perfect their position, I mentally kicked myself and made a decision to move on to something else.

By ten a.m., The Bends' usual throng of morning shoppers had pored over the wares. I took a few minutes when we weren't busy to tidy up. I adjusted three rows of old costumes and just barely heard Quinton creep up behind me.

"We've never sold any of those," he commented.

I avoided his dark eyes. After our "date," I'd steered clear of him whenever possible. I respected him professionally, but the germ-laden dead-bodies thing made my skin crawl.

"Everything in here will have a home eventually. It's all about the right shopper at the right time."

He nodded and continued to stand behind me. *Okay, creepy janitor, I should find something for you to do.*

"Did you take Mrs. Schaefer's bureaus to the back loading dock?"

"I took care of that a while ago." I knew he'd done it, but perhaps it would encourage him to remember something else he had to do. I most certainly didn't expect him to go from piece to piece like I did, searching for dust or fingerprints to remove.

Bill came to my rescue. "Quinton, I've got the customer who bought that old chest. Been waiting a year and a half to get rid of the damn thing. Take care of it, will you?"

Quinton nodded again before he left my side. I watched him shuffle away and wished I could wash our encounter from my mind. Before Neil the zombie had made his appearance, I'd learned that there was more to the necromancer, but even I had standards, such as "no sex with men who played with dead people."

Not long afterward, I had an unexpected visitor from New York. Heidi the mermaid stopped by.

When I'd actively participated in group therapy, we'd spoken often. She bounced into the room and browsed through a few tables before she came my way. Something about her reminded me of a contained supernova. From the way she walked to the cadence of her words, she held a power I didn't understand.

Every time I saw her, I expected her to look like the legends in books. Long blonde hair, pale, translucent skin. But with bronzed skin, dark red hair, and light green eyes, this mermaid in black boots wouldn't inspire anyone's bedtime story.

I approached her with a smile. "What are you doing in my neck of the woods?"

"I had to get out of the city for a while." The freckles on her face spread as she smiled. "I brought Abby along to keep me company."

The Muse, dressed in a thick cardigan sweater and jeans, stood in the corner watching others walk past her as if she didn't exist. Someone as beautiful as she was should've gotten a glance or two.

"Not sure if we have anything you like." From the way they lingered, I sensed that they needed the company of someone who could relate. "I've got a break coming up if you want to get a treat. They have tasty smoothies at the local Dairy Queen."

She nodded. "That sounds good." No matter the season, even a mermaid couldn't turn down a brain freeze–inducing Triple Berry Delight smoothie from DQ.

In the company of others, I felt safe heading down the street. The Long Island werewolves wouldn't dare attack in daylight hours, but by this point I refused to take any chances.

As we walked along the road, Abby kept glancing around as if she expected us to be followed.

"C'mon, Abby." Heidi pushed her forward. "Nat and I have everything covered."

"A werewolf and a mermaid teaming up against the psychopath author who wants my help finishing his damn book. That's not a plot I'd offer anyone." She flipped her light brown hair back and crossed her arms. We'd get nowhere if she checked around every corner. From the way she walked, everything in her world must've projected danger.

Soon enough, we reached the local ice cream place. The older man behind the counter filled our order for three smoothies. Always friendly with a smile, Phil had served the South Toms River Township since I was a kid. "You ladies must be hungry if you need three."

"Our friend is waiting outside," I said.

"Well, bring your friend in next time. You know I love to meet new people."

Heidi took a generous gulp of her smoothie before she replied, "Sure thing. Nice place you have here."

As we sat at the tables outside the shop, I couldn't help but think about Abby's existence. My life revolved around organization and cleanliness, yet she lived in a world of not only loneliness but also fear. Fear of the very same people who served as her purpose in life—her authors.

Heidi raised her face to the sun. "So glad to be farther inland. I get the blotchies when the full moon approaches. The tides kick my ass."

"Blotchies?"

She pulled up her tank top to reveal light blue dots that resembled hives along her ribs. Most likely her body's reaction to anxiety.

I asked, "Do you run away every time the tide comes in?"

"Not all the time. Just on days when I miss home."

We sipped in silence for a bit. To me, home was my family of werewolves and my things—my ornaments. To be away from them brought up feelings I didn't want to think about. "After all these years, do you still remember your home? If I may ask?"

"It's my cradle. The largest home anyone could ever have. I'd never forget it." She pushed her drink to the side and rubbed her palms against her blue jeans. "It's also the darkest, most closed-in space I've ever been in."

"Yet you want to go back." It was Abby who spoke.

"We all have to go home eventually. Whether it's kicking and screaming or swimming with the current, it's up to us." I sensed Heidi's legs swinging under the table as she spoke. "Right now I'm prolonging the inevitable. The wave is coming, and soon I won't have any place to hide."

I could relate. The Long Island werewolves were coming for us. It was my chance to make my stand. But with every confident thought came ten doubts—doubts that I could ever be worthy of the pack. Or of Thorn.

I said, "I kind of wish going home would solve all my problems. But my home is a lonely place."

They didn't speak. Only listened.

"I thought being alone would mean I wouldn't have to hear what people had to say about me, but once in a while I wish I could trade a few of my things for a lifetime of being normal."

"Normal is overrated," said Abby. "And it doesn't produce bestsellers either."

I cracked a smile. "Kind of sad when we reach the point where humor is all we have left to keep us from drifting out to sea."

Heidi reached behind her neck. "I have something to anchor you."

"I don't need anything. I just need to keep coming to therapy. It worked before."

"Here." A gold necklace slid out of her shirt with a pink shell attached. She placed it in my palm.

"No, I can't take this." I touched the faded pink shell, still warm from the contact with her skin. Like me, she radiated heat. I traced my fingers along the ridges and found them smooth with age.

"You will. You'll insult me if you don't." Our gazes locked and I slowly nodded.

I had in my palm a part of the deep sea. A part of a creature that had perished a long time ago and that represented home for Heidi. How could she give this away so easily? I would've never given it to someone.

"Whenever you need a place to stay, you two are always welcome at my place." After I said the words, I wondered how I'd managed them. I'd allow two more people to see my home? To touch my things? Yet when I looked at them, just like when I looked at Aggie, I sensed a sisterhood of chaos. Heidi and Abby weren't strangers. They'd heard my adventures during therapy. My sanctuary should be theirs as well.

"Thanks," said Heidi.

The Muse simply smiled. "This is a nice town."

We finished our drinks and watched the squirrels scurry about along the road. A few cars passed and we cracked jokes about the human tourists.

Finally, Heidi stood and I followed her to toss our cups in the nearby trash. "It's getting late and I have to take Abby home."

I turned to look at Abby, who continued to drink at a leisurely pace. "Why can't anyone see her?" I asked Heidi.

"She's a Muse. Only the writer she inspires can see her."

I frowned. "Then why—?"

"We aren't human. She can only inspire humans."

"Guess that means werewolf authors are screwed."

She laughed, her crimson curls bouncing. "Pretty much."

We parted ways, the mermaid and the Muse waving while I put on the necklace. I waited a few minutes for the shell to bring me peace, but nothing happened. I guess it only works on mermaids.

The rest of the morning went by without incident. I was glad the time passed so easily; it let me save up my energy. At lunchtime, Aggie waited for me in a booth at Archie's. Ever since the attack, she'd offered to drive me to work and meet me for lunch. I tried not to think too hard about the fringe benefits she was getting: a free lunch, and a vehicle for field trips to the store.

I slid into the booth. "Did you bake anything today?"

She rolled her eyes and headed to the line. "That was a one-time thing, Nat. If you don't want me to touch your precious kitchen, just say so."

I followed her and whispered, "You know I didn't mean it like that. You did a great job cleaning up afterward."

She plucked a snack-sized bag of chips from her purse. "I even dusted around that ugly set of figurines you have in your china hutch."

I folded my arms, trying not to think about Aggie dusting my china. "Any calls for me today?"

"No calls." I'd noticed that she'd deleted the message from her father on the answering machine. It had even disappeared from the caller ID log.

"Does anyone ever call your house?"

I tried to suppress a laugh. "Yes. The customer-service people at the Home Shopping Network. The clerks at The Bends."

She emptied the bag. "I mean *men*. The kind who leave dirty messages on a single girl's answering machine."

We gave Jake our order and sat back down to wait. Aggie didn't have a snide comment as I cleaned the table with baby wipes. Matter of fact, my partner-in-crime even wiped off the ketchup and mustard containers.

Ten minutes later, our food arrived. After our teen server's attempt a few days ago to just toss the tray onto our table, Aggie had had stern words for her.

"Is your apron on too tight or something?" she'd said.

Misty had frozen in place and mumbled, "No, ma'am." Her eyes went to the floor and she backed away.

Since then, our service had turned from sour to stellar. We got free refills, and yesterday she'd even brought us complimentary ice cream sundaes. I could get used to having a high-ranking female around.

The shrill ring of my cell phone interrupted our meal. I didn't recognize the number except for the area code— New York City.

Damn. I didn't expect Nick to actually call. How'd he get my cell phone number? "Hey, Nat, do you have time on Friday or Saturday for our exchange?"

I wish I had a glamorous enough life to say no. And I hadn't even thought yet about giving up one of my ornaments. Did I have even one I could bear to part with for a few hours? But Dr. Frank hadn't said *hours*. He'd said *days*.

Aggie peered at me with curiosity. She'd heard the whole conversation, but hadn't understood it. All this mysterious talk about an exchange must have made it sound like I was running a werewolf drug ring.

I gave him a place and time on Friday for the exchange since I had the day off. As we ended the call, I didn't detect any stress in his voice, almost as if he didn't mind parting with his property.

"Is there something you need to tell me?" She wiped her hands off after she finished her fries.

"It's a therapy assignment. I have to exchange something of value with another person in the group." A line of sweat formed on my brow, and the food, which had tasted so good just a moment before, suddenly seemed dry.

"If you're not ready to take that step, you should call Dr. Frank."

"It's just one ornament. I can do it." No, I couldn't. They weren't gifts for friends or little trinkets I shared to bring holiday cheer.

"You could always buy one at a store and give it to him," she suggested.

I laughed. "If I have compulsive-buying issues, do you think I should buy another one? And do you think I'd willingly give it up?"

"What if you bought the ugliest piece of crap the store had? You know, one of those ornaments they stuck twenty tags on at twenty-five percent, then later at ninety percent, since no one in their right mind would put it on their tree?"

I poked at my burger with distaste. I shouldn't have talked about this while I ate. "I've hunted through every place here in town. When they see me coming, the mom-and-pop stores add extra stock to keep me satisfied."

"Wow, feeding the local junkie. Damn shame."

"I'll have you know that the Better Business Bureau sends me coupons after Thanksgiving like clockwork."

She laughed as we stood to leave. I placed a tip on the table and said, "I'm a walking economy in heels."

Aggie's eyebrows went up. "You can always say no. Walk into the stores and walk right back out."

I inhaled deeply. "That's easier said than done, Aggie."

"I know. Your aunt Olga and Grandma watch commercial after commercial with all these kinds of food. Not long after, I'm sitting there as my urges come back"— she swallowed— "and then I remember what it was like when I used to binge."

I rubbed my forehead with my hand. Aggie had come a long way. I remembered the days back in college when she used to visit me. She'd escape from NYU to spend the weekend in my apartment. "God help us, we're a couple of misfits."

She returned my smile.

"To be honest with you," I said as we walked back to The Bends, "you really need to stop going to my parents' house during the day. If you keep showing up, sooner or later you'll come home engaged to one of my distant cousins in St. Petersburg."

Chapter 10

While I worked the day away at The Bends, my best friend spent her afternoons watching Russian-dubbed Mexican soap operas with my Aunt Olga and grandmother. Either Aggie had hidden the fact that she was fluent in Spanish or someone helped translate *Los Ricos También Iloran* (it's not my thing to watch *The Rich Cry Too* for hours and hours). During that time, she'd fallen into the trap of listening to Aunt Olga's stories, most of which were about her years as a beauty pageant contestant in Russia.

Aggie picked me up at five on the dot and continued to babble about her adventures during the day. "Ignore the baked goods in the backseat. We're dropping off some of your mother's masterpieces at the local church for the Cramer family baptism."

Like a true friend, she had acknowledged my quirks by laying an old blanket over the seats. Of course, the sealed Tupperware hadn't stopped Aggie from helping herself to some sugar cookies. Between bites she managed to say, "You know the Cramers, don't you?"

"They live a few doors down from my parents."

After dropping off the food at the church, we drove home. Aggie was still chatty. "Did you know your Aunt Olga did pageants for years in Russia?"

I laughed. "Yeah." I shuddered from the memories of hours upon hours of watching those pageants on tape.

Once my aunt had even tried to convince my mother to participate. Mom has the most beautiful blonde hair. But when she had Alex and me, he got the bouncy Prell-commercial locks, while I picked up the mousy chestnut curls. But every time I complained, my mom always had something kind to say. She'd stroke my hair and say in Russian, "My daughter doesn't need blonde hair to be beautiful."

We rode back to my house in silence. I tried to concentrate on the road and not think about tomorrow's exchange. How I wished I could talk to Thorn. Even with all the dirt, another run in the woods with him would feel like heaven about now.

Especially when I saw Clive and Derek waiting by my house. *Oh, shit.*

Their black Oldsmobile was parked in my long driveway, blocking the entrance to my garage. Derek sneered when he saw me approach. The memory of his words crept into my brain. "Inferior stock," he'd said.

When I braked, Aggie bared her teeth and whispered, "Stay in the car, Nat."

Did she seriously want to get out? I had no qualms about staying inside. "You plan to take them on by yourself? Are you nuts?"

"They'll just keep tracking you. That's what these kinds of people do. They weed out the weak before they all-out attack."

I glanced at the men and saw Derek taking a deep drag of his short cigarette. A trail of smoke arced across the yard as he tossed the butt onto my front lawn. The bastard.

"We're in a car. I can take us out of here." The car jostled and we looked back to see two other wolves sitting on our hood. Damn it all to hell. My head turned in her direction. "Okay, so you against four. You still want to head out there to play hero?"

"They'll kill you." She pulled out her cell phone to call for help, but then the door yanked open. One of the werewolves snatched the phone from her and threw it toward the far end of the yard. With wide eyes, I watched him wrench her from the car. But Aggie wasn't one to take punishment for long without retaliating. My door opened as she unleashed a snarl and threw her attacker into the side of the car.

Rough hands grabbed me while Aggie tussled with her fair-haired attacker. Her feisty spirit thrust my fear away. With claws unleashed, I swiped at Clive, and then at a shorter man with black hair. From the look in their eyes, they hadn't expected me to come at them snapping and swinging. I drew blood from the raven-haired man before Clive pounced on me. My back hit the ground, and my teeth rattled. I'd been holding my breath, but the fall knocked it from my chest.

Hearing the growls and barks Aggie made, I knew she'd completed her transformation and was scrambling with her prey—perhaps her attacker or Derek. My heart thundered in my chest as Clive used his crushing body weight to hold me down. In human form, the odds weren't in my favor. He barked to his cohort, "Reggie, go check on Derek!"

A familiar soft yelp from the other side of the car told me the worst had happened. I cried out Aggie's name as Clive's hands grasped my neck and squeezed. I pounded and clawed, but I couldn't break his iron grip. Dark spots danced in my vision. The sounds of the forest disappeared and reappeared. I tried to focus on Clive's face and aim my sharp talons, but my strength had withered away with the wind.

"Derek told me I couldn't keep you." His grip slipped for a moment as he examined my face. "Would be a waste to kill a sweet bitch like you." His claws bit into the soft skin of my neck, causing me to whimper. He leaned forward and pressed the rough stubble on his face against my cheek. "I can smell your sex."

Suddenly, Clive's body was lifted from mine. Something rammed his side. Hard. The man sputtered as his body was hurled upward and then landed with a sickening crunch. I coughed and rolled onto my stomach while the howls of Thorn's pack filled the clearing around my home.

Where had they come from? Who'd called them?

Disoriented, I drew the night air into my lungs. Not far away, I spotted Thorn with his tawny coat. He tore into Clive and violently shook him. The other wolves of the pack sprinted after Derek and the other two, who'd made a hasty retreat.

I tried to stand by pulling myself up on my car's open door, but my legs wobbled. Strong hands grabbed me under the shoulders and lifted me. Thorn turned me around and examined my face. Naked against the cold autumn breeze, he held me close.

"I should have moved faster," he breathed against my neck.

I tried to speak, but I could only make hoarse noises like a wounded pup. Exasperated, I murmured, "Aggie?"

He stroked the back of my head and whispered, "Will is checking on her. She put up a great fight." With ease, he picked me up and carried me toward the house.

I tried to turn my head to look in the direction of Aggie's whimpering, but my bruised neck protested.

"Don't move. She'll live," he said.

For a brief moment, I thought about the locked front door, but Thorn just kicked it in. At first I wanted to panic about him discovering my secret, but exhaustion and pain won—tonight anyway.

He ascended my stairs two at a time. Not once did he

glance at my boxes; he merely darted around them. I waited for his words as we passed through my house, but none came. Once we reached my room, he placed me on my bed. "I didn't expect them to come for you again. Why do they care so much about you?"

As he stood above me, I tried to ignore his nakedness, but in the darkness of my bedroom I couldn't resist staring. My ass had been kicked up and down my lawn, but no hot-blooded werewolf could possibly close her eyes to a sight like Thorn Grantham. His long legs were lean at the ankles, but as my eyes roamed up to his thighs, I saw where the thick yet sleek muscles clenched. Then I looked farther up, to the place I'd seen so many times in the past. The memories of the first night when Thorn had claimed me with his body caused an involuntary shiver that cascaded from my lips to the tips of my toes.

"This isn't the time or the place." He took half a step back. "No matter how receptive you are." He'd seen my roaming eye and now he could detect the hunger that lay beneath the pain. I didn't sense Erica's scent on him. They hadn't consummated their relationship yet. Did he want to wait? Was he holding out for some reason?

I averted my gaze from his well-chiseled abs to the blond trail of hair leading to his obvious arousal. With the wolf so close to his skin after being wakened by the attack, Thorn was holding on to his self-control by a thread.

He drew in a deep breath before he whispered, "I can't protect you right now. Not when you smell like this."

So that was why Clive had rubbed his nasty nose all over my face. I'd come into heat. I sighed. This whole situation shouldn't surprise me. Normal werewolves went into heat every month—just like our human counterparts. But ever since I'd gone off the drugs a few years ago, my cycle had been as crazy as my psychological problems. I stifled a laugh. Half a pill had lowered my anxiety and fixed my cycle. It had also thrown me into the path of every horny werewolf in the township. Great.

Before I could reply, he swooped in next to me and brushed his lips against mine. The feather-like touch made my stomach flip as he spoke. "I trust only one person to keep an eye on you. Albeit reluctantly, I know he'll follow my orders." He clenched his fists and put some distance between us. "And not touch you."

Slowly, he sat on the bed beside me and then remained still. His entire body tightened like the strings on a violin. Straining. Yearning. He shifted his body to capture my eyes with his own. His palm caressed my cheek. His touch gave me both pleasure and pain.

"I need to find out why they've made you high on their target list." He backed away to the door. So slowly I could count each step before he went into the night.

I woke up late, a sloppy mess of pain, only to hear Aggie giggling in the kitchen. I blinked and grimaced. Even blinking hurt. The tantalizing scent of French toast, bacon, and eggs drifted to my nose. A male voice spoke shortly afterward. The guard.

Will must have stayed behind to watch over the house. Right about now, I assumed that Aggie was sitting in the kitchen with him, wooing him with her culinary skills. I tried to rise, but my entire body protested. My neck ached to no end, and I had painful spots all over my torso.

Werewolves heal quickly, but such abilities have their limits. I have better vision, hearing, and strength, but just like humans I can be hurt badly. If I'd been human, Clive would've broken my neck.

Speaking of Clive, had Thorn killed him? I tried to recall last night's events, but the pain drove the memories away. I had to get up. I couldn't let those idiots downstairs cook a meal and leave my kitchen in ruins.

With herculean effort, I managed to reach the bathroom to clean up. The woman in the mirror stuck her tongue out. Much easier to play the part of a disgruntled werewolf than a frightened and battered woman.

But wasn't that who was staring back at me? I examined my eyes. I'd been attacked again. And why, I didn't know. I did remember, after the attack, my blissful time with Thorn.

He didn't have answers. I didn't have any either. Who could possibly care about the local cashier of a flea market? It wasn't as if I had the key to some secret government facility.

Somehow I managed to clean myself up and creep down the stairs. With each step, I knew a perfectly good workday was swirling down the drain.

From below, I heard Agatha and Will's banter.

"You wouldn't believe the crazy times we had," Aggie said.

"From the way you put it, you two made quite a pair."

"Yeah, she saved my ass a few times. I won't tell you about the time I was arrested six years ago."

"You do come off as the bad-girl type," he chided.

I shook my head with a smile. Will had to be, what— nineteen or twenty? I knew Aggie, at twenty-four, wasn't snatching pups from the local pet store window, but the guy didn't have much in terms of prospects. Aside from his winning personality, Will still had some growing up to do.

When I entered the kitchen, Aggie flashed me a smile. "I thought I heard you thundering down the steps. I can fetch crutches if you like."

I offered her a middle finger.

She snorted. "See how grateful she is? Even though I made breakfast *and* cleaned up afterward."

I checked the counter, and sure enough, it remained pristine. All those nights of watching me clean as if I planned to perform open-heart surgery in my kitchen had finally sunk in.

"There's a warm plate in the oven for you. I'm sure you caught a whiff of breakfast." She stepped up to me and examined my neck. "You need to head back to bed, Nat."

"I'll be fine." I brushed past her and opened the fridge to grab some juice.

"I'm not a doctor, but I know we had our asses smeared into the pavement last night."

It was only then that I noticed Aggie favoring her right side. They'd hurt her badly as well.

My eyes closed as a wave of pain hit me. Aggie opened my palm and placed a pill in it. "You didn't take any pain meds, did you?"

A few more steps and I could take my drink and food to the table. I reached toward the cabinet and winced. The bruise under my breast was from a solid hit. Maybe I'd even cracked a rib. Swell. "I took some aspirin."

She snorted. "That's enough for the pain associated with a pinprick. Take the horse pill."

While I backed away from Aggie, Will came to my rescue, fetching a glass from the cabinet for me. From behind him, Aggie leaned into his backside. She pushed two cups back in line from where he'd moved them. She winked at me, then escorted me to the table.

There's nothing like a comfortable chair when you feel horrible. I released a long breath and closed my eyes to block the pain. "How come you're moving around?" I downed my pill and the acidic aftertaste burned my throat. She'd given me the good stuff.

From across the table, Aggie murmured, "I've fought before. Many, many times." An awkward pause. "But that's a story for another day."

Apparently, both of us had memories from the last five years that we wanted to bury.

Will coughed. "I didn't want to wake you, so I've been waiting here to brief you on the current situation."

Aggie interrupted him with a stern face. "She's in no shape to worry about the Long Island werewolves right now."

"I'm afraid it's urgent. If she wants to reenter the pack, she should be aware of pack business." He turned to me with darkened eyes. "The attack last night was done for a reason we don't know. But now that you know you're a target, you need to be careful. You're no longer allowed to travel alone at night. With Aggie here, you'll do fine. Thorn or I will stop by from time to time at night to check the property."

The medicine coursed through my body. With a sour smile, I took a generous bite of French toast. The delicious food slid down my throat, but his words echoed in my soul. I was still a target—and they'd come for me again. "Maybe I need to leave town. I don't want to put anyone at risk by having them stay here."

Aggie huffed. "You have family here and, no matter what anyone says, I believe blood is thicker than the pack. So don't feed me a piece of your bullshit pie. I'm already full of it."

From the wry look on her face, she knew my words were empty. I'd never leave my ornaments behind. My head drooped as I concentrated on my breakfast.

Aggie continued her diatribe. "You'll stay here and continue with your life. Of course, you'll have to be more vigilant with those crazy bastards roaming around. My father told me about packs like this one. They attack in waves, but eventually if you hold them off they give up in favor of easier prey."

The shrill ring of the phone interrupted Aggie. Will found the kitchen handset and gave it to me.

"Natalya, it's Nick. Would it be a problem if we met at Archie's right now for the exchange?"

I rolled my eyes. The only direction I could go right now was up. My mind flashed to my appearance in the mirror. I looked like I'd survived a beating. How could I possibly explain this? A mugging? Eh, I didn't see a place like South Tom's River passing itself off as the mugging capital of New Jersey.

I heard burgers sizzling in the background. It was so tantalizing I couldn't help but wonder how I could pull off the exchange stress-free—and get a burger out of it.

"Nick, last night I had a break-in. This isn't the best time to visit. And anyway, I thought you wanted to meet tomorrow."

He ignored my last comment. "Are you all right? Did they catch the guy?"

"More or less. Could we do the exchange another day? I'm a mess right now."

"Would you mind if I stopped by to check on you?"

I swallowed. Either the guy was persistently kind or he didn't believe my story. "I promise I'll do the exchange. I can even put my roommate on the phone to corroborate my story."

A long pause. The sounds of Archie's faded. Damn, he'd left the restaurant. "Natalya, I've worked with Zac for months. He couldn't con me, and you can't either. When I knock on your door, you'll do the exchange."

I gripped the phone and Aggie leaned forward with concern. "Can't you tell him this isn't the best day to drop off Girl Scout cookies?"

I nodded faintly. My mouth went dry as he ended with, "I know where you live. No need to give me an address." He hung up, leaving me in a state of panic.

Aggie saw my face. "Will and I will handle him. Who does he think he is anyway?"

"He didn't believe me," I mumbled.

"What's going on?" Will asked.

Aggie turned to him and explained that I attended

group therapy—therapy that included a pushy wizard who'd been ordered to exchange an item of value with me.

"So what's the big deal?" He gestured to a stack of boxes. "Give him an ornament and call it a day."

Icy shock gripped my stomach, and my mouth dropped open. Aggie stepped in quickly. "She went through major stress last night. I think you should tell this guy to come back another day."

A loud knock on the front door nearly stopped my heart. How did Nick reach my place so quickly?

I just couldn't give away one of my ornaments. Not right now. All the strength I'd had just a few days ago was gone. Aggie held my hand while Will answered the door.

A few seconds later, Nick's voice floated from the foyer into the kitchen. "Is Natalya home?"

"This isn't a good time. We had some problems here last night." It didn't take keen werewolf senses to detect Will's distaste.

"Is she safe?"

"She has friends here to watch over her."

"I want to see her."

"Don't push me, Wizard. You're in my territory now."

"Be that as it may, I will see her to verify her safety."

I stood and stalked into the foyer before a fight ensued. "Enough, you two."

When I'd first met Nick, he'd smelled sweet, like cinnamon, and he'd had a rough edge that made me curious to know the mystery behind his black irises. But now, frowning, his eyebrows lowered, he gave off an overwhelming scent of burnt cinnamon that made my eyes water. He'd held back before, but not now. Now this wizard stank of power.

"Calm down, Nick. As you can see, I'm fine."

The odor faded with the next breeze that passed through

the doorway. Will moved aside as Nick approached me with wide eyes.

"So it's true. What happened to you?" Dressed in his black trench coat, he resembled a 'forties gangster without the tommy gun.

"Like I said on the phone, I had some problems."

He glanced at the stacks of boxes in the foyer and grinned. "So this is what you wanted to protect from me, huh?"

Aggie entered the foyer. "And you can come back tomorrow to pick up the ornament. She's in no shape to do the exchange today."

Nick assessed me with his black eyes. I couldn't resist falling into them. They twinkled for a moment, and a wave of warmth cascaded through the small space. A dose of delicious magic like Dr. Frank's, but much stronger. A white-wizard spell of some kind. The warmth from his magic caressed me, from my forehead down to my toes, like a gentle lover's hands.

"Holy shit!" Aggie released a sharp breath. "Did you do that?"

Even Will sensed it. He took a step back and gulped.

"You should feel a bit better now." Nick reached into his pocket. He paused as if deep in thought.

"Nick?" I asked.

Reluctantly, he pulled a long-stemmed rose from his pocket. He rubbed his fingers against the thorns and stem. The sweet scent from its petals hypnotized me, and my blurred eyes followed the rose as if it were a beacon.

From far away I heard him blurt, "Sorry about that." When my vision cleared, I blinked. He was stroking the petals, completing some kind of spell.

Will growled deep in his throat, and anger boiled to the surface of his skin. I didn't blame him—this wizard clearly had powers we didn't understand. At times like these I understood why my mother was suspicious of spellcasters.

Nick turned to Will, unafraid. "Don't worry, I mean you no harm."

With two werewolves ready to pounce on him, this wizard was still keeping his cool—he had balls the size of snow globes.

"This is my offering for the exchange." For the first time, through his nonchalant visage, I saw a sliver of his anxiety. He didn't want to give me the rose, but he'd come all this way and was determined to make good on his word.

I peeked at the nearest box, the dilemma of the moment gripping me. This exercise should be simple. I'd open a box and hand him one of the ugly ornaments. (Hey, even they needed love.) Perhaps I'd give him a big bulky lawn ornament with enough beeps and annoying lights to drive Christmas carolers away.

A line of sweat formed on his brow. He continued to hold out the rose while his heart beat rapidly. How long would he hold out?

"Natalya, take the rose," he whispered.

The first footstep toward the stack lasted a lifetime. One step. And then another with more confidence. I opened the box on top. A wave of nausea hit. I couldn't do this. These were my friends. Damn it! I lowered my hand into the box and pulled out the first thing I found. I couldn't look—I simply handed the ornament over.

The rose stem tingled in my hand after I took it. Even though I gripped it tightly, the thorns didn't bite into my palm. I snuck a peek at the flower while Nick handled my ornament. How could he give something so powerful and beautiful away?

Somehow, Nick placed the ornament in his pocket. I tried to think, *Out of sight, out of mind.* But the whole experience left me exhausted. I slouched forward and tried to resist the siren call of my bed.

"I'll see you next week at Dr. Frank's." He turned around and touched the doorknob. "Plant it at the perimeter of your property. Sprinkle it with frankincense, and the flower will protect you from those who mean you harm." And with that, he left.

Chapter 11

I slept for the rest of the day. I had to recuperate before I could cope with everything that was happening. The next day I'd have to go to work no matter what, since I'd taken today as a sick day. Bill didn't care whether I walked in limping—he wanted goods sold. So there was no way, with his money-grubbing habits, that he'd just give me a couple of sick days. I could hear him now, "I thought you werewolves healed quickly. You've had a few hours. Just walk it off."

After that, I'd open myself to an all-day lecture on how it used to be in the Dark Ages. "Back in the day, you took a spear up your butt and you moved on. I could have half a leg torn off and I'd still show up to work. Do the same, Natalya, and you'll go far." I wondered how many college students would find inspiration in such words during a commencement speech.

It was also true, though, that even if Bill wanted to play the patron saint of employers and let me take tomorrow off, I'd still find a way to sneak in to organize things.

The next morning, I crept out of the house so I could avoid Aggie's complaining about me heading into work. On my way out, I noticed a rose among the bushes along the edge of my property. While I'd slept, Aggie had planted it. The vibrant red flower stood starkly against the deep green of the bushes. The beautiful bud was a persistent reminder of the exchange with Nick.

Unexpectedly, the workday wore on without any problems. Aggie called to berate me for leaving her at the house alone. But I reminded her that she was the so-called guard who'd slept through her charge's departure.

"I'll see you at lunchtime," she'd grumbled over the phone.

How she'd get to town I didn't know. But since Aggie didn't mind taking cabs, I knew that, come hell or full moons, she'd find a way to show up promptly at 11:50 a.m.

And indeed, by lunchtime, Aggie was waiting for me at Archie's with a frown. A tourist had taken my usual booth. For years I'd picked the one that was farthest away from the busy door and had the cleanest tabletop. I took a nearby seat so I could stare him down. From the way I glared at the man in the booth, Aggie knew I was about to make a fuss.

She plopped down into the seat across from me. "Do you really want me to kick an elderly man out of your spot?"

"He has two bites left. At the rate he's eating those sliders, the Long Island werewolves will have kicked my ass long before he's done."

I couldn't contain myself any longer. I stood up, thinking that if I brooded beside him and asserted my ownership over the booth, he'd flee. I was tired of being the most submissive werewolf around. I had to one-up someone, even if it was just a human.

"Don't do it!" Aggie just missed grabbing my purse to drag me back.

I strolled over and parked myself next to the tourist, an elderly man in a bright green visor. He smelled just like every other tourist, but he'd smell even better at one of the tables on the other side of the place. Okay, time to try being nice. "Hi, I work at one of the local companies here and I just wanted to thank you for your patronage."

The man's head bobbed but not enough to indicate that I had his attention.

"And, as a local, I enjoy eating here. I bet you're enjoying it, too."

Still he ignored me as he chewed his meal with his oversized dentures. I was close enough to discern the scent of his Dentu-Creme from the heavy layer of Old Spice.

"OK, let me cut to the chase," I snapped. "This is my table. Are you almost done yet?"

"Nope. Piss off."

Instead of reaching for the panic button, I took a deep breath and returned to Aggie. She was grinning. "I'm proud of you."

"Whatever for?" I put my elbows on the table and rested my face in my hands.

"I thought for a second there that you'd tackle that guy and get arrested for assault."

I shrugged and laughed. "My parents told me to try to respect my elders. Key word 'try.'"

Even though I didn't get my preferred table, I'd definitely maintained my dignity and managed to subdue the raging urge to follow my routine.

She chuckled while we took our places in line. "Can you pay for my food? I used the last of my cash to get a ride into town an hour ago."

"Why so early? Standing guard outside The Bends?"

"Naw, I went job hunting." She sighed, eyeing the fries on another table. "But this place doesn't have much in terms of white-collar work right now."

"You're too good for retail?"

"If I had to work at McDonald's or something, I'd do it."

Jake took our order and I paid. "They do have managerial positions at those kinds of places." Once we returned to our table, I said, "Mrs. Hawkins from the flower shop down the street said something about Barney's hiring people."

"The pickle place? No thanks."

I laughed at her. "You too good to serve *long* green pickles to people?"

Misty arrived with our food—and served it with a smile, no less. Good girl.

Aggie tore into her sandwich. "Yes, I'm too good to stand behind a counter and place pickles on plates like they're eight-inch dildos."

"Well, they're hiring and you need a job." I glanced at my bare wrist to examine my imaginary clock. For some reason I'd forgotten my watch today. "I have a few minutes before I return to work. I think I'll go fill out an essay or two at Barney's on my past experience as a rich Manhattan socialite."

When I came home from my Saturday shift, I found Aggie sitting in the living room wearing a nice blouse and dress pants. Of course, she had a snack in her hands.

"You look—nice."

"Thanks to your glowing application and recommendation, I was called in this morning for an interview."

I plopped down on the couch and wrestled her bag of Doritos away. "That fast?"

Aggie flipped back a thick strand of her hair. "Apparently, I work well with others and have an aptitude for teamwork. Where did you pull that shit from?"

"I can be imaginative when necessary."

"Oh, yes, it's from your new book, *The Guide to Being a Smart-Ass*. We should use your old New York connections to get it published."

I tried to imagine what my coworkers in New York would think if they saw me now. Not all my memories of them were pleasant. Back in the day, one of them had grumbled about me from another room, "I should invite her to the Christmas party, but she's way too creepy. I heard from somebody that she's at work *all* the time—and that she wears the same clothes every day."

At times, werewolf hearing royally sucks.

Chapter 12

With the Long Island werewolves on the prowl and all those kids hunting for candy, Halloween didn't have the same exciting vibe as usual. At least I knew someone planned to visit my house for something other than slitting my throat. I tried to harness some positive thinking while I sat in the nest with the rest of the cuckoo birds in Dr. Frank's office. I wasn't doing too well.

I had a few more days until the full moon. The tides roused the wolf's hunger in my blood. The animal under my skin writhed and eagerly awaited a chance to spring forth. I hoped Heidi was managing the changing of the tides better than me.

The beautiful rose, wrapped in parchment paper, rested in a bag over my shoulder. As I was getting ready to leave the house, I found myself wishing Thorn would stop by. We hadn't spoken to each other in a while, and I wished I was bold enough to just call him. With resolve, I closed my bag instead of picking up the phone.

Aggie offered to escort me into the city, but I declined. "The last thing I need is for you to witness the freak show I attend."

"I'm sure they're just regular people who have— problems. Hell, I can't talk with the way I eat every fifteen minutes."

I glanced at her clothes. She'd borrowed one of my dressy shirts and pulled her hair into a professional bun. Agatha McClure appeared . . . responsible. "And don't you have to report in to work or something?"

"I can call to tell them I'll be late."

I headed into the kitchen to fetch my keys. "You'd be more than late. I have to drive into Manhattan and stay there for the afternoon. This isn't a casual day trip."

"As your friend, I'm not comfortable with you being out alone. We were attacked, and I expect my father to find me sooner or later, which means even more trouble—"

Someone knocked on the door. Aggie paused and raised her nose in the air. "I didn't hear them approach."

"Neither did I." My claws itched to come out, but I got a knife from the block in the kitchen instead. My reindeer blade wasn't exactly menacing, but I hoped it might frighten them anyway.

Aggie peeked through the keyhole and groaned. "It's the wizard from last week."

Nick? What the hell was he doing here?

Aggie headed back into the kitchen and I opened the door.

The wizard, dressed in his usual black ensemble, stood outside with a smile.

"Is something wrong?" I asked. "I have your rose if you want it now."

He raised his hands. "Oh, it's not that. If I remember right, you said you'd had some werewolf trouble, so I thought I'd make sure you reached the city safely."

How did he know I was leaving now? My eyebrows rose. "Did Aggie or Dr. Frank call you about a ride?"

Aggie's voice floated in my direction from the kitchen. "I didn't say a thing."

"Look, I don't need help today. Head on back to the

city and I'll see you in a few hours." I checked behind him, but I didn't see a car. "How did you get here?"

He grinned and folded his arms. "I have my own transportation. Are you sure you don't want a free ride into the city? I'm even willing to offer you lunch. I'm assuming you'd have to stop and eat."

"I don't know." What did he mean by "transportation"? That materialize/dematerialize thingy he'd performed back at Dr. Frank's office seemed all sparkly and flashy, but I'd seen *Star Trek* movies. Some people didn't make it back when Scotty beamed them home from the monster-laden planet.

He opened his black trench coat. From one of the pockets he pulled out my ornament. "I didn't want to use this little guy as an incentive." He examined the round green ornament with plastic rhinestones around the middle. The sunlight reflected facets of forest green on the walls. "You could have this back in your hands much sooner."

I took a step forward, transfixed. "Or you could give it back to me now." I reached for it, but he put it back inside his coat.

My heartbeat quickened and I couldn't suppress a growl. "You shouldn't tempt a wolf by dangling a bone. Especially a shiny one."

He laughed. "Well, if you went with me, we could accidentally stop by a few stores. And I won't tell Dr. Frank if you won't."

By the time Nick said, "I won't tell Dr Frank," I'd grabbed my jacket and bolted out the door.

"I have a ride, Aggie."

Before I slammed the door shut, I heard Aggie yell, "You better come back empty—" With my hearing, I caught every word she said, but perhaps she meant something else.

We walked across the porch to the front lawn, where I asked how we'd reach the city.

"We need to walk over to the field across the street from your place."

"I thought wizards waved a stick or something and then they magically teleported places."

He chuckled. "I can do short distances, but those are restricted to teleporting myself. Since you're my guest, I'll have to use a jump point."

Now, as a werewolf, I shouldn't allow magic and its associated intricacies to surprise me. I mean, on every full moon I sprouted fur and hunted wild rabbits. "What's a jump point?"

We began to walk across the lawn. The brown, red, and orange leaves crunched underneath our feet.

"In the past, the world was covered in forests, which were full of magical places and towns. As time passed, larger towns and cities were built over those magical spots. Man built buildings and paved roads, but the magical points remained. Whether it was a great wizard or a fairy who charmed those places is unknown."

I nodded to encourage him to continue. He had a charming look in his eyes when he explained things.

"Wizards like me can use these magical places as 'jump points' to teleport between locations. Some of us have staffs and wands to increase our natural spellcasting ability, but the quality ones are hard to come by."

"Expensive too. We stock that kind of stuff at the flea market. I know we've got something rare when the witches turn into crazy vultures."

We reached the road and walked across. With the lack of traffic, we didn't need to watch out for cars, but a thicket of trees slowed our progress toward the field in the distance.

"How do you work at The Bends without feeding your habit?" he asked.

I opened my mouth and snapped it shut. I'd never been

asked that question before. "I don't know. I guess I'm too busy doing my job. In the beginning when I started working there it was really hard."

He parted some branches for me to cut through. "Yeah, I work at a pawnshop in East Village. I'm not really helping my hoarding either."

"I'm not a hoarder."

He paused before he turned back to reveal half a smile. "Ah, yes, you're a collector."

"Hoarders have filthy homes with a bunch of garbage. My home is clean."

"We're almost there. So that's your definition of a hoarder, then? Dirty people?"

"No, they're not all dirty people." I paused for a moment. The *collector* in me wanted to deny that I should be labeled a hoarder. If I was a hoarder, then I had to be like all those people I'd heard about on TV or in the paper. I'd never be *that* kind of woman, who's discovered by the police lying under a heap of her own stuff.

"We're almost there." He dropped the subject, but a part of me felt ashamed. I knew he had an anxiety disorder. He hadn't told me or the therapy group what kind it was, at least not while I was there. So far he'd treated me with respect and kindness. (Even after taking my ornament away.)

Beyond the thicket of trees a mile of plowed farmland loomed. The remnants of cornfields lay in the rich soil.

"Are we close?" I asked.

"The jump point's over a rock near the edge of the field." He directed me to a five-foot limestone rock that jutted from the ground. My nose couldn't detect anything magical or otherwise amiss.

"So this is your magical rock, huh?"

"Well, you obviously can't feel it, but this entire field is charmed. Perfect farming grounds. The farmer even

used this land, even though there's this troublesome
rock in the middle of a plowed row." He took one of my
hands with his dry, yet warm fingers. Then with his
other hand he reached for the rock and touched it.

A strange humming vibrated in my jaw and slithered
down to my toes. The sensation left me with an uncomfortable chill that raised the hairs on the back of my neck.
I yanked my hand away and mumbled, "That's weird."

He nodded. "This stone's imbued with magic. It's most
likely that whoever placed it here masked its scent to
keep curious supernaturals like your kind away. I would
too if I created a teleportation point here." He took my
hand again and whispered words in an unfamiliar language. The vibrations began again and spread through-
out my body. Just when I thought I'd wrench my hand
away and pull his arm from its socket, my body jerked
and then somehow I *shifted* into another place, almost
like walking down a path and failing to see a cliff in the
distance. Well, I plunged right off that cliff.

The brightness of the day vanished and turned into
darkness. I blinked twice as my eyes adjusted. Within
the folds of the shadows, Nick stood beside me. A strong
stench of decay cascaded over my nose in waves. My
face scrunched up. All this dampness, mildew, and ver-
min made me squirm. Where the hell had he taken me?

I turned to him and paused in surprise. In the dark,
his skin looked different, almost ethereal with a slight
glow. When I calmed enough to take a step forward, he
walked toward an arched doorway on the other side of
the room.

"We're in an office building basement in Brooklyn. All
we need to do now is head upstairs to leave."

"So you're saying we're in New York? Right now?"

"That's what jump points do. They teleport people to
different destinations."

I couldn't resist smiling. How neat.

Nick reached into his coat and pulled out something that appeared to be a marble. Without much light I couldn't discern its exact shape. But after a few seconds the marble quivered and bright light enveloped the room. I squeezed my eyes shut from the glare.

"Hey, could you be careful with your flashlight there?"

He chuckled. "Sorry about that. This basement has cockroaches and all sorts of nasty things."

My nose had told me the place wasn't clean, but after he'd turned on the light, I wished he'd turn it back off. Every corner of the basement was filled with boxes—covered in mold.

I covered my mouth and tried not to retch. "I thought I smelled mold, but I didn't know it was this bad. Oh, my goodness, it's everywhere—"

We weaved around the maze of boxes until we reached the end of the storage room.

"Couldn't they . . . move the jump spot?"

"For my sake, I wish they could. But this building belongs to a warlock who doesn't appreciate others casting spells in his domain. He's been kind enough to allow me access."

I huffed. "So you're saying someone willingly lives like this?" I reached into my purse and pulled out a baby wipe to use on my hands. They weren't dirty, but I still felt soiled. I offered one to Nick and he gratefully used it.

"When you see where we are, you'll feel better." Eventually we emerged into a lobby, a rather clean one, at an office. I watched as men and women emerged from the *Greenpoint Gazette* building to head out for an early lunch along Nassau Avenue.

We walked out into the street and I gazed at the buildings. How I missed New York. I immediately recognized the location—the Greenpoint community of Brooklyn.

So many scents, both welcoming and repulsive, but a cornucopia of richness for me to absorb. I noticed many places we could have lunch, whether we wanted American or Polish food. Archie's was great, but even I knew a little variety never hurt.

"From the look on your face, you're hungry. We could eat before we head to Dr. Frank's."

"I'd love to."

We strolled for ten minutes. Eventually, Nick pointed out a pizza place, but I declined.

"But they're owned by werewolves. I've had their pizzas before and they're not too bad. I thought you'd feel comfortable there."

"Yeah, but just because they're clean doesn't mean they can make pizza. Werewolves make the worst pizza."

He shrugged. "Your choice. But unfortunately the rest of the places nearby aren't clean to . . . our standards."

I hadn't expected my escort to cater to my needs. From the look in Nick's eyes, the werewolf pizzeria would offer a sane place for us to eat.

"Lead the way. We have time to eat and do a bit of shopping. I want to be on time."

After we entered the place, I knew I'd come back again. It was pristine and well organized. A hostess in a black dress greeted us at the door. "Ready to eat? Booth or table?" She wasn't a werewolf, but she smelled of magic. Perhaps she was the daughter of a supernatural and a human.

"A booth, please," I said. I hated tables and sat at them only if I had no choice. Tables offered points of vulnerability.

With only the workers who were having lunch early roaming about, we had no trouble finding a perfect booth.

As we sat down I said, "This has to be a dream." The jade-green seats were comfortable and wonderfully clean.

"Yeah, I eat here often. The owner is . . . like us. He's pretty strict about cleanliness. I think he's won awards from the Department of Heath for the cleanest kitchen."

I ran my finger over the table and just about purred. Perfect. Just the way I like it.

"He told me a few weeks ago that he'd had some Department of Health trainees come through to see how he runs his business."

A waitress appeared to bring water and take our orders. While I perused the menu, Nick struck up a conversation. "So you lived in New York before?"

"I lived here a little over four years ago." My voice trailed away as I scanned the listings. Nick had entered dangerous territory.

He paused for a moment and folded his arms across his chest. "And? Most people live in the city for a reason. You moved back to New Jersey to work at a flea market?"

"People leave the city all the time. I had a job that didn't work out for me."

"In what way? I'd have thought you'd crack working in a city like this."

My grip on the menu tightened. "Over the past few years, things in my life have changed in many ways. Some of them haven't been good."

He took a sip of his water. "And that's why you're seeing Dr. Frank."

I nodded. "Yet again. I guess I finally want to get my life back on track."

"I fell off the track and I've been off it for years." He cocked a grin. "Perhaps too long to climb back on."

His positive nature was infectious. "So you're going to work at a pawnshop for the rest of your life?"

"I wish I could. Dr. Frank tried to take me on as an apprentice but that would require a few years of medical school."

"I think you'd be a great therapist. That calming spell is divine."

He chuckled. "Sometimes we wizards get a thrill from the exchange too—if it's with the right person."

I tried to hide my smile as we sat for a bit. Was he implying that he got as much from using his magic to calm me as I did?

To end the silence I asked, "So, are you a goth wizard or something?"

"Goth? Whatever made you think that?"

I pointed to his death-march clothes.

"Oh, I guess I would give that impression. No, I prefer to wear black. If there were any dark stains it would be harder to see them, and my whole wardrobe looks the same, so there's less stress."

Every once in a while, Nick stole a glance at my face. The whole encounter didn't bother me at first—I'd had men check me out before. But it was unnerving the way he stared at the contours of my face as if he found me interesting. His heart rate hadn't changed, nor did his scent indicate that he was aroused. Thorn never examined me like this. He would've undressed me with his eyes by this point. Suddenly, I couldn't stop my cheeks from reddening. Was Nick using glamour to hide certain things from me? To me, the world is a place of smells indicating the state of everything, including whether someone was sick, aroused, or angry. A scent revealed everyone's true nature, but somehow the man in front of me showed me one thing but told my nose something else.

Not a bad trick if it was true, especially if it meant that someone wanted to reach out to me. I wouldn't mind hooking back up with Thorn, but he wasn't free. And with all the burdens I had to bear, a little calming magic on demand wouldn't hurt.

The continuous line of customers distracted me from my thoughts, in particular the shape-shifter couple that entered the restaurant and sat across from us. They nodded briefly in Nick's direction and ordered from the waiter.

We watched the other customers until our food arrived. Now, most folks might think that werewolves growl and snarl when they consume their meals. But, well, as someone with an obsessive disorder, I eat like I'm dissecting my meal in a biology lab.

I ate my pizza with a fork and knife to keep my hands from getting greasy. If I'd ordered the lasagna, I would've cut every piece for the perfect fit in my mouth. At Archie's I'd gotten eating a burger and fries down to an exact science of cleanliness.

Across the table, Nick did the same. A wide grin spread across my face. He smiled too and added a wink. For once, I didn't feel self-conscious about my actions. *Great minds think alike.*

The therapy group went well—the first three minutes anyway. Besides Nick and me, the gang from before was there: Abby, Raj, Tyler, Heidi, and Lilith. Dr. Frank used the first three minutes of the session to prepare us for the arrival of our newest member.

"Now I want you all to take a moment to feel calm and prepare yourself for a new member." As in the last session, Dr. Frank worked his white-wizard magic to woo us into a serene state.

I wished the man bottled the stuff so I could hoard it.

"I wanted to wait until everyone was present and seated before I introduced you to Starfire Whimsong."

Oh, this had to be good. A few people here would need more therapy just to get over the stress caused by parents who couldn't just name their kids Will or Betty.

Mr. Whimsong, as I shall call him henceforth, came in after Dr. Frank left the room to fetch him.

The appearance of our newest member elicited a laugh from Lilith; she covered it with a hand. Apparently, even the desperate had standards. Mr. Whimsong was dressed in a Hawaiian shirt and jean shorts. Never mind that the weather outside was cold enough for a jacket. With his cheeks rosy from the outdoors, a bright smile, and a long mane of blond hair, Mr. Whimsong resembled a husky Norseman. From where I sat, I immediately noticed his hands, or should I say, the lack of hygiene they exhibited. A layer of black dirt was caked under his uneven nails. Accompanying him into the room was the scent of forest magic—on top of his deodorant-free "natural smell." Heidi scrunched her face. Hell, even the mermaid knew he stank.

He nodded to everyone and went around the circle trying to shake everyone's hand. Not the smartest choice with this group.

"Hey, thanks for letting me come by." He held out his hand to Tyler and the dwarf shook it with an uneasy smile. Heidi and Abby didn't have cleanliness issues, so they shook his hand and mumbled their names.

Then Mr. Whimsong came to poor Raj. Our visitor reached for the Indian deity's hand, but Raj's didn't move. "Nice to meet you," Raj mumbled with a nod. His gloved hands gripped the box of antibacterial wipes I'd recommended. From the look on his face, he appeared to have high hopes of not needing it.

Mr. Whimsong chuckled. "Oh, that's all right, man. Some folks like their personal space in this universe."

I could've avoided the handshake like Raj, but I wanted to be cordial like my grandmother had taught me. I briefly shook Mr. Whimsong's hand before he took the empty seat between Dr. Frank and Raj. Thank goodness I had some hand sanitizer.

Watching me apply a generous amount of Purell to my hands, Nick gestured for me to toss the bottle. I pretended I didn't understand.

Dr. Frank said, "Starfire is here with us today to begin group therapy. I appreciate you taking the time to welcome him." He turned to Mr. Whimsong. "Feel free to tell the group whatever you like. We have a supportive atmosphere here."

From across the group's circle, Nick gestured again with a growing frown. I mouthed the word, "What?"

Our little exchange didn't prevent Mr. Whimsong from telling us his harrowing story. "I'm glad to be here with all this positive energy. I mean, man, this city is practically overwhelming, with the pollution and chemicals. But then I come in here and all I see is positive people trying to help each other."

The mermaid sighed in agreement. From across the room, Nick flicked his fingers and the antibacterial bottle flew out of my hands.

"I thought the east coast would be a good place to work—whoa, flying stuff there." He chuckled again and then continued. "You wouldn't believe how hard it is to be a nymph with all those companies poisoning the environment. All these dying kids without food, the melting icebergs—all of this has gotten to me, and I'm kinda having trouble coping."

We all fell silent and nodded in sympathy. Even supernaturals deserved to live free from their anxieties. My problems seemed trivial in comparison; poor Mr. Whimsong had the weight of every melted iceberg on his mind. (Should I be a good girl and not mention the growing global warming problem?)

"Have you taken any steps to lower your anxiety?" Heidi asked.

"I spent some time in India to find my center and refocus. But it didn't work." His head swiveled to Raj. "Awesome country you got there, brother."

Raj rolled his eyes and suppressed a laugh.

But Nick couldn't hold his laughter in. He covered his outburst with a cough as Lilith chimed in, "I agree that finding your center doesn't work. Have you tried to let it go and tell yourself that shit happens?"

All of us turned to Lilith with wide eyes. I guess she didn't see Mr. Whimsong as a potential date.

Dr. Frank said, "What we'd like you to do today is talk through your problems, and then talk about the solutions you can find to face them."

Mr. Whimsong lowered his head. Now his long blond hair covered his rosy cheeks. "I face these problems every day, man. I head out there and try to bring down those greedy corporations."

"I think he meant facing your problem via non-protest-related activities," Lilith said.

Nick leaned back in his seat. "Could you shut up for ten minutes?"

"Now, now, Nick. Lilith, are you having a rough day today?" Dr. Frank asked.

She grinned and revealed a line of toothpaste on her teeth. "Actually, no. I have a date for tomorrow night."

"God help him," I mumbled.

After that, each of us discussed our exercises and offered support—real support that let us laugh and even allowed Abby to cry. It's amazing how baring your soul to a small group of people can make such a difference.

After the session, I declined to talk further with the new representative for SETA (Supernaturals for the Ethical Treatment of Animals) so Nick could escort me home. According to Dr. Frank earlier, we'd successfully completed our exercise and were now ready for our next one.

"I think you're both ready for another exercise. But I need you to be on your best behavior this week," Dr.

Frank said. He eyed us both with suspicion. Did he know about the Statue of Liberty commemorative ornament hidden within the folds of my purse?

"You guys need to head over to a pawnshop in Brooklyn this week or the next. Nick needs to face the prospect of returning an item, and Nat, you need to resist your urge to acquire new things. I think this will be a low-stress exercise, since you aren't being asked to remove anything from your home."

I bit my lip. *Sounds easy enough.* And it wasn't as if the pawnshops in Brooklyn even stocked halfway-decent ornaments. (Should I tell Dr. Frank that I'd already scoped out most of the establishments on a biyearly basis? Nope, I thought not.)

Dr. Frank gushed with approval. "Great work this week, Natalya. I'm proud of your forward progress. Nick told me how cooperative you were when he wanted a piece of your property."

Then it would be wise not to tell him that I wanted to bite Nick's hand off when he refused to return the ornament.

As we headed back to the building in Greenpoint, a feeling of dread came over me. "Do we have to go into that room again? With the bad smell?"

"Unfortunately, we do. That's the jump point that takes me directly to your home. There are other jump points to Jersey, but we'd have to hike for a while, and I don't think you'd want to do it in those shoes." For some reason, I had a feeling Nick took pleasure in my pain. I knew he didn't like the jump point, but he tolerated it much better than I did. From the way he vigorously used the baby wipes and alcohol I had in my purse, he hated germs about as much as I did. So he either used his magic to hide his fear, or he'd somehow conquered his anxiety over filth. Perhaps it was a guy thing.

As we entered the building, he asked, "What do you think Dr. Frank will ask you to do next?"

"I'm sure it'll be something even worse than giving up an ornament. I suspect that I'll have to buy something and return it, or else I'll have to give you an entire box."

He opened the door to the basement. "Are you ready to do that?"

Fear bit into me. So far, I felt like I'd made progress in recovering. But my voice shook a bit. "I think I've improved a bit. I've done things this month that I wouldn't have done on my own."

Our footsteps echoed on the rough, dirty metal stairs.

"I'm glad one of us has improved," he said after a brief laugh. "By the way, you can keep my rose."

He reached for the doorknob and I stopped him. In the receding darkness, I saw his eyes. Apparently, he wanted to do the right thing. He hid his anxiety behind a wall, and I couldn't smell it. Fear has a scent similar to body odor. Depending on the person, it either excites me or fills me with anxiety. In this case, I didn't know how to react.

"You don't have to do that. I have friends around."

He opened the door. "With the rose on your property, you'll be protected. I can stand my torment if it means you'll be sleeping safe and sound."

From the way his stern voice echoed through the room, I knew he meant for me to let it rest. Apparently even wizards felt a need to swing their magical staffs around and exert some kind of machismo.

I covered my nose with one hand—as if it helped. The room's smell bordered on putrid. "I think it smells worse now."

Nick placed his hand on my stomach and pushed me back. "Someone else is using the gate." His voice lowered to a whisper. "Back up."

"I don't smell anyone."

He pushed harder. "If you could smell it, you'd be dead."

His fingertips on my body tingled, as if he was preparing to do something. I searched the darkness for movement. But all I could discern were shadows along the walls. Then a slight movement at the end of the room startled the wolf within me, but it was only a mouse.

We were slowly stepping backward when I felt the hair on the back of my neck rise. A growl tickled the back of my throat, but I clamped down on my panic. This wasn't the time to fight. Nick had some serious powers, but if he was running, it had to be bad.

"Shit!" he muttered.

"'Shit' what?"

He stopped me ten feet from the door. "They've surrounded us."

"They? You haven't told me what we've run into. How about a clue so I can defend myself?"

Something slithered toward us and knocked me in the mouth. I stumbled backward but Nick caught me before I hit the floor. I touched the side of my mouth and tasted blood. From every corner of the room we heard grunts and hisses. Something inside me snapped and I growled. No one hits a werewolf without consequences.

"Not now, Natalya."

My body shook as the urge to change gripped me.

"Clamp it down. This is not the place. I can't control both you and them."

He placed a hand on my heart. The cool sensation flooded my senses again. Wave after wave of calming energy brushed against my cheek and caressed my torso. Meanwhile, he used his other hand to reach into his trench coat and pull out a long black staff. He flicked it and the room burst into flames. Swirls of orange, red, and yellow danced around the room torching the boxes and anything that hid around them. So bright, yet so deadly. I closed my eyes when the light became too much to bear.

As soon as the fire disappeared, the room fell into the silence of a tomb. I tried to back away from the smoldering boxes around us, but Nick grabbed my hand and pulled me toward the gate.

Smoke filled my lungs, yet Nick managed to stumble toward the jump point and activate it. He coughed, then leaned over me. Within seconds, our bodies were whisked away from the burning basement into the field near my home.

With a wet plop, we landed in mud next to the rock. Rain fell on our soot-covered clothing. I touched the sore spot on my face and then reached for Nick. He lay facedown and didn't move. How had a trip to New York for therapy turned into an attack?

"Nick?" Faintly, I heard his heart beating. I turned him over and watched for the rise and fall of his chest. Slow yet steady. The man sure knew how to scare the crap out of people.

I never thought I'd have to actually *carry* a man home, but with a mighty heave, I picked Nick up and hauled him across the field. If he'd been a suitor, my mother would've been proud to know I'd finally snagged a man.

When I reached my front yard, I found Aggie watching from the porch with worry in her eyes. "I tried to call your cell phone but you didn't answer."

She sniffed the air, and then she noticed the bundle on my shoulder.

"What the hell happened?"

"I got attacked by something and Nick rescued us."

"If he rescued you, then why the hell are you carrying him?"

Once inside, I laid Nick on the couch—though not until

after Aggie had thrown down a blanket. (She had proved a quick study in how much I hated filth.) "I wonder if he's hurt, or if casting the spell just drained him after he rescued me."

Even with me safe and sound back at the house, Aggie continued to appear worried.

"Did something happen while I was gone?"

"It's Alex. He's disappeared."

Chapter 13

It was clear that either a gang of nymphs had kicked my brother's ass or something had gone down with the werewolves. I put my money on the latter.

"Your mother called and said your brother hasn't been answering his cell phone. So they checked on him at his apartment, and that's when they discovered that he's missing."

I used a clean towel to dry my hair before I glanced at Nick again. His pulse was much stronger and I could sense that he'd awaken soon.

"How long ago did they call? Did it look like a were-wolf attack?"

"Your mom didn't say. She sounded distraught. I was scared you'd fallen into the same mix when you didn't answer your phone."

This wasn't good. Perhaps the Long Island werewolves had switched targets.

"We need to go." I grabbed my purse and phone. The darn thing was dead so I left it on the charger.

"What about the wizard?"

I gazed at Nick for a moment. A lock of his black hair had fallen over his forehead. Perhaps he shouldn't play hero so often. "We can leave him a note. He's a grown man. He can figure out how to open the door and leave by himself."

I was rather disappointed in myself. Why hadn't I re-membered to charge my phone? For someone as anal as I was, a dead battery was uncanny. Perhaps everything that had happened over the past few days had distracted me so much I was coming undone.

Fifteen minutes later, we reached my parents' home. When we walked in, I was reminded that, when things weren't going well for my family—not counting me, apparently—the Stravinskys banded together for their brethren. Grandma and my mother sat on the sofa, wait-ing in silence. Aunt Vera brought out several cups of hot tea.

"Mom, what happened?"

No one moved, as if I'd asked the worst question possible.

"Sasha's missing." My mother whispered the words and lowered her head.

"Are we going to look for him?"

Mom managed to nod. "He should've stopped by to take your grandma to the store, but he didn't."

All I could do was stand there hoping my mother's words weren't true. Maybe he'd show up any minute now and knock on the door. My parents would chastise him for a few hours, and then everything would be as it was before.

But I couldn't completely reassure myself. Perhaps my brother had fallen into some woman's bed, but some-how I doubted it. Alex would never forget an obligation to our grandmother. After all, the wrath of his aunts would be never-ending. They'd bark, "Shame on you, Sasha! You left your poor sad grandma waiting for you on the curb." Of course, they'd embellish their remarks with every guilt-inducing statement they could muster. Alex had made mistakes in the past, and I expected him to make many more in the years to come, but he always put family first. That was why the unanswered calls and empty apartment raised the alarm.

Minutes turned into an hour. Finally, all the Stravinskys filled the house, the women preparing meals for the search party. Grandma had finished her tea. To occupy herself she murmured prayers every few minutes.

Meanwhile, the men huddled together trying to form a plan. First, we'd sweep the township. I had another idea, though. "Have you tried Karey?" I asked Mom.

"Yes. She hasn't answered either." My mother ran her fingers through stray curls that had escaped her ponytail. She always seemed composed, but this afternoon, after she'd taken a few shots of bourbon to calm her nerves, the calm Russian woman I once knew had vanished. In her place sat a mother with worry etched into her face.

"I can't believe he got caught up with a nymph. For all we know, she's enchanted him and they're frolicking in the woods while we worry about him."

"Oh, Mom. Alex would never do that."

My mother snorted. "I find that hard to believe after a pregnant nymph showed up at our door."

I shook my head, but I let her rant. Better for her to assume that he was with Karey than captured by the Long Island werewolves.

"While you were in college in Pittsburgh, he had so many girlfriends I lost count. Though actually, your aunt Vera did start counting all the girls he cavorted with." From across the room Aunt Vera nodded. "While you managed to stay with one man, he couldn't wait to sample every flavor in the fruit basket, if you know what I mean."

"Did those two witches ever find out about each other?" my aunt asked.

"Those poor girls never had a clue."

I suppressed a chuckle. Those girls had likely met each other, all right. Both in the same bed, with my brother.

Mom shook her head. "I'm not sure how it happened, but my homebody husband and I gave birth to a ladies' man."

She continued to unravel. "If those dirty wolves have touched my boy—"

Aunt Vera brought my mother another cup of hot herbal tea. She murmured in Russian, "Don't worry about him, Anna. I'm sure this is all a misunderstanding."

The phone rang and Dad rushed to answer it. We all stopped and waited with expectant faces.

But then he frowned. "This isn't the time, Yuri. No, I won't put your grandmother on the phone."

Mom and Aunt Vera groaned at the same time. If I hadn't found my cousin's timing slightly amusing, I would've done the same. After a few curse words, and a threat to have his mother take away his car privileges, the conversation ended.

A few minutes later, the phone rang again. This time Dad checked the caller ID and quickly picked up. But the hope in his brown eyes faded as he turned to us and briefly shook his head. "No, Stan. Thanks for checking out those places for us."

He turned to my uncles, rubbing the small balding spot on the crown of his head. "Looks like the time to go out and hunt for Alex has come."

I stood and followed the men outside. No one questioned my decision to join them. All this time Aggie had remained at my side, quiet and solemn. Once outside, everyone divided into teams. Aggie joined Aunt Vera to head west. Dad pushed Mom in my direction. "Look after your mother, Natalya. Search the lake and the surrounding property." My mother headed for my car, but my father tugged on my arm to speak to me privately.

"You won't find anything there. Just keep her busy. She's starting to think the worst."

I had the same fears, but I buried them under resolve. It was no time to release the wolf straining to act on my mother's words. I wanted to hunt. To track and find him.

When I reached the car, I found my mother in the driver's seat. "Are you sure you want to drive? You've had a few drinks."

"Be quiet and get in the car."

I shrugged and got in. Dad had wanted me to distract my mom from the hunt, but I suspected that those distractions shouldn't include getting pulled over by the cops.

We drove northbound for a while, heading toward Highway 9, which would take us to the lake, but instead of taking the entrance we continued through town.

"Mom?"

"I know what I'm doing, Natalya."

"Are you sure? We're supposed to go to the lake."

She ignored me, so we just sat there for a while as she drove. I tried to figure out where we were headed, but I didn't have any friends on the north side of town. Then, after a certain point, South Toms River Township turned into Toms River. Where the hell did she plan to take us?

Mom twisted and turned through a subdivision, and then pulled up in front of a three-story brick condo building.

I leaned closer to the window. "Who lives here?"

"You'll find out soon enough."

Did my mother know something about the kidnapping that my father didn't? "Is Alex being held here?"

She pulled into the parking lot. "I have my suspicions."

Of all the ideas my mother had ever hatched, this wasn't the smartest. We shouldn't be here. Not alone anyway. But before I had a chance to stop her from leaving the car, she jumped out and made a beeline for the building. I slowly followed her, pausing to catch the scent of other werewolves. Only one scent lingered in the air like a faint whisper.

My brother had been here. Matter of fact, he'd marked the bushes outside the apartment. In werewolf form.

"I smell Alex."

Mom nodded, but she didn't speak. She simply walked inside the building. No glancing around. Almost as if we were visiting an acquaintance.

A cramp hit my gut. "I don't like walking into unknown territory."

As we passed the mailboxes, I noted one in particular: Karey Nottingham. So the nymph lived here. We marched up the stairs, only to have a nymph meet us on the way.

With a pixie haircut and freckles covering her nose, she looked us over warily. Her light blonde eyelashes fluttered as she said, "Karey isn't here."

I stared the girl down, searching my memory. There was something about her. Unlike Karey, this one's scent reminded me of springtime after a rainstorm. But it wasn't her smell that triggered the memory. It was her face. This was Karey's getaway driver from my parents' house.

"Are you friends with her?" I asked.

"I'm her roommate."

"Where is she?" asked my mother. Her voice was even.

"She said something about needing to find Alex." The nymph's lips formed a sneer. "You're his family, aren't you?"

Somehow my mother warped space and time to make herself three inches taller. "Yes, we are. Have you seen my son?"

The nymph's confidence receded. "No, I haven't." She swallowed two times. "But Karey should be back soon."

Mom nodded. Her eyes darkened. She didn't trust the nymph. "I would hope so."

With the conversation concluded, my mother backed down the steps, then twisted to walk away. Mom never presented her back to an enemy. All these suspicious occurrences set me closer to panic overload. I hissed on the way out, "What's going on?"

Mom continued through the parking lot and darted to a lone Toyota Camry. She circled the vehicle with me trailing after. My nose told me that magic covered the car from the bumper to the driver's seat. Forest magic from the wood nymphs.

I peeked into the backseat—and just about passed out from the car's contents. These wood nymphs were preparing for *something*. But their preparations didn't include a car seat and other baby stuff for Karey's impending birth. Oh, no. These nutcase nymphs had littered the backseat with rope, pink duct tape, towels, and rubber bands. I clutched the hood of the car, ready to rip the door open. Who the hell carries around this shit? Mom said things in Russian that even I refused to repeat.

Had my father been mistaken about who'd taken Alex? Had the nymphs kidnapped my brother? We reached the trunk and eyed each other before I touched the lock. Part of me didn't want to open it, but I had to know. Even if his scent didn't linger here, we had to explore all the options. Would that crowbar-wielding nymph be crazy enough to kill my brother in cold blood?

My panic rose and my blood boiled. I broke the trunk's lock and wrenched it open. And then I gasped.

No one lay trapped inside.

But the nymphs had left more supplies for their planned heist inside the trunk. Five more rolls of pink duct tape. (What store sold that much pink duct tape?) I rifled around and found three pairs of scissors, a packet of magic markers, shaving cream, a razor, and pink nail polish. Oh, my God.

My mother's mouth moved but nothing came out.

I was just as speechless. In the back I also found some makeup, a platinum-blonde wig, and a disposable camera. To top it off, there was also a bag of cheap cat food. Like a sorority of deranged woodland creatures, they had likely planned to kidnap him, hold him somewhere, and then dress him up Marilyn Monroe–style with cat food in a bowl as a backdrop.

Mom touched the multipack of pink duct tape. "I don't think they have him."

I wrinkled my nose at the disgusting cat food and slammed the trunk shut. "I agree."

"We need to go home. If I stay here any longer, I'll do something I'll regret."

Formerly the epitome of the suburban mother who cooked for local church groups and the PTA, Mom's yellowed eyes and twitching fingers now indicated that she hungered for blood. But she seemed conflicted too. If Karey was truly carrying Alex's baby, Mom would never harm her, even if she'd planned to capture my brother and humiliate him.

I drove back to my parents' house with the radio turned low. Over and over in my mind, I kept picturing how the nymphs would have run him down. The woods around his apartment's parking lot had plenty of hiding places. Trees with leaves beginning to turn color. Their scents would blend into their surroundings. They'd giggle in the shadows with smirks, ready to pounce. The whole thing seemed like a B-grade horror movie with zombies and papier-mâché swamp creatures swooping in to attack. By the time we pulled up to the house, I didn't want to continue imagining my brother's embarrassment at having the Knocked-up Patrol take him down.

During the short time that we'd been gone, my father had returned. I tried not to get excited at seeing his car in the driveway. Why had he returned so early? Had the search for the Long Island werewolves taken a turn for the worse?

We found Dad inside sitting on the couch—alone.

Mom asked, "Fyodor, have they found my boy? Where is everyone?"

"*Nyet*. Nothing at all." He perched on the edge of his seat, staring at the phone. "But I did get a call from that girl Karey. She's coming here in a few minutes."

Mom left the room. When she gets stressed out, she either has a generous serving of her friend Jack Daniel's, or she found solace in her kitchen. From the sounds of slamming cupboards and banging pans, I guessed she planned to use culinary therapy to keep herself from attacking wood nymphs in the night.

"What will you say to her? Will we hold her here?" I asked.

"Your father wouldn't do such a thing," said my mother from the kitchen. "He may have battled the Bolsheviks in the thirties, but he wouldn't hurt a harmless pregnant woman."

"Harmless? Based on the contents of the nymphmobile, Mom, I don't think Karey's as harmless as she seems." *Should I call Supernatural Family Services now or later?* I wondered.

The knock on the door came right on cue. I could smell the nymph from my spot on the love seat. But a new scent accompanied her. It belonged to a man who towered over her, his gaze scanning the room.

Thorn had arrived.

Karey waddled into the house, her forehead wrinkled with worry. She sat down on the La-Z-Boy while Thorn took a spot next to me on the love seat. He swallowed the space and glanced at me twice, but I refused to meet his eyes. I didn't want him to see me like this. To see me teetering on the edge of a panic attack. They had my brother and they wanted me. For some reason, other than extermination, they wanted to kill me. But why? I kept asking myself the same question over and over again: *Why did they want to kill me now, after all this time?*

"I heard from my roommate Lydia that you'd come looking for me." She clasped her hands over her belly. Though her eyes remained focused on my father, everyone else's went right to the shiny rock on her finger.

Her ring finger. *Alex, you responsible little devil.*

She continued with, "Thorn told me I needed to come here to tell you what I know. Especially since I meant Alex no harm."

I snorted. Kind of hard to believe that, with her trunk's contents. My father shot me a warning glare.

"Alex proposed to me this morning." She twisted the ring as her voice lowered. "He told me that he'd call me after he took his grandmother to the store. He never did."

After what I'd seen I wanted to be upset with her, but now it was rather hard. Alex had proposed. Somehow—maybe with bleach and heavy scrubbing—I might be able to wipe away the nagging fears that she'd hurt him.

"I have more news," she managed, "from the fairy folk."

News from the fairies? The most I heard from a fairy's mouth was from Bill's every day. As a goblin, he sure as hell wasn't a true fairy, but a backwoods cousin, as he called it. He'd blurt tidbits once in a while—that he spotted brownies, or hob goblins, poking holes in people's tires in the parking lot or about the irate fairy manager down at the Cracker Barrel. Just like Bill, they roamed the countryside around unsuspecting humans. Pretty much any kind of news I learned was never good.

"The fairy folk have been speaking in whispers about the outsider wolves lurking among the trees."

"The Long Island werewolves," I said.

"Yes—" She licked her lips and gripped her belly as if labor pains plagued her already. But in her eyes I detected the pain of loss. "The crazy dark elf who works at the 7-Eleven told me they've taken Alex. They plan to kill him unless you give up Natalya and surrender the South Toms River territory."

Chapter 14

Nothing in life can prepare you for a vicious hit from reality like this one. That painful swelling in the chest when everything goes wrong. The feeling, like a burden of a thousand bricks stacked one on top of the other. All I could do was endure. Hope my body could fight the desire to claw at my throat for air.

I gripped the side of the love seat and leaned forward. I could deny the facts again and again all I wanted. But they'd taken my brother. And now they wanted me in his place. Nothing in the universe could set things right. Nothing except for the death of every Long Island werewolf who dared hurt my brother.

Thorn touched my shoulder. Somehow his words bled into my thoughts.

"I've spoken to our pack leader about the matter." He paused. I refused to look into his eyes. "And he has made his decree. One life should be sacrificed for the good of the many."

"No!" I stood up, fists clenched. "Don't give me that bullshit, Thorn."

My father boiled, but he didn't move. His furies were always contained. Anger that I've never seen unleashed. His mouth formed a thin, twitching line.

The kitchen had gone quiet. Without a sound, my mother entered the room and approached Thorn. The blank look on her face made the hairs on the back of my neck stand up.

"I wish Farley would come here and say those words to my face," said my father, his voice even.

Thorn took a deep breath before he spoke. "Fyodor, Alex is pack. He's my friend."

"Then why didn't you tell Farley we need to find him?" I asked.

"I did speak for him."

"Yeah, right. Old Farley doesn't care about anyone but himself."

Thorn's voice rose. "He is still pack leader and my father."

I walked away from him to sit next to my father. Why sit next to Thorn if he didn't care about me? "Some leader."

My father broke in with, "Be that as it may, my family doesn't need the pack to go hunting for my son." He stood with a straight back. "We will search for him and bring him home."

Thorn ran his fingers through his hair. "I can't let you go out there alone."

"You just told us my brother is expendable—"

"Damn it, Nat. Have I ever listened to my father? Time and time again, he's ordered me to do things I didn't want to do. But this time all he ordered me to do was relay the message. That's done. Now it's time to get the bastards who took Alex."

I swallowed, trying to ease the rising constriction in my chest. This whole situation left me weakened and bitter. "How long until we leave?" I managed.

Thorn's face resembled stone. "You're not coming with us. Not this time. You're in no condition to take this on."

Somehow I laughed. "You think I plan to sit here? This isn't pack business anymore. This is my—" Suddenly, I couldn't find the breath to speak. My throat went dry and only a moan escaped. Thorn took a step forward with his hand extended to touch me, but I shrank back.

"This isn't open for negotiation. If you think you're coming, you're mistaken."

I attempted to stand my ground. "You. Can't. Stop. Me."

"I know you. And that's why I'm giving you a direct order. Sit down on that couch and don't move." He advanced a step. His eyes glowed with warning. A warning that shoved me into the seat.

As I watched Thorn follow my father out of the house, I tried to think what I could do to make this all better. But nothing came. Only the overwhelming stress of my brother's kidnapping and pending execution. I ran my fingers over the fabric of the love seat. A flood of memories collided with my pain. The past always came back to haunt people. This particular room held devastating memories. I knew that most of all.

The three months after Thorn left me resembled a white dwarf star collapsing into a supernova. The raw wounds from my broken heart seemed fresh and all-consuming.

I distinctly remembered the day when I left New York and moved back in with my parents. As I sat in the living room with Grandma, she tried to cheer me up with a gift. Inside a beautiful brown box lay my first ornament: a papier-mâché farmer boy holding a Christmas wreath. On his beautifully painted face, he had a bright smile that held promises of the future.

"My child," she said, "hold on to him. He represents love. My beloved Pyotr fixed him for me after your aunt Olga tried to break him in half."

The spring air turned into the heat of the summer. I remained in the house helping Aunt Olga take care of my grandmother. With the pocket money Grandma gave me, I bought more ornaments. That was how it began.

Hours and hours of watching TV with soap addicts had been my downfall. In between the reruns of *Ryan's Hope,* which I translated for my grandmother, we watched the Home Shopping Network or QVC to look at the clothes. At first, I found these channels boring and mundane.

But then again, in my depressed state, I found everything tedious. But even as I was lost within my boredom, I didn't want to escape into the haze of my medications. I didn't want all those side effects the wolf hated. Who in their right mind would want to have fits or experience strange random patches of fur?

And after all, what was there to be anxious about, when I already had a broken heart?

My parents didn't notice the growing pile of treasures in my closet. I held them close, like a secret stash of drug money. The tiny box of Precious Moments from the Precious Percy collection. A deal at $10.99 apiece. (Well, at my current budget, it was a deal.) Right beside it I hid an envelope of antique-like Christmas cards and a tiny dove ornament made in Waterford crystal.

Back then, Grandma was my constant companion. At least until my father announced that particular July day that I would accompany the family out to the forest.

"Get washed up and get dressed." My father crossed his arms and waited by my doorway. "We're heading out as a family to Hope Park."

"But how can we go out? We don't have any food to bring," I said.

We never went to a gathering of werewolves without my mother cooking some large beast of burden.

"We'll pick up something," he grumbled before he left my room.

"Pick up something?" I peered out of my room, wondering at the sacrilege we were about to commit. My mother *always* cooked.

As it turned out, my mother still managed to prepare

a chilled dish. She scraped together an instant cheese-cake topped with fresh jam, with time to spare. It wasn't the big meat dish she would have preferred to bring. But from the way young pups approached her, I knew they smelled a winner—especially compared to old Mrs. Halverstein's pea soup.

An hour and a half later, the whole family reached the park to find all the werewolves gathered together for fellowship and food.

I sat at a picnic table, next to Grandma. Of course, I searched the scene to see if Thorn would come, but as far as I could tell, he wasn't there—I saw only Will and Old Farley. The Holdens, minus Erica, brooded at their table next to the Granthams.

Werewolves are all about hierarchy, even at a picnic. The closer a family's table was to the Granthams', the higher their place within the pack.

The lowest families surrounded the more important ones under the gazebo roof. Luckily for my grandmother, my family had a comfortable spot in the shade.

From the way my father shook hands and chatted with the others, I wondered what was up. Compared to the grumbling leader of the pack, he seemed jovial.

And I didn't expect my father to approach Farley Grantham halfway into the meal. My heartbeat quickened when my father glanced back in my direction and smiled. What the hell was he doing?

I clenched my fists and couldn't suppress the chill that ran down my spine. It spread across my chest and constricted my breathing.

"Natalya." My father gestured for me to come to him.

I didn't move so my grandmother nudged me. "Listen to your papa, Natalya."

With unsteady feet, I stood and walked over to my father. I had to force every step forward. The scraping of my shoes against the cement thundered against the back of my skull.

I joined my father, who now stood next to Rex. Thorn's childhood friend grinned at me as his eyes roamed over my form.

Good God, no way.

"As you can see, Farley, my daughter would make a fine mate for Rex." My father placed his hand on my shoulder and paused when he detected my rapid heartbeat. His eyes narrowed and the side of his mouth twitched.

My lips parted as my hands began to shake.

I'd recently lost Thorn and now they wanted to pass me along to Rex as if I were some bowling ball that could be traded among teams?

Farley examined me as well. His brows lowered while he sat back against the lawn chair. Not good.

I wanted to vomit. I wanted to purge my body of the contents of my stomach as well as the fear and angst from my loss. And now my family was prepared to toss me away in hopes that marriage with Rex would heal me.

"Nat?" Rex leaned toward me with a frown.

I took a step back. "No! Don't touch me! Stay away from me!" I hissed.

"What's wrong with you, girl?" Farley snapped.

Light-headed and ready to hurl the cheesecake my mother had made, I continued to step backward until I fell on the kids' table. I collapsed on their plates of food, knocking everything to the ground. My mouth refused to blurt apologies. I had to flee. And anyone in my way, including my mother, would be pushed aside.

"Stop it, Nat! Calm down." My father tried to placate me. To hold my arms as I flailed and jerked. The whole moment felt surreal, as if I stood to the side and watched another person fall over the edge and plunge into darkness.

When I woke up at home on the couch, our home was full of tension. I expected to find my grandmother close to me, but only my father and mother waited. Each of them sat in chairs and peered at me. From the trail of her mascara, I knew my mother had shed tears. Whether it was from the embarrassment of what had happened or from the personal pain she felt over my full-blown panic attack, I didn't know.

I sat up with my chin touching my chest. After one glance I couldn't look at them anymore. The wave of disappointment from my father doused me like ice water.

"I honestly thought when you came home that your brief bout of loneliness was due to Thorn leaving. A beautiful girl like my daughter would pick herself up. I mean, she had a job in New York, a career." He sighed. "All those events from your childhood, I thought you'd gone past that."

But I hadn't. My coping skills had failed, and the husk that was left was a broken woman who didn't want a new man.

"Farley called me after we brought you home. He told me you're no longer welcome in the pack."

Even though I sat on the couch, the floor left my feet. The delicate string that attached me to the other wolves in the pack had been severed. Not only had I lost Thorn, but I'd lost my pack as well. I'd lost the special bond that tied me to the men, women, and children of South Toms River. Thanks to Farley, any respect I had as an adult had been wiped away overnight. I was no better than a rogue.

The next morning everything changed. Upset over the shame I'd brought on my family, my father didn't speak to me or acknowledge my presence. My mother followed my father's lead, albeit with slight reluctance. The only two people who treated me the same were my grandmother and Alex. Now that I think about these events, I completely understand why I left. How it happened that, a year after that fateful summer, I had my cottage and a position at The Bends. With my ornaments around me and a job helping Bill organize his place, I'd found a crutch.

A crutch that had held me up, however precariously, until Thorn had returned to South Toms River.

Chapter 15

Alpha males like Thorn could order me around all they wanted. Face-to-face anyway. But as a rogue werewolf, I had a distinct advantage that I could exploit. I didn't have to follow the pack—unless I wanted to. No words could prevent me from leaving the house twenty minutes later. No one could stop me from jumping into my car and driving south via the Garden State Parkway.

My father had taught my brother and me tracking skills. Fyodor Stravinsky might've lived in the suburbs for the last few years, but before that, he'd rubbed hairy elbows with some shady individuals—powerful men and women who needed werewolves to do the dirty work humans couldn't do. Why pay three men as bodyguards when one werewolf could do it?

After Thorn and my father left the house, I expected them to meet my uncles and a few cousins at the local truck stop north of here. When we needed to round up the troops, we'd gather our supplies before heading out.

The Four Winds Roadside Eatery was a family-owned business run by wind witches. As I'd grown up I'd never enjoyed the Eatery's "rustic" charm, but the Stravinsky brood loved the generous portion sizes at this supernatural establishment. Any werewolf who could tolerate the conditions of the place always left with a full belly.

Unfortunately, I'd crossed it off my tolerable list a long time ago.

I pulled into the parking lot and made a beeline for the restaurant.

I scanned the place, spotting an array of both humans and supernaturals. The decor bordered on eclectic, with a mishmash of red and green seats and worn white tables. The witches had tried to appeal to their supernatural customers by hanging enchanted paintings on the wall. Why bother watching the old TV they had when you could stare at a raging sea battle? The rest of the wall space had vases, jars, and containers full of who-knows-what on haphazard shelving. Their creative wall scheme still didn't make me want to eat here.

The wind witch hostess tried to offer me a booth, but I declined.

My uncle Boris always wears the most disgusting after-shave; it has the same effects as pepper spray. Whenever I tease him about it he replies, "Hey, I haven't heard any complaints." I tell him that maybe the fog of death around him keeps everyone too far away to complain in the first place. Uncle Boris had been here recently, but they'd left already. Based on the strength of the stench, I guessed that it had been about ten minutes ago.

Two messy tables, which had been pushed together in the back, caught my eye. One plate had a half-eaten pastrami sandwich with toasted bread and an overflowing cup of mustard on the side for dunking. Yep, my dad had been here.

Time to check in with the locals. I approached a waitress named Gertie who worked the busy counter. As the eldest of three sisters, gray-haired Gertie had a generous waistline that she miraculously managed to fit behind the counter.

With a grimace, I squeezed in at the counter between

a greasy warlock drifter and a wizard truck driver who also needed a shower.

"Hey, Gertie. Long time no see." I pushed a smile onto my face.

"Natalya. It's been years." Her eyes brightened. "Have a seat and I'll get you the Hairy Navel special."

The Hairy Navel special? I'll pass. "Thanks, but no thanks. Has my dad been here recently?"

"They came in, all right. Didn't leave much of a tip, though."

I slid a ten-dollar bill across the counter. They'd definitely been here. My uncles still thought 10 percent was an adequate tip.

She grinned and dropped the money in her shirt pocket. "I do recall hearing about a park south of here. Wharton State Park." A customer asked for ketchup, so she briefly left to fetch it. When she returned, she offered a final piece of information. "One man in particular, a handsome fella, said something about the swamps along the Batsto River."

The pack had run in the park a few times in the past. Not often, though, since we have closer places. As the largest state park in New Jersey, Wharton has plenty of hiding places—over 100,000 acres of lakes, swamps, and thickets of trees. Far too big for me to sweep alone. Especially in my condition. But my brother's life was at stake. If I had twenty panic attacks, I was prepared to face every one of them while traipsing through the swamps. I had to move quickly to keep track of the men.

The whole trip would take an hour at the current speed limit down the Garden State Parkway. But since I was in a hurry, the speed limit might slip my mind once or twice. Time was a luxury I couldn't waste. The men would likely enter along the access road to the south. From there they'd eventually reach the river. If I gave them too much of a head start, I'd lose them for good.

An hour and a half later, I sat in the car, with the setting sun at my back.

I found not a single clue the entire way. None of the gas stations had a discernable scent. The gas station clerks hadn't seen anyone either. I gazed out the window to see campers driving by. They all moved with a purpose, a purpose I wished I possessed. I didn't want to find Alex by myself.

I tried to take cleansing breaths. To remember how much I loved Alex. How I would endure anything for him. My gaze went to the pines and cedars beyond the unpaved road.

After a few minutes, I opened the door and climbed out of the car—only to find Thorn leaning against the side. Clad in a jacket, T-shirt, and jeans, he crossed his arms over his chest and stared at me with an amused expression.

I rolled my eyes. "How nice of you to join me."

"One of your cousins kept telling me you'd never follow us." He slowly approached, his gaze never leaving mine. "But we both know how stubborn you can be when you can't control a situation."

"We've already discussed this. Don't act surprised."

He laughed, revealing a smile that set my heart pounding. "I never said anything about being surprised. I know you, Natalya. Matter of fact, you're pretty predictable by now."

We didn't have time for this little chitchat, but I refused to let him have the high ground. "If I'm so easy to read, why haven't you read me yet? Besides predicting my next move, why not predict what I want? What I need?" I closed the distance between us. Close enough for our lips to brush if I wanted them to.

He didn't budge. Thorn never backed down from my challenges. I dared him to speak. We stood nose to nose. Eye to eye. All he had to do was ask me to follow him into the forest and I'd surrender to him. He refused to do the same for me.

Finally, I managed to whisper, "You're a coward."

"Cowards choose to run." His warm breath fanned my face. "I'm still standing here."

Five years ago, this type of standoff would've ended with me naked and ravished on the ground. He'd close the distance between us with a kiss. An endless, dizzying embrace where hands reached for buttons, tore open shirts—anything to end the separation. But now that wouldn't happen. I closed my eyes. When I opened them, he'd resumed his spot leaning against the side of the car.

The wolf within me whined. Unable to placate my hunger, I got my backpack from the car, all the while trying not to think about Thorn. "Where's the search party assembled?" While I stuffed a few things into the bag, I tried to cool my heated blood. "Perhaps if you'd been around instead of hiding out at the Grantham cabin, my brother wouldn't have been kidnapped."

I expected him to be angry, but his voice was that of a protector. "You may not see me, but I'm always around."

My grip on the backpack faltered, but I managed to grab it and head for the trees. Thorn followed close behind.

Any minute now, he'd tell me which way to go. Especially since I didn't know which parts of the park he'd already visited. But I suspected from the way he strolled behind me that he expected me to turn and ask for directions sooner or later.

My gaze went to the damp ground to look for tracks or a hint of a scent. My father always said, "Keep your eyes and nose on the land and your ears alert for danger." Right now my only danger walked behind me.

Ten minutes later, I picked up the trail. It wasn't too difficult, since the men had taken a narrow path right off the muddy road. Their level of stealth included discarded cigarette butts and two beer cans.

Less than an hour later, darkness surrounded us as we left the trail and entered the forest. The moon disappeared under the cloud cover. At first, I cringed every time my tennis shoes stepped into squishy mud. This whole place squirmed with life. Everything was wet and the rain-soaked earth stank. Small animals scurried about. A family of beavers prepared their winter lodge to the north of us. The chill in the air had driven the insects away, but anything nocturnal like wolves would lurk in the shadows hunting for prey—like us.

By the time we spotted my father's camp, the sky had opened to pouring rain. With no moonlight, the shadows around us deepened. The trees provided minimal protection. I'd packed an umbrella, but who the hell used an umbrella in the forest? Thorn paid the rain no mind while I threw on a poncho. The weather slowed our progress. The damn wind, bitter and cold, stung my face as the lights from their lanterns grew brighter.

Before I could make out their forms, Thorn grabbed my poncho. "Don't!"

His low hiss pierced me as he pushed me behind a tree. A fresh scent came from downwind. My hands clenched into fists while my body threatened to initiate the change. Our enemies' scent, very faint, brushed against my nose. The Long Island werewolves had anticipated our attack and infiltrated the camp. *Oh, shit.*

For once I was proud of my uncles—they'd picked a position that we could approach from downwind. I tossed the backpack to the side. Time to play.

Thorn sank against the thick oak tree, his hazel eyes darkening. He slinked along the ground with his back arched and I followed suit. The rain muffled the sounds of our approach. After ten more feet, I could make out the Stravinsky men.

Their captors had tied them up and set them in a single-file line. My younger cousins sat hunched over as the rain pelted them, but my father and uncles stared down the Long Island werewolves. They'd been caught by surprise. From the way they'd tied my father with painful silver-threaded ropes, they meant business.

The sight of my brother was my undoing. He lay bound like an animal not far from the rest of my family. They'd tied him in the manner used by warlocks. A small number of those black magic–wielding nuts collect werewolves as protectors and in the worst cases use us for spells. As I looked from the oversized muzzle covering his mouth to the enchanted ropes that bound his wrists to his ankles, I could hear my mother cursing the men who'd constructed the bindings. They were all magical tools to harness and constrain the raw power of my kind, to the point that even if Alex transformed, he wouldn't be able to escape.

My canines filled my mouth as the cold rain hit my poncho. How dare they do this to my family? My gaze swept over the Long Island werewolves. Our two against their six didn't look good. I paused. A sliver of fear clamped down on my legs. The forest around me spun in circles as my chest tightened. Not now. Not now. A part of me screamed that I didn't belong out here. What the hell was I doing out in the forest, in the rain, crawling through the dirt? I wasn't ready for this. My fists clenched like tightly coiled rubber bands and threatened to snap as I prayed for release. I'd pushed myself too hard, too soon.

Suddenly, the pain retreated. The wolf took over, preventing the human inside from cringing away from the mud and brush I crawled through. My claws sank deeply into the grass as the lust for revenge seeped in. My slow pace increased. I moved closer and closer to the light. From between the trees, I spotted Thorn ahead. Shirtless. In less than a minute, he'd discarded his shirt and shoes.

One man in particular stood taller than the others and his stance exuded power. Slick black hair flowed down his back. His eyes glowed light green in the darkness. That had to be Luther, the Long Island pack leader. Why would he come all this way? Something about his face tugged at my memories. I always remembered faces. I'd seen that chin before. That sneer. But this wasn't the time to dwell on past acquaintances.

Luther gestured to his men. Their stench filled my nose. From the shadows under a set of bushes, I could make out the fine details in Luther's clothes.

The Long Island pack leader approached my father. "It's been a long time, Fyodor. Far too long."

Luther gave a sinister grin before he stepped on Alex with a steel-toed boot. My brother groaned in pain and my body jerked with the urge to run to him. Not yet. I had to wait for Thorn.

I didn't need to be close to smell the wave of rage from my father. His wide shoulders resembled a tightly strung bow waiting to be released.

"You should've stayed in Atlantic City," Luther said. "I would've found work for a cold-blooded killer like you." Through the rain, I could barely make out his whispered words. "Especially one with a mate as beautiful as Anna." He added weight to his foot and I strained to move. I could question my father later about his past transgressions. The time to act was now. What the hell was Thorn waiting for? My mouth watered with the possibilities. Claws extended, I could take Luther out and end the conflict tonight. From the far right, I saw golden eyes blink in the shadows. Thorn was ready.

"If I didn't want to kill that sweet little daughter of yours, she would've made a fine pet." Luther laughed.

"Perhaps I should seek her out all by myself for an up-close-and-personal introduction?"

My father lurched forward, but caught himself in time as the silver-threaded ropes bit deeply into his skin.

Luther approached my father. Close enough to taunt him into jumping again. "I could just as easily kill your son instead of your daughter, but that won't give me what I want from her. Will it?"

"Take me instead of them. My life has more value than theirs."

Luther laughed again as his cell phone rang. Before he picked it up, he said, "You have nothing to bargain with, Stravinsky. I've heard plenty about you. Enough to know that once I control this area, both you and your boy will belong to me."

The Long Island pack leader turned his back to them to talk on his phone.

C'mon, Thorn. Stop pissing around!

As he snapped his phone shut, Luther barked at his men. "Stay alert, boys! I have more urgent business." Then he smirked at my father before disappearing into the brush. Disappointment turned into rage. I'd waited too long and now Luther had escaped. Six were now five. Thorn wouldn't wait too long. And when he struck I had to be ready. Ready for the chance I'd been seeking to make them pay for their attack at my home. Their attack on me and Aggie.

The wind whipped through the trees to my right. Everything in the forest came alive. The time had come.

The trees parted. Thorn burst out, leaping through the air. I sprang a half second later toward the two men holding my father. They'd sensed our arrival. Thorn lashed out at the two men he'd crashed on, tossing one into the trees behind him and breaking the other's neck.

But the carnage wasn't over yet. The two werewolves I confronted were far larger than me. They both scrambled from underneath me and tried to pounce. Their blows were both fast and brutal—no mercy for a female. My head snapped back as one punched my face. Hot blood ran down my cheek. Since I was still in human form, the pain was amplified. But I didn't falter. I didn't pause. I lived in the moment—I lived for freeing my family. The only option was to win—to kill.

Meanwhile, Thorn had released two of my cousins from their bindings. With two more Stravinskys at our side, I continued to fight the two Long Island werewolves while my cousins sprang into action. One raced toward my father, while another ran to free Uncle Boris.

Another werewolf confronted Thorn. Derek. That bastard had stood back and let the lesser wolves attack while he waited with the prisoners. Hisses and barks filled the air as they clawed at each other.

The wolves I fought wrestled me to the forest floor and stomped on my back. I had a lifetime of drive and spirit, but two against one were too many. And my rain-slick poncho didn't provide any protection. Their claws ripped right through the thin material. One grabbed the back of my neck and slammed me into the damp ground. The other tried to subdue my kicking legs. As I tried to free myself, I could make out the sounds of struggle. Fists flying. Wolves growling and whining. Could Thorn defeat Derek?

In a flash, the wolf on my back vanished. A second later the other yelped as hands grasped and shook him violently. I looked up to see my father standing over me, the limp bodies of the two werewolves in his fists. He tossed them to the ground and offered his hand. When I couldn't get a firm grip, he pulled me up by my shoulders.

"Well done, daughter." He touched his forehead to mine.

The fight was over.

Uncle Boris and my cousins tried to free Alex from the

enchanted ropes, while a short distance away, Thorn checked on the fallen Long Island werewolves. Best to make sure we didn't have any stragglers to throw a surprise our way. Five bodies lay silent on the wet forest floor. There should've been six, but I'd take five for now.

The rain had trickled to nothing, but drops of water continued to fall from the trees. My entire body ached. Every movement, every step, resulted in sharp pain. I touched my bruised lips and tried not to think about what had happened. Whose blood I had on my hands.

I limped to my brother's side. From the way the men were struggling, it would be a while before Alex was free.

"Looks like we got a tight spell on these. Damn warlocks." Uncle Boris spat on the ground. "My shitter's got more purpose in life than those bastards."

Finally, they yanked off the muzzle. I peered at Alex's swollen face. Purple bruises marred his eyes and cheeks. What the hell had they done to him?

With gentle hands, I knelt next to him and touched the delicate skin on his ear. One of his eyes twitched. I traced my fingers lightly along a bruise on one cheek. He didn't wince or draw back. He knew my touch was meant to soothe.

"I'd ask why they did this to you, but that's a dumb question."

"Yeah."

"So what's the damage?"

A set of ropes dropped away. Alex hissed in pain. "Well, one of my ribs is broken. They broke it to slow me down. I think my ankle's sprained too."

I managed a painful grin and tried to think of a less painful topic. "I heard you made an honest woman out of Karey."

"Yeah. It was time." His face turned serious as the others worked around him. "I had a talk with Grandma about it."

"Grandma? Why not Dad?"

"Dad's pretty easy to figure out. I wanted a woman's perspective."

I feigned a hurt face. Not too difficult since I had blood running down it. "So why didn't you ask me?"

"I think you need a consistent dating record before I come your way with life-changing questions." I flicked his forehead with my finger. He chuckled with clenched teeth.

I couldn't resist looking for Thorn. He sat propped against a tree nursing a wound to his shoulder. He gazed out into the forest, with thoughts I wished I could see. After everything that had happened tonight, the only things I knew for sure were that my brother was safe— and that the Long Island werewolves were still coming for me.

Chapter 16

Aggie grumbled, "I want to choke this DJ. Who in their right mind would think it's a good idea to play 'Singing in the Rain' over and over again?"

The rain continued to fall for the next two days and made everyone miserable. Thank goodness I had the weekend off to recover from the kidnapping. Of course that didn't stop me from checking in at work. Aggie had tagged along for the drive.

"It's the best radio station in the area," I replied.

"You mean it's the only station you want to listen to."

"That too, but their commentator has years of experience."

"Years, my ass. He's as boring as a hot date between two tax lawyers." She pulled one of those miniboxes of cereal out of her pocket. I found it rather disturbing to watch her munch on it like it was potato chips. "Did you see the note from Nick?"

We'd forgotten about poor Nick after Alex's kidnapping. He'd left a note to say thanks for the ride on my back.

I gingerly touched a sore spot on my back where one of the Long Island werewolves had kicked me repeatedly. "Yeah, I hope it's the last time a man thanks me for a lift." I gestured back in the direction of The Bends. "I can't believe Bill told me that the neighborhood kids don't look as beat up as I do right now."

She patted my knee. "You don't look beat up." She snorted. "You look like you got your ass handed to you."

Should anything that came out of Aggie's mouth surprise me anymore?

"You don't look as bad as this one drunk chick I used to know at NYU. Picked fights all the time with other drunk folks. She looked horrible. And she still never took an ass kicking as bad as yours."

Even PETA had more tact.

"I just wanted to go in to check on things. After all this time I thought he wouldn't mind if I looked a bit under the weather," I said.

Even though I was driving, I could sense Aggie rolling her eyes. "Why do you care? It's only a few days."

A few days for me meant pure torture in terms of "what-ifs." What if some idiot had messed up our stock? What if one of the clerks—a chain-smoking fire witch— had finally managed to burn down the joint?

We pulled up to Aunt Olga's place. Once in a while Grandma spent the day here instead of at my parents' house.

I groaned. "Why did I come here with you again?"

"Because if you stayed home you'd be asking for a second helping of kick-ass quiche."

"I'd be fine. If they really wanted me dead, they would've come in with guns blazing."

Not that guns mattered. Werewolves rarely used them. Instead of a .45, the Code told us we should use our bare hands.

"You think of everything, don't you?" Aggie laughed. "If I obsessed over things as much as you do, I'd become a stockbroker."

"OCD does not mean I have savant-like mathematical

skills." I snatched the only umbrella before she had a chance to take it.

Before I left the car she asked, "So is there anything good about it?"

I didn't know how to answer that. Every day, with every decision I made, I faced my condition. If there was something good about having my disorder, that perk had better show itself soon.

Since I wasn't welcome at work, I followed Aggie up the sidewalk to my aunt's town house. My aunt lived close to my parents' home to allow her to easily walk back and forth, since she was Grandma's caretaker during the day.

We trooped up to the door, and I knocked.

But Aggie just reached for the doorknob and waltzed on inside. "She told me I didn't need to use the doorbell." She shrugged at my surprised expression. "It's not like she wouldn't hear us come in."

"With the Long Island werewolves roaming about, I don't think it's safe for her to—" I paused when I saw the sawed-off shotgun on Aunt Olga's coffee table. Whoa. I guess the Code didn't apply at this house today.

From the kitchen, she called, "Make yourself comfortable, girls. Alex is resting and Mama's watching TV. I'll be out with tea soon."

Aunt Olga had a flair for the dramatic. Other than the rough edges of the shotgun perched on the ornate table, her home displayed a well-kept European elegance. I locked the door as Aggie entered the living room and we both greeted my grandmother. She sat on one of the cream-colored couches with her hands in her lap, watching some trashy morning show. With gentle hands, she gingerly touched the bruises on my face.

"You need to be careful," she whispered.

"I always try, *Babushka.*"

I hadn't visited my aunt's place since I was a young

girl, but not much had changed. Compared to my mother's practical home, with its lived-in furniture and cheap-looking plastic plants, my aunt had the home of a woman with style. Unfortunately, the style was stuck in 1980s' Soviet Russia.

Aunt Olga entered the room with a tea service. She placed the tray on the coffee table and began to fill the cups. I had to admit, she moved with a grace I rarely had. Her chestnut-colored hair with strands of white fell to her waist in soft waves. With narrow wrists and feminine hands, she handed each of us a cup. Aggie spied the slices of coffee cake and promptly helped herself.

In a thick accent, Aunt Olga whispered, "Two more people to join in the fun will be nice. Won't it, Mama?"

Grandma nodded between sips. The backdrop of people yelling and arguing on TV took the tranquillity of the tea away.

"Aggie said you wouldn't mind if I stopped by for a bit," I said, standing up to go in search of my brother. I didn't even need to ask which room he rested inside—my nose led me to the second bedroom.

On the way I spied some of Aunt Olga's belongings that I hadn't seen in a while: the cabinet full of her gleaming beauty pageant crowns, right next to her expensive china. Weathered ribbons curved around plaques and photos. I remembered one distinctly: "Miss St. Petersburg 1979."

From past conversations between family members, I knew pageants in Russia were held in high regard. We'd watch tapes or satellite feeds of the Miss Russia Pageant when I was a young girl. Aunt Olga would drone on and on about how the girls lacked poise or sophistication. "Look at that dress! What kind of mother would allow a nice girl to dress like that on the stage? Still, I bet she wins and heads on to Miss World."

I didn't bother to knock, simply opening the door to

peer inside. Tucked in Aunt Olga's guest room, my brother lay under heavy quilts, lightly snoring. The guard, Rex's brother Pete, sat next to the bed with a motorcycle magazine and an open can of beer. Nothing like a brewski and half-clothed dames on bikes to pass the time.

Pete looked up from his magazine, grunted, and then went back to his entertainment. I didn't know whether he made much of a guard, but Thorn wouldn't have chosen him unless he was someone my family could trust.

From a free spot at the side of the bed, I checked my brother. He looked just as bruised as he had a few days ago. The boyish features that made him so handsome now appeared worn and frayed. Just looking at him made me want to get back at the Long Island werewolves for what they'd done to him. Even when I'd been closest to a breaking point, Alex had always been there for me, supporting me. If there was anything within my power—however limited it was—that I could do for him, I would.

He shifted under the covers and I left him to his rest. From outside the room, I could hear Aggie enjoying Aunt Olga's food while my aunt entertained both her and my grandmother with her long, drawn-out tales.

As I sat down next to Aggie, I grabbed a napkin and a small piece of cake, taking only a few nibbles since it hurt to chew anything bigger. My aunt grumbled to me, "Unlike your hungry friend here, you appear to have impeccable manners."

Through a mouthful of cake, Aggie mumbled, "But it is quite good, Olga. I mean, you baked this knowing I have a soft spot for the stuff."

Aunt Olga ignored Aggie and glanced my way. "Legs crossed at the ankles. Good. Your back is stiff as a board, which gives you height. But there is something else about you." She frowned.

I peeked at myself, not realizing I'd been put on the spot as if I were some kind of pageant participant. Bruises and all.

"You need to act like the confident woman I see on the outside." Our eyes locked for a moment and I turned away.

"No!" she snapped. "Never turn your eyes away from someone unless they have proven their superiority to you."

Well, that was easier said than done. I'd run into far too many werewolves who shoved their superiority down my throat. Like any respectful girl who knew her place within the family, I'd assumed Aunt Olga was my superior within the pack. But to my surprise, this pageant addict had put me in my place. In an unexpected way. She wanted me to believe in myself.

Before I could ask why she'd said what she did, I sensed footsteps outside. A familiar scent, a member of the pack. Pete emerged from the second bedroom and opened the front door.

"Were you expecting company?" asked my aunt.

"Just got a call that I had some chow coming." The door swung open to reveal his drenched youngest brother, Melvin, clutching a grocery bag in his arms. With only a nod and a mumble of thanks, Pete took it and shut the door. I hoped Melvin had managed to snag some food, since Pete evidently lacked the manners to offer any. Seemed like "asshole disease" was contagious in town.

Pete made a beeline for the bedroom, but of course, with someone like Aggie in the house, he didn't make it far.

"So you planned to eat all that food and not offer any?" Her nostrils flared. "You'd be a little more hospitable and less of a dickhead if you shared."

Perhaps Pete thought Aggie had filled herself up with Aunt Olga's coffee cake, but he should have known better. Before he could reply, Aggie took a bold step forward and snatched the sack. Aunt Olga stood and followed Aggie into the kitchen. "That does smell good. I think I'll help myself as well."

I shared a secret smile with my grandmother before turning to watch a new show on the TV. My mind drifted for a bit. The show was of no interest to me since the commercials didn't offer any Christmas sales yet. From the galley kitchen, I heard Pete complain about the generous portions Aggie put on her plate.

"That's my food. Do you mind?" he grated.

Aggie chortled. I could imagine the expression on her face. "How about I call Thorn and tell him you're working under the influence?"

Pete had the common sense to realize Aggie was not the kind of woman he wanted to tangle with. He emerged from the kitchen with a small portion of food on his plate and anger glittering in his dark eyes.

Aggie and my aunt ate their food at the dining room table off the living room. I took a seat next to Aggie and couldn't help but say, "You could've tried to be nice."

She pushed a small plate of Chinese takeout in my direction. I shook my head since the food reeked of a strange scent, strong and bitter, like mushrooms. I didn't want to tell her about my paranoia regarding the local Chinese buffet earth witch chef. She took natural foods to the next level. I'm all for pesticide-free food. The cleaner the better. But herbs that came from earth demons promising to cut you a *deal* if you release them from the third level of hell don't count. They sure as hell didn't have an FDA-approved stamp on their backsides.

Aggie beamed like a proud pup with a fresh kill under its paw. She added my share to her plate with a "more-for-me" sigh. "Olga told me that I did it in the most refined way possible."

Refined as a pit viper, I thought.

Aunt Olga offered my grandmother a plate of sweet-and-sour chicken, but she declined too. As she'd gotten older, I'd noticed that she wasn't as adventurous in her food choices. So I fetched some chicken noodle soup to share with her.

Not long after we ate, the late morning turned into a lazy early afternoon. Like glazed hams stewing in their juices, Aunt Olga and Aggie leisurely watched TV while my grandmother knitted. She'd done a fine job of converting the sweater she'd planned to make for Alex into a blanket for the baby.

Grandma loved to knit, and encouraged my mother and me to try it out, even though we always turned her down. What little time we all had together was precious, so we took a few minutes sorting through colors in Aunt Olga's room. Once she was settled, we returned to the living room to watch some more TV.

Not long after, I noticed that my grandmother had finished her soup, so I picked up the bowls and put them into the sink. When I returned to the living room, I saw Aggie fast asleep on the couch, with her arm holding her head up. Her hair fell over half her face. Aunt Olga, ever the lady, had curled up to sleep on her side.

"When did this happen?" I asked Grandma with a grin.

"I don't know." The rapid movements of her hands slowed down. The needles had occupied her for most of the day.

I plopped down on the couch next to Aggie. She didn't budge. Matter of fact, she flopped forward and landed in a heap on the floor.

I wished I'd reached for her instead of yelping after I watched her fall. The side of her head hit the coffee table with a cringe-inducing thud. For several seconds, I sat there, my mouth flapping like a goldfish out of its bowl. The whole scene seemed twisted. Aunt Olga unmoving on her side, Aggie lying prone on the floor. Neither of them woke up when I shook them hard. This wasn't good.

Grandma whispered, "Alex?"

I jumped up and rushed to the second bedroom.

The curtains had been drawn, so my eyes had to adjust to the only light source, a single lamp in one corner of the room. Pete's food caught my eye first. The rice and colorful stir-fry had spilled on the carpet. A dirty hand, palm up, lay a few feet from the pile. Pete's chest was the only thing that moved. I stepped over him and checked on my brother.

I gently shook his shoulders, but he didn't respond. The only sound in the room was the pitter-patter of the rain against the windows. I leaned close to his face, pulling up his eyelids to examine his eyes. Unfocused irises stared back at me. With each deep breath he expelled, I caught the scent of the Chinese food.

Oh, shit. Oh, shit. Oh, shit.

The food.

I staggered to stand, my stomach twisting again and again. My body froze while a thousand thoughts crossed my mind. Who had done this? Would everyone die from the drugs they'd been given? How had they poisoned our food?

"Natalya?" My grandmother interrupted my thoughts from the doorway.

"They're both alive," I managed.

Time to call in help. I spotted a phone on an end table and picked it up. There wasn't a dial tone, only the sound when another phone in the house has been left off the hook. The faint hiss of someone listening on the line.

"You planning on making a phone call?" a male voice asked.

"Who is this?" I whispered.

The voice laughed, deep and low. "You thought no one would notice the Long Island pack in the area?" Silence filled the line while he waited for his words to sink in. "A beaten-down dog's always easy pickings. I wonder who gets the spoils first?" A disturbing sound—the thud of a dropped phone—and then the line went completely silent. Not good. Not good at all.

Now, stuck in a town house whose only occupants were me, my knocked-out relatives, my wounded brother, and an elderly werewolf, I was the only one who could defend us from a whole new threat: a different pack of werewolves closing in on their vulnerable prey.

Chapter 17

Every second that I wasted freaking out gave me less time to achieve my goal: protect my family.

After hearing a faint creak from below, I rushed to the kitchen and slammed the basement door shut. It was clear, though, that the flimsy lock wouldn't hold. I scrambled through the galley kitchen. The chairs weren't the right size to wedge under the knob. Nothing in the drawers of value. No screwdrivers to jam in the door. I couldn't find anything to help me—even though the woman's kitchen held every knickknack you could imagine.

Footsteps thundered up the stairs.

I just about laughed when I spotted the fridge right next to the door. With three mighty heaves, I shoved the ancient thing in front of it. Not long after, the burly Frigidaire shook.

Instead of waiting around to see the carnage of spilled food, I hauled my butt into the living room to find my grandmother waiting for me.

"We're leaving," I told her. "Right now."

First things first. I tried to find my purse. A few quick calls should get family and friends over here. I searched around the coffee table for my purse or Aggie's but couldn't find them.

When I saw the barren coffee table, the sight hit me like a punch in the gut. Not only had they disabled the phone, but they'd also taken the shotgun. I glanced from Aggie to Aunt Olga and wondered how the hell I could get them both out of here. Maybe break a window, toss them outside?

While millions of scenarios danced inside my head, Grandma wrapped a handkerchief around her head. Then she wrapped a blanket around Aunt Olga. The constant slams against the door jolted my senses. No time. I had no time to fall apart.

I picked Aunt Olga up and threw her over my shoulder. The sharp bones of her hips jabbed into me. I hurried outside and pushed intruding thoughts away: the way her slack body flopped, the rain soaking into my pressed clothes, and the aches and pains from my deep wounds.

Once I reached the car, I used a backup key I'd stowed away in a crevasse under the car. I rarely forgot my key, but keeping a backup handy ranked high on an anal retentive–preparedness scale.

I hoisted my aunt into the backseat and then ran back inside.

A loud clatter as more of the fridge's contents fell to the floor. *Hold door, hold.* I stepped around shattered glass. Tomato juice gushed from a bottle like blood from a wounded victim. I checked the door. The fridge tilted forward, and the doorframe appeared cracked. Between curses and growls, a set of clawed hands slipped through the seam and tried to push the door open.

One down, too many to go. I hoisted Aggie over my shoulder. She weighed a little less than Nick, but I'd been stronger the day I carried him. My body protested with each step.

"Grandma," I hissed. "Let's go!"

She poked her head out of the room where Alex and Pete lay.

Okay, Thorn you can show up and be the hero any time now.

But only the rain greeted me as I ran outside. More cold rain that plastered my hair to my scalp.

I added Aggie to the backseat. "Get in the car, Grandma." I shifted to look out the window and squint through the murky downpour. No Grandma.

From my line of sight, the light of the door beamed like a beacon. But nothing inside would offer a safe haven.

I ran through the rain, expecting to enter a house in turmoil. Instead, the silence in the house raised the hair on the back of my neck. I crept through the living room and searched the kitchen. The fridge lay on the floor. Crushed food littered the place, revealing where the intruders had stepped. It was clear that several people had passed through.

Lightning flashed outside the windows. A few seconds later the dull crash of thunder filled the house.

The urge to call out for my grandmother tickled the back of my throat. Did they have her? Had she managed to find a hiding place? My steps quickened. If they touched her . . .

From the kitchen, I headed to Alex's room. I wasn't as stealthy as my father could be, but the carpeted floor muffled my approach. And I didn't detect any foreign scents in the hallway connecting the bedrooms. Only a trace that my grandmother had been here. When I opened the cracked door, I expected to find what I'd seen before, both Alex and Pete asleep. Anything but the sight before me.

A man crouched on the side of the bed, hovering over my brother. The man had a narrow back with damp black hair streaked with green. His dirty leather jacket shook as he bent forward.

When I saw what he was doing, I was so shocked it felt a like a sledgehammer slamming into my kneecaps.

He was holding a pillow over my brother's face.

My hand twitched first. Then my entire body erupted into a black rage. All-consuming. Boiling until my anger spilled over and I roared. I unleashed myself on my brother's attacker, grabbing the back of his neck. Again and again, I slammed my fist into the side of his face until he fell backward on the floor. I sprang on him, not caring where I scratched, where I bit.

"Crazy bitch!" the werewolf spat. He angled his elbow under my neck to keep me from clamping my mouth down on him again.

Pete and his discarded food tumbled around us, filling the room with a haze of sweat, blood, and take-out Chinese.

We wrestled for control, but I managed to grasp a handful of the intruder's hair. I yanked his head up, then slammed it back down on the carpet. Bits of noodle and vegetables clung to the side of his face.

Harder and harder, I knocked his head against the floor until I couldn't see his face anymore, only his hands on Alex's pillow. The attacker was lucky I didn't carry a gun.

"That's enough!" The roar from the door entered the din of my haze. "Get off him!" the other man warned. "Now!"

I glanced up, my hands still clenching the man's hair.

The other man had my grandmother. He filled the gap of the doorjamb with wide shoulders and menacing black eyes. He was overwhelmingly tall, too tall for the low ceilings in this house. Something about him pecked at my memories. I'd seen his face before. At a gathering of packs for the state of New Jersey. From which one I didn't know.

"Stand up slowly before I do something to Granny here." My grandmother winced as Tall Man roughly shook her shoulder.

The wolf inside me wanted to tear him apart. To initiate the change and rip his limbs off. If I had my way, he'd never leave this house. Somehow my grandmother remained silent and stoic.

The man beneath me groaned as I backed away from him.

"You okay, Burt?" Tall Man asked his cohort.

"I'll be fine," Burt gurgled. "Got a bunch of stars in my eyes." His thick Jersey accent slurred the words.

I continued to sit on the floor staring Tall Man down. My hands quaked, itching to attack.

Tall Man laughed. "You're more of a firecracker than I'd expected." His eyes formed slits. "Quiet field mice shouldn't bite cats on the prowl."

I wanted to tell him I had rabies and planned to share with him, but I kept my mouth shut.

Burt managed to stand not far from me. "Wish we could take out the trash instead of adding to our ranks." He pounced on me, grabbing a handful of my hair. With a vicious yank, he forced my back into a painful arch.

He continued to twist my hair around his fist, trying to pay me back for what I'd done to him. For good measure, he kicked me forward, placed his boot on my back, and pressed down.

A grimace stretched across my face. The pain across my torso amplified, with electric shocks running down my legs.

"Not so tough now, are you, bitch?"

I wanted to tell him that I wouldn't mind an introduction of my foot to his ass, but I was too busy straining to look at Tall Man.

"We got three of them. I see no reason I can't stay and play with this one before I put her to sleep along with the injured one." Burt continued to leer in my direction, perhaps thinking he could promise me as much fun as Clive had.

Tall Man sneered. "Derek said the Long Island pack

wants her, but that doesn't mean she can't be taught a lesson or two. I don't have time for old women, so I'll take care of this one in the living room." He turned away and said over his shoulder, "Do what you want with her."

The time between when Burt grabbed me by the throat with his other hand and when Tall Man prepared to drag my grandmother out of the room flashed by in seconds.

Burt's grip on my throat tightened. The air in the room *shifted*. The scent of ozone filled my nostrils. Nothing smelled the same—as if my perception had been twisted within the space of this room.

Tall Man glanced down at my grandmother. He murmured, "No fuckin' way."

First, her lips moved as if she was whispering to herself. Then her body rapidly expanded like lava rushing out of a tunnel, surging and ready to explode. Nothing like the bone-cracking and form-shifting of a young pup. This metamorphosis bordered on beautiful—and then horrific when her body grew. Far larger than any werewolf I'd ever seen. Enormous. A thing of nightmares, with a massive snout bulging with teeth. Bristly gray hair extended from her back and spread to become black hair down her muscular legs.

The creature, which stood on its hind legs where my grandmother had been, seized the wide-eyed Tall Man between its large-clawed hands. With her body concealing the carnage, I could only hear Tall Man gurgling while she tore at him. Thunder muffled the loudest of his screams.

The man who held me mewled like a frightened child. He released me and stumbled to the corner. The foul stench of his released bowels hit my nose.

When Grandma Lasovskaya turned around, the creature that peered at us oozed hunger. A hunger to savage anything in its path. Yellow eyes stared at Burt and me. Waiting for one of us to move.

Fear pulsed through my skull and locked my lungs. Even if I'd wanted to move, my body prevented any action. Survival mode kicked in.

Her height prevented her from completely standing, so she crouched with the remains of Tall Man in her hands. She took a step toward us. Then another.

I closed my eyes and remembered all the times my grandmother had held me, soothed me. The scent of her skin. The warmth of her touch. How she'd do anything to protect me. This monster wasn't the beautiful wolf I remembered from when the pack ran during those long-ago summers. Was the creature before me really my grandmother?

My lungs burned for air, but my body refused to move.

Burt broke the standoff. He bolted from the corner like a frightened rabbit and scurried toward the window near the foot of the bed. His arms flailed, grasping at anything so he could hurl himself through the window.

She snatched him before he reached the windowsill.

When my vision dimmed, I managed to suck in a mouthful of air. Panic built in my belly first. The surge was overwhelming. I didn't need to run. I didn't need to escape. I didn't need to look. My body rocked while I tugged at the worn carpet. I was unable to swim out of the death spiral toward the depths of the abyss.

I opened my eyes after an unknown expanse of time. Had my panic attack lasted a few minutes? Longer?

Blood and the remains of two bodies littered the floor. No sign of my grandmother. Poor Pete would awaken in this mess.

Somehow, I managed to creep to the bed and check on my brother. I watched the rise and fall of his chest with relief. Burt hadn't killed him; Alex would survive to become a father.

I dreaded the trip back to the living room. Would I find my grandmother, waiting there to end me? A beast that would then escape the house to wreak havoc on a neighborhood full of unsuspecting humans? The overturned lamps in the corners remained lit, casting light on the floor—and revealing a single form, lying curled on its side.

Even over the sound of the rain, I could detect my grandmother's shallow breaths, and could see the slight movement of her chest. I wanted to cry from relief as I rushed to her side.

I touched her face. Her skin was cold and dry. "*Babushka*, are you all right?"

But when I shook her, she didn't awaken.

Chapter 18

After Thorn and my family arrived, I spent the rest of the day at my parents' house. I wanted to remain by my grandmother's side, but my mother forced me sit in the living room.

So I sat there and watched. I watched my uncles carry Aggie and Aunt Olga into a bedroom. And then I watched my father carry my grandmother inside. Aunt Vera hovered over them, wiping away tears as she followed. When my mother finally sat down, I asked her in a hoarse voice, "Mom, what's wrong with Grandma?" I didn't want to think of the worst, but I had to ask. "Is she dying?"

"No, thank the good Lord." She gazed at the cold coffee in her hands. "I tasted old magic in the air at the town house."

"Old magic?"

"I don't know what happened at that house. Who attacked whom. But werewolf magic is against the Code."

Again and again, my mother had spoken about how she hated magic and those associated with it. Long ago, when she'd told me that werewolves couldn't cast spells, I'd taken it as the truth. Why wouldn't it be? I had no inherent spellcasting abilities. Nothing mysterious happened when I handled magical goods at The Bends. None of my werewolf relatives or friends ever talked about old magic— perhaps due to the Code's restrictions on the matter.

I rubbed the beginning of a growing ache in my forehead. Good God. Grandma Lasovskaya had transformed into something other than a werewolf. Was my grandmother's unconscious state the reason werewolves shouldn't cast spells?

My face must've betrayed my thoughts. "What did you see, Natalya?" my mother asked.

Visions of the transformation flashed before me in my mind, from the creature's hunched-over back to its jagged teeth. To me, the werewolf form represented power and beauty—it wasn't an exaggerated killing machine.

A large hand touched the top of my mother's head. "Leave it be, Anna," my father said. "What's done is done."

"Nothing good comes from such poison," she spat. "Magic's meant for warlocks and witches." Father stroked the crown of her head while she ranted. "We've survived for millennia without their so-called tricks."

She shrugged his hand away. Dropped her coffee cup on the floor and snatched my hand. "What did my mother do to those men?" Her wide eyes searched mine for answers.

When I didn't respond, she whispered, "Just do what you always do. Go back to your little world and your little *things*."

Before I could cringe as if slapped, a few sharp knocks on the door pulled us out of the moment.

Thorn entered and nodded my way. "I need to speak with Natalya."

My mother released my hand so I could stand. She refused to face or acknowledge us. As a higher-ranking werewolf, he could have commanded her attention, but he chose not to. As we left I wanted to shout that it wasn't my fault we'd been attacked. It wasn't my fault that Grandma had defended us. But I knew my place and remained silent.

Thorn motioned me toward the front door and I followed. Thankfully, only a light drizzle was falling now.
I buttoned my jacket while he walked ahead of me. How
easily he endured this weather, despite the pain from his
wounds.

We weren't alone. Five men trailed after us. Three
walked on the other side of the street while two followed
in a car.

"So this is what things have come to."

He grunted in response. "The pack in Burlington sniffed
us out. Rather quickly."

I wanted to touch the back of his head, but I'd grown
tired of always making the effort to reach out to him.
Perhaps it was for the best.

"This was a calculated attack on pack members at their
homes. These guerilla tactics were a surprise." He shook
his head. "My father had never heard of anything like
this before. Since I've never defended a territory before,
this situation is much more complicated than I'd expected. No wonder he tells me I'm of no use to him. I
guess the feeling is mutual."

He slowed his pace, but even so I couldn't catch up. It
was almost as if he wanted to literally put some distance
between us. "I hope you've had enough time to catch
your breath, so you can tell me exactly what happened."

I pondered what to say while we walked down the
damp sidewalk. A laugh escaped my mouth. "Hell opened
up and swallowed us," I began. I then recounted everything, from my arrival at Aunt Olga's and Melvin's delivery of the food up to the point when I discovered Burt
trying to suffocate Alex.

"So someone poisoned the food?" he asked.

"Yeah. Took about an hour before it hit."

"How come you didn't fall asleep?"

I snorted. "Have you seen the local Chinese buffet?

Since I don't like to be doubled over with stomach pain, I passed."

He cast my comment aside. "I think I need to have a talk with Melvin."

"He just delivered the goods. One of the men who attacked us said that the Long Island pack wanted me. I bet Derek and his cronies had someone tail me."

"That I understand, but why would they plan such an elaborate attack with a rival pack?"

I hesitated. "Maybe Luther promised the Burlington pack some land or something else valuable for helping them bring us down."

We reached the end of the subdivision and continued down the main road. I waited for the real question about what had happened, but it never came.

"You're not going to ask me about my grandmother?"

"I'm not as ignorant about old magic as the others. I learned a thing or two in San Diego."

"So do you know what she'd become? What my grandmother turned into before she killed those men?"

The SUV that was tailing us pulled up to the curb. A window rolled down and a man shouted out, "We caught one of the Burlington boys on Dover Road!"

Thorn said, "Tell them to do nothing until I get there." Then he turned to me and took my hand, "Before I came inside, I heard some things. What your mother said—"

"Don't worry about it," I blurted. "She's upset about Grandma."

"Yes, but that's no reason to take it out on you."

"Leave it be, Thorn." I yearned to feel the warmth of his hand for a moment longer. And for him to take me into his arms and tell me that this nightmare would end soon. But instead, he simply released me. "Get in, Nat." I followed him into the SUV, thoughts swirling around my head.

This was all because of me. The nightmare would end soon, but I feared it would bring the end of me as well.

"Ugh! What did I hit my head on?" Aggie rubbed her bruise. "I can't believe we got attacked and all I did was hit my noggin on a coffee table. Did I at least trip someone?" I rolled my eyes. "Don't give me that face, Nat. You don't have a hangover from hell."

Aggie glanced at the closed bedroom blinds. Slowly, she eased herself over the side of the bed. "How long have I been out?"

"About seven hours. It's dinnertime."

She grinned. "So that's what I smelled."

"This is serious, Agatha McClure." I handed her some water and aspirin. "I don't know if it's safe for you to stay here anymore."

My best friend shrugged and flipped her hair out of her face.

"What if your dad finds out about what's going on here?" I asked.

Her face darkened. "You let me worry about him. Is everyone all right?"

"Aunt Olga and Pete woke up a while ago. They're not hurt or anything. Alex is still sleeping."

Aggie noticed my hesitation. "What about your grandma?"

I'd left out a few things when Aggie had woken up. Guess now was as good a time as any to give her the gory details.

"She did all that? To the bastards who attacked us?"

"It wasn't pretty. They'll need a Hazmat unit to clean that town house up." I tried to sound upbeat, but my final words broke as tears began to well up.

Aggie took my hand. "Is she okay?"

"She didn't eat the food, so it's not that. It's something else. We don't know when she'll wake up. Or *if* she will."

After that night, the days stretched out. Somehow, I managed to work—under guard from one of Thorn's men. Maybe it was my job that kept me functioning even while my grandmother continued to sleep. One day turned into three.

My distracted mind leaked into my daily tasks. Bill couldn't help but notice when I drifted away at the cash register. "Nat, even the guard Thorn posted here is getting more work done than you. Wake up!"

Bill, the ever-manipulative goblin, had convinced my werewolf guard that instead of holding the wall up, he could make a few bucks helping Quinton haul furniture around.

If the guard was such a great employee, I didn't see why Bill didn't keep *him* around to negotiate with conniving harpies. For the first time in a long while, I didn't care that much about my work. Perhaps things were different now that I might not have someone who I knew loved me unconditionally. My grandmother had always made me feel that way.

Before I had a chance to bury myself in cataloging a set of gaudy enchanted capes, Will came into the store. He scanned the floor until he found me.

"Good news, Nat."

He seemed a bit happy so I asked, "Did the South Toms River pack manage a truce?"

He shook his head and motioned for me to follow him to a quiet corner. "Unfortunately, no. But Thorn called to tell me your grandmother woke up."

A smile broke out on my face. That is, until I realized that my family hadn't called me with the news. "How long ago?"

"About two hours. Thorn said he paid her a visit once he got word."

"Thanks for letting me know." My voice didn't sound as confident as I wished it did. I'd had time to heal, but I'd been broken down in more ways than one.

Will leaned against the counter and bit his lower lip, as if he had heavy thoughts. Compared to Thorn, he seemed too young to shoulder the burden the alpha had to carry.

"There are other things we need to discuss—before we see my father. You and he need to talk about what happened at Olga Lasovskaya's home. In particular, why the Long Island pack has targeted you as a key person in their takeover."

Will's forlorn face said it all, but his words dug the blade deeper into my heart. "Natalya, I have no choice but to bring you before Farley to face judgment."

Because of my actions, innocent members of the pack had fallen into danger. If they'd surrendered me already, maybe no one around me would've been in jeopardy. The Long Island werewolves sure as hell would have continued their takeover of the South Toms River territory—but I would have been one less problem for Thorn's pack, and for my family, in the whole scheme of things.

I clenched my fists to keep myself from reacting. I tried to remember my aunt's words and looked Will in the eye. "What time do I have to be at your house?"

"We could go now if you want."

"What time do I *have* to be there?"

He swallowed deeply. "Before sunset is fine."

I shifted to show him that I wanted to get back to work. "I'll be there then. See you around, Will."

But despite my brave words I didn't want to see his father anytime soon.

When, a long time ago, I'd made this same trip to the Grantham cabin, I'd resembled a frightened girl who was hoping for the best. That frightened girl remained—but now she felt like a lamb waiting for slaughter. In my stunned state, I climbed into my car with the guard and drove to Old Farley's place.

I'd waited until the last minute to leave The Bends, cleaning up my station and everyone else's.

The guard merely grunted when I told him we needed to go to the Grantham cabin. It wasn't as if he didn't frequent the place. I watched the landscape while we drove into the woods. South Toms River had been my home since my birth. This town had been through blizzards, blackouts, droughts, and even recessions. But through them all, the werewolves had remained, and even thrived. We'd huddled together in our homes and weathered storms, together, as a pack. I tried to remember these things as I passed the ice cream shop where I'd been recently with Heidi and Abby the Muse. And then Archie's place, where I ate lunch every workday.

As I drove farther, I kept pondering what judgment Farley would pass. Would Luther be waiting there for me? Would Old Farley give in to his asshole ways and surrender me to our enemy for the sake of the pack? But surely, even though Thorn wasn't the alpha, he'd never let his father do such a horrible thing.

I hit a checkpoint before the long driveway to the house. With the Burlington and Long Island packs at our throats, we couldn't take chances anymore.

The circular driveway in front of the Grantham cabin was full of cars. Most of them likely belonged to the guards posted there to protect the pack's leader.

When I stopped the car, my eyes drifted to the woods where I'd run with Thorn, then over to the house. The sun slowly drifted toward the horizon, casting a reddish purple haze on the sky. Would this be my last sunset?

Chin up, girl. I straightened my clothes and marched

up to the house. I might've been cast aside, but I'd been born a Stravinsky. I had the blood of Slavic warriors, however diluted it was in my case, and I would sure as hell try to show it. Key word: *try.*

The guard didn't follow me. Before I had a chance to knock, the door opened. A man I remembered from high school stood there. He hadn't changed much over the years.

"C'mon in, Nat. Farley's been waiting for you." His voice sounded like he was ready to prepare me for the roasting pit. "Have a seat in the living room. I'll let him know you're here."

I took a seat on the sofa next to Farley's La-Z-Boy. To my disgust, I noticed discarded potato chips and pretzels in the seat. Good thing the pack leader wasn't chosen based on cleanliness.

The big-screen TV had been left on. A western was playing, with a night-time gunfight. Not the best thing to watch while I waited for Farley, but I didn't have the balls to change the channel. And besides, the remote control, just a few feet away, was covered in crumbs and grease.

The sounds of a conversation from the ground-floor bedroom drew my attention. Though the thick walls kept me from catching the words, I could still make out a heated conversation. Was Thorn here too? His scent lingered everywhere, leaving me wondering if he planned to intercede on my behalf.

The door swung open and Old Farley lumbered in. His expression looked almost soft—until he caught my gaze. Then the old coot sneered. His smile told me I was in for it.

Just behind him, I spied a floral pattern and then a wrinkled face. My grandmother had spoken for me. What had brought these two together?

I rose and took a step in her direction. Of course, Old Farley stamped down on our reunion by slamming the door shut behind him.

"No need to stand on my account," he barked. "Have a seat."

I immediately averted my eyes and resumed my place on the couch. His hard gaze burned into me while he shuffled with his cane to his seat. All the while, I detected a subtle shift around me. The guards, who'd remained hidden in the shadows, now emerged to protect the alpha.

When he sat, I heard a soft crunch from the snack food. He grabbed the remote and turned off the television.

I tried to strengthen myself as my father would expect me to. No matter what punishment Farley gave me, I'd still have my home, my job, and my life. If I had to kowtow to his whims, I'd do so. When he opened his mouth to speak, I held my breath.

"I told you the weakest link brings down the pack," he said slowly. "But you didn't listen. Not surprised, though. You're like your grandmother in that regard. I thought you'd make it easy for us when they kidnapped your brother, but I can see you don't hold the pack's safety before your own." He leaned forward and scratched his bum knee. When he didn't speak right away, I glanced at the window, wishing I could see outside.

"Since you're a liability to the pack, I have no choice but to force you to leave our territory." His gaze drifted to the room from where he'd emerged. "But out of respect to the Stravinskys, I'll give you thirty days to leave."

I sucked air into a chest that refused to expand. The red curtains behind him filled my vision. I had to leave?

"If the Long Island and Burlington packs aren't driven off by then, you must leave—or you'll be marked for execution by our pack." His gaze burrowed into mine. I waited a split second too long before I glanced away. "I'll execute you myself if necessary."

Silence enclosed the room in a blanket of ice. My body shivered. Whether it was from the chill of the coming winter, or the shock of my world collapsing around me I didn't know.

"Is there anything I can say in my defense?"

He cackled. "Like what? Luther not only wants to conquer our pack, he has a vendetta against *you*. Are you keeping something from me?"

"I'm no one. Why would the leader of a powerful pack want me?"

"That's exactly what I want to know. But since you have no answers, I have no choice but to cut you off. You're a diseased limb that must be severed from this pack."

I clenched my fists and dug my claws into my palms. Tight enough to draw blood. The blood's warmth slid between my fingers and dripped on the floor. I refused to look at him and give him the satisfaction of seeing how far he'd ground me into the dirt.

"I remember there was once another wolf like you," Farley whispered. "It was a long time ago. He was the alpha's—my uncle's—guard. For years, the man seemed quiet enough. Didn't speak unless spoken to. He knew his place, kept the alpha safe when attacked.

"Then one day my pa found him at his place, talking to himself. He'd talk to the furniture, the houseplants, any piece of crap he had around. Of course, Pa just shrugged it off. After all, the man lived alone with no family. But when things mattered most, my uncle learned a hard lesson." He turned to me. "Can you guess what my uncle's guard did?"

I shook my head.

"One day, a rival pack leader came by to challenge the

alpha for leadership. That's how they did it back then—none of this sneakin' round and slittin' throats in the night.

"Well, the guard flipped out. Just when the rival leader almost had my uncle subdued, the guard went apeshit and started killing pack members indiscriminately. It was as if he'd lost his mind, grabbing people without thought, not listening to the commands of his alpha."

He remained silent for a bit until a fit of coughs shook his frame. After he composed himself, he continued. "What I'm trying to say is that I refuse to let that kind of thing into my pack. I refuse to allow anyone who might be unstable to get close to me."

"It's not as if we have movie nights together, Mr. Grantham," I whispered.

"I'm not stupid, girl. I can see the way my boy looks at you. You're more than a liability to the pack. You're a liability to *him* as well." He snorted. "I can't believe he tried to defend you. Defend what you *are*. A bunch of words about what you've done in the past won't help us now. We're vulnerable, and we don't need your kind around here."

My kind?

"May I leave now?" My voice quivered.

Old Farley grabbed the remote control with one hand and flicked in the direction of the door with the other. "Be sure to escort your grandma home. I'll let you take one of my guards along—for her safety." He guffawed. "*Her* safety. That's a good one."

The blaring roar of the western filled the room again. I walked to the door, my limbs numb and rubbery. When I opened the door, I expected to see her waiting alone. Instead Thorn sat on a chair next to her, holding her hand.

I managed to blurt in Russian, "It's time to go home, Grandma."

From that point on, I didn't look at Farley or Thorn, even though he held the door open for us and followed us out into the night. When I headed to the car, my grandmother tugged me toward the road. "Come walk with me, Natalya. We need to talk."

"It's cold outside, Grandma. I don't want you out here like this. Especially after what happened to you."

She ignored my words, gently pulling me along. Thorn stayed out of earshot, yet didn't stray far.

"There's nothing to talk about. We both know I'll have to leave."

"Absolute nonsense. That man is still young and doesn't know any better."

I snorted. "If he's too young to know any better, then I must still be considered a werewolf toddler."

"In many ways, you're still Anna's little girl, but that hasn't stopped you from growing, from learning. Some people never accomplish that much."

We stuck to the gravel road and avoided the muddy puddles. Grandma told me about when she'd first met Old Farley. How he'd been as much of a jerk then as he was now. I loved listening to her speak. She had a soft lilt to her voice that rocked and lulled me.

"Did you come to Farley's house alone?" I asked.

"You know who brought me here."

I glanced over my shoulder to see Thorn walking along the tree line. He kept his gaze on the open road. When I dared to stare a second longer, our eyes met.

"Why did he help us?" I said. "He doesn't care if I'm driven away."

"You take those words back, Natalya Fydorova Stravinsky." She gripped my hand more tightly while her voice became stern. "You weren't in the room to hear what he said to his father about you. From your vantage point, he might not be worthy of your affections right now, but he'd give up everything if he could guarantee the pack's safety *and* have you by his side."

I bit my lower lip as my face reddened. I sensed Thorn's eyes on my back. "What do I do? Farley wants me to leave."

"Thorn told me he'll do everything in his power to end the conflict. What you and I will do is what we always *should* do. Pray and hope for the best. I've been through wars and enough pack rivalries to tell tales until dawn. What they all have in common is that they eventually end. When this fight ends, you'll see that this short span of time is only a sliver of your long life to come."

I nodded but couldn't keep from interrupting her to learn the truth about what had happened that night. "Grandma, why did you do what you did the other night?"

We walked a bit before she answered. "Would you do what I did if you knew such secrets?"

I quickly nodded. "Without hesitation."

"Then you do not need to ask why. What you want to know is how I did it." In the darkness, she had a sly smile on her face. A twinkle in her brown eyes.

"Mom said the old magic's forbidden."

"Your mother was always a city gal. She doesn't know the old ways of the countryside." She sighed. "What I sacrificed these last few days will be with me for what time I have left. But it was worth it. My family is everything to me."

I thought I'd been emptied of tears, but more now flowed freely.

"One day, you'll learn what I know," she said. "See what I see. There's more to our world than the Code. And in the end, some prices are worth paying."

Chapter 19

The day of my brother's wedding to the crazy local wood nymph should've been a day of unhindered celebration. But they rushed into the ceremony, in the atmosphere of turmoil and fear that gripped the community. Only two weeks after the attack and Farley's proclamation of my banishment, we decided to hold the wedding. Thorn had urged my family to postpone it until spring, but Karey balked. She refused to have, as she called it, "a bastard werewolf baby."

"Natalya, stop staring out that window and get me another pan. This one's boiling over." If my mother had had her werewolf snout, she'd have literally nipped at my heels.

She continued, "We should be safe for now. The sooner I finish cooking, the sooner we can head over to the church."

We finished the task of cooking rack after rack of food. As the parents of the groom, my father had offered my mother's services as a short-order cook. Little did those nymphs know they'd be getting enough food to feed the entire werewolf population of South Toms River. I stirred a pot while my mother sealed containers of casseroles and Cornish hens. A well-glazed ham—okay, *seven* well-glazed hams—sat steaming in pots, ready to be carried to the family minivan. My mother refused to use my father's truck—which was always filthy—to transport her fine fare.

As Karey's maid of honor, I had to be at the church early. But with my mother cooking food for everyone and *their* mother—and with me drafted as her assistant—I was worried I'd show up late.

My father hauled the food to the minivan, where my grandmother was situated comfortably in the front. Since I was the lowest member on the totem pole, I got to sit in the back, holding a Crock-Pot with the au gratin potatoes.

"You know, I could always go in *my* car."

My mother flicked her hand. "No need. You're heading to the wedding, we're heading to the wedding. Why waste gas?"

I rolled my eyes. I wasn't a child anymore who could be conned into thinking I wasn't cheap labor. I was expected to help bring the mountain of food to the church.

Her bitter words the night of the attack had been buried. After Grandma had woken up, Mom had relaxed a bit, though she refused to talk about my upcoming banishment. Since I didn't want to think about it myself, I was perfectly fine with that. Why dwell on it when I could enjoy my brother's wedding?

The church looked more like an office complex than a place of worship. But that didn't stop my family from giving their respects. My great-grandmother and grandma had attended the Russian Orthodox Church, but once they came to America they fell off the wagon and lost the horse in the process. But like any devout religious believer, my grandma paused to cross herself as she entered the church—even though it was a nondenominational one.

I wish I could've seen the pastor's face when my brother approached him: "Excuse me, I'm a werewolf, and I need to marry the pregnant wood nymph who scratched up my custom truck." I knew Alex had more finesse than that, but I didn't see why he didn't pick a venue like the local banquet hall. After all, Karey was most likely a practicing pagan.

I made my way to one of the back rooms, where the bridal party was sequestered. The matron of honor and another bridesmaid perched near the round bride and prepared her for the event. As the only werewolf in the room, I felt like a misplaced brown egg among the white ones in an egg carton. So I played with the bouquet a few feet away.

Even after seeing the party-in-a-trunk Karey had been planning, and her artwork on Alex's truck, I tried not to hold any of it against her. I would've been totally justified in having an attitude, but since I was leaving soon anyway, I thought it would be best to try to be nice.

"Are you sure you want to do this, Karey?" a waif-thin bridesmaid asked. She wore a frown that marred her delicate beauty. She was so thin I stifled the urge to feed her some of my mother's food. The poor thing looked like one of those stick-thin models who subsist entirely on energy drinks.

"Stop asking me, Arielle. I love him. Even if he *is* a nincompoop. No offense, Natalya."

I shrugged. After today, she could call him every name in the book and it wouldn't matter. They were about to be married, and, no matter what, the child she carried would be part of my family. I'd give my life for the child. I'd even protect the young scrapper no matter how much its nymphlike skin glistened in the noonday sun.

I was already wearing my bridesmaid dress—pink taffeta and lace—so I sat there quietly while the others applied their makeup and tended to Karey's needs. Her roommate stopped by to ask if we needed anything, but we pretty much had things covered. To pass the time, I opened a paperback book and read.

After all, they didn't need my help to thrust Karey's full belly into the slim-fitting white dress she wanted to wear. I myself thought a loose-flowing gown would've been more appropriate, but she planned to walk down the aisle telling the world that my brother had not only sampled the cow's milk but had produced a calf too.

I realized it would be a big change for Alex. No more partying or carousing for him. He'd have to live a responsible life as a father and provider. I snorted and the cheesy grin on my face caused the bride, matron of honor, and Arielle to glance in my direction.

"It's a funny book," I said. But not as funny as this whole wedding would be.

While I waited, a question bugged me to no end. I had to ask. I had to know.

"Karey, this may sound like a weird question, but how did you know Aggie and I were eating dinner with Alex the night you," I paused to think of something nice to say, "visited the house?"

She brushed off the question as if she'd never keyed her fiancé's car with a deadly tool. "The weeping willow on your street never minds its own business. It blabbers gossip to every tree in the subdivision. So it was just a matter of time until I learned about the dinner."

And I thought the movie *The Birds* was creepy enough. Now I needed to worry about the malicious intent of the foliage watching me like Big Brother. Note to self: *Every bush and tree is a blabbering traitor, and nymphs can talk with them.* I went back to my book. Nothing like some international action with Dirk Pitt via Clive Cussler to wipe away memories of my conversation with Karey.

Soon enough, an usher arrived to tell us it was time to walk down the aisle. I tried to stay positive and paste a smile on my face. Sinking into misery would've been easy to do. But this whole experience would be good for my brother and the rest of my family. A new baby would bring joy to my mother and her sisters. And Alex would finally no longer have my nosy relatives playing matchmaker.

But would it be good for me? After all, I'd be the banished, unmarried sister who watched from afar.

The wedding procession went like clockwork. Well, my role in it went like clockwork. I entered the sanctuary to see my brother waiting at the altar. To my left, the guests of the bride included every nymph, pixie, kobold, and goblin in the area.

Even Bill was one of the bride's guests. Perhaps he was a distant relative. I prayed they weren't actually related. On the groom's side, my family filled the seats. Even with just a couple of weeks to plan this shindig, my mother had managed to invite every relative this side of the Garden State Parkway. I nodded to Auntie and Uncle Petrovich from Connecticut as well as my distant cousin Yelena from Maine. The youngest Stravinsky was about to be married, and everyone was here to send him off.

Eventually, I reached the end of the aisle and stood off to the side. My brother beamed in my direction. He didn't look too shabby in his black suit and tie. For once he even appeared, well, *responsible*.

The matron of honor came next. I thought she'd stroll as we'd done in rehearsal, but instead she danced down the aisle carrying a small urn of myrrh. The overpowering cloud of ancient perfumery made all the werewolves scrunch their noses. And I had no idea how old she was, but her thin white gown wasn't exactly modest. What had happened to the bridesmaid outfit she'd had on earlier? Aunt Vera's mouth dropped open in horror as the men watched her with hearty grins.

It was the first sign that a traditional wedding wasn't what the nymphs had in mind. Now their devious plan went into effect. This included see-through gowns with breasts bouncing around in them like jelly doughnuts in a Krispy Kreme bag.

Finally, the matron of honor reached the altar. The musician, a pianist from the local church, had managed to keep playing even though he'd tilted his head twice to catch a glimpse. I bet the teenaged boy hadn't caught that much boobage since he'd tried to sneak a peek into the girl's locker room.

Still, with as much dignity as he could muster, the pianist switched the tune to the bride's song. Karey entered alone, without an escort. She waddled down the aisle with a large bouquet of white roses and daisies. Alex grinned at his bride. As she entered, everyone rose, and I thought the wedding would proceed as planned.

But that was before Karey paused in the middle of the aisle and whipped out a dead marmot.

She squatted, as well as an eight-months-pregnant woman could, and then proceeded to build an altar in the aisle. Aunt Vera made a move to intervene, but my mother grabbed her arm. Mom suppressed a chuckle as Karey shouted, "I stand before you today, oh great Hera, with my sacrifice! May I prove worthy!"

I bit my lower lip and tried not to follow my mother's example. No wonder the nymphs hadn't shared their plans with us. Aunt Vera wouldn't have allowed a dead anything in the church. It's not as if she didn't tolerate other religions, it's just that a dead marmot doesn't exactly create the best impression on the other werewolves in the room. Or the pastor.

My cousin Leonard, who happened to be the photographer, darted out into the aisle with his fancy camera and took several shots. I assumed he was doing it to piss his mother off and not for the couple's wedding photo album.

The rest of the ceremony, including the vows, went as planned. Thank goodness. The poor priest knew we were werewolves, but the sacrifical display had still surprised him. I tried to imagine Aunt Vera explaining it to him and couldn't see how it could possibly go well.

After they smooched, the pastor introduced to the room Mr. and Mrs. Alex Stravinsky and they stood before a pleased congregation. (Well, the werewolves were mostly pleased because they knew they could finally eat.)

The reception took place next door at the local men's club. My mother had already used my younger cousins/ minions to decorate the space with gaudy ribbons and white table covers. The band was in place making preparations.

The wedding party's table was at the far end of the room and I couldn't wait to have a seat. The matron of honor continued to parade around in her semitransparent outfit.

Werewolves don't mind nudity—after all, it was often a necessity of pack life, because of our transformations. But it just didn't seem necessary to expose the entire fairyland population to her hooters and hips. As she took her seat her nether regions disappeared from view and I wanted to applaud her for finally sitting down.

As expected, when the buffet-style meal began the werewolves were first in line. Steaming plates of food passed under my nose as I watched the parade of family members sit down to eat. Thankfully, Aunt Vera appeared with plates for the wedding party.

"Here you go, ladies. You'll love the ham, Arielle. My sister's a wonderful cook."

From the horrified look on Arielle's face, you would've sworn we'd run over her cat in the night and served it to her. "I don't eat swine. As a matter of fact, I don't eat meat, period."

How rude! Especially saying it to someone who'd brought you the damn food in the first place. Ever the lady (well, today anyway), Aunt Vera replied, "I'll fetch you some fruit and sauerkraut. Perhaps some potato salad?"

The nymph sighed and rubbed her temple. "I'm sorry if that came out wrong, Vera."

Too late for that one, sister.

She continued with, "I've been awake for days preparing my sister for the wedding. In between the wedding and my own children . . ."

Vera simply nodded. "I have children as well. I understand." She glanced at me and snorted before she returned to the buffet table.

The vegetarian issue turned out to be a widespread one with the fairy crowd. Most of the fairies in line chose nonmeat options. Not Bill, though. The goblin piled his plate high with *olivie* and roasted chicken breasts. I'd never eaten with my boss, so I didn't know he had such a healthy appetite.

Alex entered a few minutes later as I ate.

"Where's Karey? Is she all right?" I asked.

"She said something about arriving later. I don't mind. I could eat a woodchuck, whether he could chuck wood or not." I was almost relieved to hear that, right after the whole ceremony, the old Alex was already back. I didn't expect their relationship to be Ozzie and Harriet. More like Felix and Oscar.

By the time I'd eaten a second helping, Karey had made her grand entrance to everyone's applause. (Before the matron of honor left to sit with her children, all five of them, she explained to me that the bride entering alone was part of the ritual.) While Karey sat down beside her husband, I watched everyone eat. All the guests had smiles and the bride and groom appeared pleased. Since everyone at my table had what they needed, I decided to get up and spend some time by myself back in the kitchen.

By the time I entered with some empty bowls, most of my mother's helpers had left to enjoy the festivities. A perfect time to decompress. The place wasn't in that bad of shape, so I pulled on some rubber gloves and decided to start rinsing out the bowls in the sink.

"How you holding up?" Aggie stood in the doorway with a plate in her hand. She took a bite from her food, which of course I wasn't surprised to find with her.

I chuckled. "You know, you could've left your plate on the table."

She rolled her eyes. "Oh, c'mon. Instead of saying, 'Why, thanks for the concern,' I get read the riot act for carrying a plate of food with me?"

"Well, you could've waited until you finished to come find me."

"Werewolves don't leave leftovers. So back to my previous question. How are you doing?" Her last question was a little garbled due to an additional bite of sauerkraut.

"I'm handling things. The dress makes me uncomfortable, the odor from the urn during the ceremony made me want to pass out, I can't stop thinking about the banishment, and Thorn didn't come to the wedding. But other than that I'm super."

There, I'd said it. Thorn hadn't come. Aggie's date, Will, had, so I'd kept hoping that Thorn would too. But so far, there'd been no sight of him. The words he'd whispered in the forest constantly played in my mind.

You may not see me but I'm always around.

Just not today. Not when I actually needed someone who was more than a friend to me.

"You don't smell anxious. I'd say you're hanging in there," Aggie said.

I stared at the dirty utensils and bowls in the sink. The urge to clean them thoroughly beat against my skull. To push the temptation away, I took off my gloves and turned to Aggie. "You never told me what happened to you after we stopped hanging out five years ago."

Until now, I hadn't wanted to ask her anything. From what I could recall, one of my aunts had asked her once and Aggie had never really answered.

"There isn't much to say. I went back home to my dad's place."

"Yes, but something else happened to you, Aggie."

"Why do you want to talk about it now? We're at a wedding." She placed her food on the white counter and leaned back against it.

"Seems like a perfectly good time to me. After all, you're not going to run away, not while there's so much food around. And, well, your father called again and left another message."

She glanced at me for a moment and pursed her lips in thought. "Did you talk to him?"

"Yeah, I told him I hadn't seen you."

"Thanks."

"Now that you owe me one, what happened to you?"

She stared at the gray tiles on the floor and I waited for her to speak. "Not long after you left, my father arranged a marriage for me. And not a good one either. A rather shitty one."

I touched her hand. "Oh, Aggie."

"His name was Victor. Some rich asshole out of Pittsburgh with connections all over the place. My father hadn't discussed it with me either. During dinner one evening, Victor showed up with flowers and an engagement ring."

I couldn't speak since I thought I knew what direction this tale would go. Unfortunately, I could sympathize.

"Out of respect for my father, I didn't say anything when Victor placed the ring on my finger and kissed me. He smelled like a cold eel dunked in Brut cologne." She snorted. "He was quite the character, with his black suit and slick black hair. I even thought him handsome—until he opened his damn mouth."

She paused, so I pressed her. "But what happened after you two got married?"

"Victor told me that, ever since my father had sent him my picture, he'd loved me. Said he had a thing for redheads. Before I moved in with him, he showered me with expensive gifts the likes of which even my father never gave my mother. But all of it was bait—bait to chain me up in his penthouse as his breeder."

In shock, I clutched my dress. Her mother had lived such a life. Aggie had never let me forget that fact during camp. While everyone else opened up about their problems, Aggie was too embarrassed to talk about the dirty little secret among the more affluent packs—the practice of forced breeding for the high-ranking females. In an ideal situation, many strong sons would create a powerful legacy, but for Aggie's mother years of miscarriages had left her a bitter woman.

"So you ran away from him."

"I ran away from what he represents. Control. A wife who was no more than a mate, who would stay trapped in an ivory tower and breed his bratty pups."

I nodded. I didn't want to push anymore to learn of her life at Victor's penthouse, but I was curious about something in particular. "And the fighting? The arrests?"

She laughed softly. "So you heard me when I told Will, huh? Those were rebellion. Rebellion against the control my father exerted. Against the control Victor tried to have over me. You'd be surprised how far you'll go when people tell you what you can and can't do."

I reached for her and pulled her into my arms. At first she was stiff, but eventually she hugged me back. For a second, I wasn't sure what to say. After everything that had happened to me, I'd come to depend on her. How I hoped I wasn't holding her here—indirectly controlling where she'd go.

"You can stay as long as *you* want," I whispered. "Not that you're safe here, but I do like the company." I hugged her tighter.

"Are you sure you don't need this hug more than I do?" Her voice was quieter. A bit sadder.

I never answered her. For a moment, it felt easier to just worry about my best friend and not myself.

The party ended a few hours later with werewolves dancing with full bellies. And a bit of liquor made their dancing much more lively. According to my aunt Olga, it improved with every beer.

I tried to join in the festivities, to laugh at the jokes, but my heart tugged painfully. I'd been cast out of the territory. Unless the pack members came to visit me, I'd never see them again. For that reason, I never got up to dance.

At the end of the day, the immediate family stayed behind to clean up the mess. As we gathered up the soiled plates and vacuumed the floor, I realized how the event had come together.

"Peter, could you fetch me another garbage bag?"

He headed into the kitchen and returned to hand it to me. Then he went back to work with no snide comments. I hadn't even thought about it until I mumbled, "Thanks."

"No problem."

After all I'd been through, Aggie was right. Things had taken a turn for the worse, but things had also *changed*.

And it was up to me to continue down this path and make my life better—with or without my family.

The last of us trickled out of the club. The sun hung low in the sky and cast an orange glow over the building. I strolled out and spied a man in black leaning against a car. He waved.

I couldn't help the grin that snuck onto my face. I pointed to myself and mouthed, "Who, me?"

He rolled his eyes as if to say, *"Duh. How many were-wolves would have a wizard show up at a wedding they've attended?"*

As I strolled up to his rental vehicle, I couldn't help but feel a bit pleased to have someone waiting for me. My face warmed. Was that the reason I walked faster, touched my upswept hair to see if anything was out of place?

I noticed something different about him too. For the briefest moment, before I approached him, I detected his quickened heartbeat. A few pitter-patters before he slammed down a wall of magic.

When I came close enough to see his eyes, I tried not to feel insulted by his behavior. As long as I could see through his ruse, he could play the dark knight all he wanted. With a stern voice, he asked, "How long do you expect to skip out on therapy?"

"When I'm no longer getting assaulted by rival werewolf packs, I'll be ready to laugh it up with my therapy group."

He ignored my comment. "I'm not letting you back down from your exercise with me. When things slow down for you, I'll be back."

I rolled my eyes, yearning to get out of my bridesmaid dress. "It's not safe to be with me right now. I'm in a bit of a bad place." My gaze darted to the empty street around us, searching for danger.

"You let me worry about our safety."

Was that before or after I had to carry him back to my house from our last trip?

"I mean it, Nat. Even if I need to come armed, I'll escort you to your therapy." The wizard had a look in his eyes that dared me to question his power.

I sighed. Other than packing for my departure, what plans did I have? Maybe therapy would help me move on with my life. "Let's get this over with. Pick me up at my place tomorrow."

Chapter 20

The next dreary day, a white wizard, dressed in black, knocked on my door. I wasn't surprised that Nick didn't suggest using a jump point. With a smile, I noted the car in the driveway. "No jump points, huh?"

"Even I'm not dumb enough to tempt fate again." Nick jostled the keys in his hand. I never thought I'd see a wizard with a Mazda Miata. The small roadster didn't exactly fit with the whole gothic-wizard thing he had going on.

"A wizard with a car. I guess magical folks need rides too."

Through the downpour, we rushed to the car. I waved goodbye to Aggie, Will, and another guard, who stood at the door.

"Just because someone has magical powers doesn't mean they don't try to live normal lives. You act like I spend all my time in a dungeon turning frogs into slaves to help me cast spells for world domination."

"Frogs?" I said. "I don't think they'd make the best slaves. I suggest rabbits. Much more agreeable as slaves."

I didn't expect him to open the door for me, but he did. He also didn't have a drop of rain on his body.

"You don't have an umbrella," I murmured.

"I don't need one."

He climbed into the car on the other side. The vehicle

had that new-car smell and made me wonder if it was a rental. Then a rental company flier on the floor confirmed my suspicions.

"What's this about a guise of normalcy? How can you say magical people want to be normal? After all, you just showed me you can stay dry in the rain."

"So what you're saying is, you *like* the smell of wet wizard?"

"Wet wizard? Like wet dog?"

He shook his head, and flashed that smile of his. I couldn't resist smiling back. Even with the head-to-toe black, he had an easy way about him that made me feel good.

At first, our ride into Manhattan was silent but we eventually eased into a conversation, and a topic I hadn't expected to talk about: my previous jobs.

"You've had all kinds of jobs, but you're saying you'd never work in a fast-food restaurant?" he asked.

"As someone with cleanliness issues, working with dirty pans and greasy food would be a panic attack waiting to happen."

Along the roadside, I saw the signs of the never ending rain—the gutters flowing with water and leaves covering them. He adjusted the windshield wipers as the wind picked up.

Nick said, "For two years, I was low on cash so I had to work in a restaurant. It was the only job I could find."

"Why not just use magic to make money?"

He rolled his eyes. "There are limits on what wizards can do. Unlike warlocks, who can perform black magic, white wizards are restricted to selfless deeds of heroism."

"I guess that rules out my master plan to make counterfeit money with you."

"Yep, and anyway, most shop owners have these cool markers now that can detect fake money. Next thing you know, the markers will be able to detect fake magic." He smiled. "So, like I said before, I worked at those horrible places. I tried to find employment at stores that sell magical stuff but they didn't have anything for me. Most of the magic folk got hit in the early nineties during the magical recession."

"Magical recession?" Now, this was news to me. I sold goods to supernatural creatures, but none of them talked too much about their own world. All this new information about a magical economy drew me to learn more. For all I knew, they had a stock exchange and their very own branch of the IRS to screw them over.

"I'm sure you've seen some filthy restaurants. Well, the one I worked at had a clean area up front for the customers, but the back was another story. How they kept the roaches and bugs away from the tables . . ."

I cringed and scrunched my nose. As my mind formed images of Nick standing horrified in the kitchen, it was clear that the story was heading to a bad place.

"My first night was the worst. The night-shift manager made me the dishwasher. While I was cleaning food off the plates, I saw roaches scurrying across the floor."

I mewled and squirmed. "Oh, that's just wrong." A wave of unease crept up my spine.

"I nearly dropped the plate I was holding. I'd seen the filth—the dirt on the counters and the dried-up food on the floor—but I'd hoped they kept the place at least clean enough to stay up to code."

"Did you leave right then and there?"

"I wanted to, but I couldn't afford it. I had an apartment and bills to pay. And by that point, I had so much stuff I didn't want to move it."

I gazed at his profile. He had an inner strength I wished I possessed. "How did you survive your first day?"

"I prefer to avoid medication. But back then, I needed it to feel like a normal person. Either way, sometimes you have to face your inner demons. You know what I mean?"

I nodded and turned away. He had a valid point. But facing *my* demons meant trying to find a way back into a pack with a leader who didn't want me. At this point, I saw any efforts I could make as futile.

I contemplated my situation in silence as we rode across the bridge into Manhattan.

By the time we reached Midtown, it had stopped raining, and the sun peeked from the cloudy sky, warming us, though only briefly. The chill of autumn had reached New York.

"I've already picked out a pawn shop in Brooklyn, if you don't mind," said Nick.

"No problem. If it's someplace new, that'll be for the best. I know the stock in my favorite stores too well." Especially whether they had any new ornaments. I tried to shove my dark thoughts aside and prepare myself for the exercise.

I'd forgotten what it felt like to drive around New York. After spending so much time in the country, the place felt uncomfortably alive. But I still missed it.

After driving around the block twice, Nick finally found a parking spot between two delivery trucks.

We left the car and headed toward the shop. Along the way, we passed several other stores. Even with the doors closed, I could smell the inhabitants inside. My senses drove me nuts on days like this. As we trotted past an Asian food store, I salivated as a clerk wrapped a duck behind the counter. I could imagine the succulent, gamey meat on my tongue.

"Hey, you coming?"

I hadn't realized that I'd slowed to a near stop in the middle of the sidewalk. I caught up with Nick and murmured, "It's that time of the month."

"Oh," was all he said.

"Not like that." I tilted my chin to the sky. "It's that time of the month for all werewolves."

His mouth formed another "O" and nodded. Why did every guy—the ones who knew I was a werewolf, that is—assume when I said it was that time of the month that I meant a woman's monthly cycle? Well, it wasn't as if I mentioned the subject very often. When I said it to Bill, he simply nodded and replied, "So that's why Mrs. Ferguson kept sniffing the other customers."

We turned on a side street I hadn't ventured to before. Brooklyn is a large borough, and I hadn't explored every nook and cranny. When I'd lived in Midtown five years ago, I'd seldom left Manhattan.

Earl's Fine Antiques had an old wooden storefront with an awning covering the sidewalk. Two large, junk-filled bins sat in front of the window. I thought leaving containers out there was just begging people to steal stuff, but as I approached I detected the scent of magic in the air. The owner had placed a protective ward on the bins. It was a mental push for customers to behave. The heavy scent of cinnamon left me wary, instead of eager to pick up the merchandise.

But once we entered the shop my mood changed. I knew the feeling all too well: It was the eagerness to buy something new, the delight in finding an untapped source, new territory in which to find gems for my collection.

Even with the low lighting in the store, I could still see the superb quality of the merchandise. No castoffs like The Bends. Fine leather-bound books lined the far wall, while another had tall glass goblets full of potions. A few bubbled and gurgled as I passed by.

The wonders continued as we walked deeper into the store. I spied a section with a glass case of jewelry. Not far away, a marble chess set moved on its own. For a second, I wondered if I'd ever see an ornament—until I caught the glint of shiny baubles on a circular table.

When I reached out to touch an ornament shaped like a cupcake, Nick crossed his arms. "You can wipe the smile off your face now. We're here as an exercise. Remember?"

"Of course. We're here only to look—and to resist temptation." I sighed and glanced at the Christmas lights on display. It wasn't Thanksgiving yet and they'd already put the Xmas signs up. I guess the magical world likes to hit its customers nice and early too.

As we ventured on, I tried to quell the rising joy in my belly. My eyes roamed everywhere, searching for more. I didn't care if Nick said this was an exercise. If I came upon another ornament, he'd have to pry my claws off it.

Nick led the way with his arms crossed. He appeared calm and stoic but I sensed urgency under the surface. From the drop of sweat on his temple, I knew he wanted to shove me out of the way and dart to the checkout line.

When we'd first entered, I'd envied his demeanor. He walked around like he didn't have hoarding tendencies. But our progress came to an abrupt stop when I ran into his back.

"Hey!" I turned to see what had caught his attention.

A beautiful antique sconce. Perhaps Victorian, from the style of its cover. A closer examination would reveal its origin. I couldn't suppress a grin. It was about time he revealed a chink in his armor.

"Do you like Victorian antiques?"

He nodded faintly and moved on. *Wow, I wish I had that kind of willpower.*

I was about to follow when I heard the clerk in the front blurt, "I'm sorry, pal, but to buy back your watch you'll have to pay $499."

I angled myself so I could see the exchange without moving.

A man near the counter shook his finger and said in a slurred voice, "I'll pay the $499—after I fuck yo mama."

I ambled to a better location to get a look at the drunken satyr slumped against the counter.

The clerk, a wizard who appeared to be in his late forties, rolled his eyes. From behind me I heard Nick whisper with sarcasm, "These kinds of customers make a pawn shop owner's day."

The clerk frowned and glanced at his phone. "If you're going to use that kind of language you need to leave."

"I'll leave all right." *Belch!* "After your mama is good and ready."

I tried to suppress a laugh. I'd met my share of crazies at The Bends, but this was a good one for the scrapbook of memories I kept in my head.

"This is my first satyr," I whispered back. "First *drunken* satyr, that is. Wow, he's got the goat legs and the human body—so that's what that combo looks like."

Nick's eyebrows rose. "You mean you can't tell he's a shapeshifter?"

To my nose he smelled like a goat dunked in a barrel of bourbon. Low-quality bourbon at that. "What's a shapeshifter supposed to smell like?"

"Well, to your nose, another shifter like you would smell like the form they've taken. But to me, a shapeshifter is boundless energy without form. To think that he can change into anything is mind-boggling."

"He's like me?"

Nick offered a small smile. "Oh, no. To my eyes you're something entirely different."

My body warmed from his words as the drunken satyr/shapeshifter continued his diatribe about the clerk's mother. "She wouldn't be proud of a useless son like you. So she'll come to a real man like me." He thumped his chest with his index finger hard enough for me to cringe. "And I'll give it to her right."

I covered my mouth to keep my giggles to a minimum. I'd take this guy over the harpy in a heartbeat.

I feigned a frown at Nick as he pulled out his phone. "Oh, come on. He just wants to fornicate with the clerk's mom and not pay $499 to get his watch back."

Nick rolled his eyes and said into the phone, "Hi, I'm at Earl's Fine Antiques and I need a drunk-bus pickup for a shapeshifter."

I faintly heard the voice over the phone saying she was with the Supernatural Municipal Group. They had a drunk bus? First I learned about a magical recession, and now about secret buses for drunken supernaturals. What a smart way to stay organized and keep drunken magical beings away from unsuspecting humans.

As Nick finished his call, I joked, "Do they have a holding center for crazy banshees too?"

He began to amble toward the front of the store. "Banshees are the one thing you don't call for help about—unless you have a powerful warlock on speed dial."

My lips formed a smirk. "Are you saying you can't win a fight against one?"

"I can hold my own." He offered one of his rare smiles. "But after encountering one a long time ago, even I know when I can get my ass kicked."

"What happened?" I'd never seen a banshee before. Not that I wanted to meet one, but, hey, even a werewolf can find other supernatural creatures fascinating.

"Another time. I'm more worried about our friend here."

The shapeshifter took a swig from his bottle, which was in a brown paper bag, no less. When I glanced his way, he looked me up and down and said, "Meow, my pretty." His eyebrows moved suggestively.

I bit my lower lip to stifle a laugh. Then I said to Nick, "I'm going to wait outside for the transport."

After five minutes, the drunk bus appeared. Not exactly what I would call a bus, per se, but a delivery van with a large logo on it: Linda Leeks French Breads. Was the Supernatural Municipal Group actually using a bread company as a front for its operations?

A gangly man stepped down from the driver's seat. He wore a green jumpsuit with the bread company logo on his shoulder, and had beady eyes, and stubble on his chin. He stepped up to me and briefly sniffed. "Stay out of trouble tonight, Wolf."

I crossed my arms. "Your pickup is inside, Warlock." I had no idea if the man was a wizard or warlock, but the word felt appropriate. I could've said "jerk" or "asshole"—which was probably even more appropriate— but I wasn't feeling that bold.

I followed him back inside, to see that the satyr had already left. In his place stood something else—a werewolf. The poor drunk shifter must've not only lost the ability to keep his mouth shut but I guess he was having trouble controlling his shape-shifting abilities too. What's next? Puff the Magic Dragon? Wait, a drunk dragon? Not a good idea.

The character in question continued to slump against the counter. The bottle of bourbon lay outside its sack on the floor, empty and forgotten. The metamorphosis into his werewolf form, the very same one I'd take on tonight, was not yet complete. Instead, he stood there with clawed hands, long snout, and foul bourbon-laden breath. I shook my head while I assessed the scene.

"Mel, you can't keep doing stuff like this," said the guy in the green jumpsuit. "This is your fourth notice for public intoxication this month."

"I'm busy right now, Mike." He then issued a cough-ing snarl worthy of one of my intoxicated uncles. "This guy won't buy my watch. That's . . ." He searched for the word in his drunken haze. "Discrimination."

Buy? I thought he wanted to buy it *back*.

The clerk rubbed his face with his hands. Nick leaned against a wall, amusement shining in his dark eyes.

"Look, Mel, it's time to go. You're usually so peaceful when I ask you to come down to the center. Let's go."

Mel snarled. I took a half step back as the hairs on the back of my neck stood on end. How fast could a shifter fully complete his change? And was there really such a thing as a "peaceful" drunk shapeshifter?

Everyone stood still as Mel's claws ground into the wood. Since my nose and eyes thought he was a true werewolf, my body reacted in turn. My fingers twitched. Deep within my belly the thirst remained, and I was eager to hunt. Eager to call Mel to my side. But this wasn't the place, and the human side tried to quell the wolf that writhed under my skin. Then Mel jumped onto the counter. He continued to focus on Mike.

"Natalya." A brief whisper from Nick. He'd watched me this whole time. He shook his head once. What had he seen me do?

A surge of power blossomed in Mike, and the clerk took a step back. From my position I couldn't see any changes, or dancing light. All I heard was a hum in my ears that grew until it made me scrunch my forehead in annoyance. Ready to strike, Mike stood still. I glanced at Mel and made a subtle gesture.

"Come to the van, Mel. You shouldn't stay here with these humans."

Heads swiveled my way in shock. I purred, "You answer to the moon now—and to me. You will come with me to the van so that we may hunt." I hadn't known I could speak like this. I drew his gaze as I took a step back toward the door.

"Nat, what are you doing?" whispered Nick.

The change lingered on the surface of my skin as Mel perched, ready to pounce. I didn't know how fast spellcasters like Mike were. But I suspected they needed to be quick on the draw to catch a crazed shapeshifter.

"Don't come near me," Mel growled at Mike. "I know what you warlocks do to people like me." He blinked twice and shook his head. Then he shifted his attention to me. "What are you?"

Who'd have thought our little exercise in restraint would take such an interesting turn?

"Mel, I'm like you. It's time to go now." When I said the words I couldn't believe how authoritative I sounded. Only an alpha would dare to use such a commanding manner.

Mel slowly stepped off the counter. For each step I took out the door, he took one too. Just behind me, I heard Mike murmuring words. Suddenly, a veil of heavy magic flowed out like thin curtains in a summer breeze. I briefly closed my eyes as the sensation cascaded over my body. I wasn't sure what Mike had done to us until a couple with their dog walked past us without freaking out.

Five more feet and I'd reach the van. Almost there.

"Get in the van and sit down." He paused for a moment. Had I lost the edge I thought I had? I lifted my chin. No time to second-guess myself with pedestrians walking around. "Inside. Now." I snarled for good measure.

Mel entered the van through the back and sat down quietly. Mike came up behind me and shut the doors. With a curt nod, he said, "Thanks, ma'am," and pulled away.

I stood there for a few minutes trying to absorb what had happened. The other Natalya I knew would've just stood by and watched the whole event occur.

Nick walked over and touched my shoulder. "What you did was crazy. You should've let Mike take care of it."

"I know. I guess I had to do something since he was in werewolf form."

He nodded. "Mike's pretty powerful. He could've handled it. You could've been hurt badly."

The look of concern on his face made me feel guilty, but at the time it had seemed like the right thing to do.

Nick said, "Anyway, it's time to leave. Even though I don't think you learned your lesson."

I shook my head with a snicker. "I don't think I did either."

"I need to grab something to eat. Are you hungry for lunch?"

"Yeah." The scent of food along the street made me realize that I was, even though Aggie had made a generous breakfast that had nearly cleared out my fridge. "I need something substantial though."

"I wouldn't expect anything different." He chuckled. "Do you mind if we make a stop at my place? I need to pick up something, and if we eat at Ralph's, I can drop it off."

I smiled at the great memories I had of Ralph's. Most supernaturals knew about Ralph's food cart. As a *magical* traveling cart, though, his shop tended to appear and disappear in various places. When I'd worked in New York, I used to visit his cart often for the werewolf specials. Not that the other awesome carts here in the city didn't have their merits. By all means, like anyone who'd lived in New York City, I could appreciate a good cupcake, piece of pizza, or even a fresh gyro. They were also much easier to find with websites, and die-hard fans flocking to them. But there was just *something* about the taste of Ralph's food.

"I can practically taste his meat sticks," I said.

Nick nodded as we strolled back to the car. "My place is not too far from here. After that, I need to cast a spell to find Ralph's cart."

"I envy you spellcasting folks. Most of the time I had to rely on my nose to find him."

"Yeah, I always make sure I catch him a few times a year too since I love the sandwiches."

After a short ride, we pulled up to a street full of brownstones. "Nice neighborhood."

"I've lived in this area for a few years now. I used to live in Long Island but the commute didn't work out that well."

"Long Island? That's where Aggie's family lives. Why did you live out there?"

"I used to have a job out there as a wizard's apprentice."

I scrunched my nose. "How many jobs have you had over the years?"

"More than I want to admit."

We walked up to one of the buildings as Nick pulled out his keys. "The building is divided into a few studio units. I live in the one upstairs."

"It's nice and clean outside."

He rubbed his fingertips against a set of metal keys. "You can wait in the car if you like."

"Wait in the car? Why?" I'd seen guys' apartments before and knew what to expect. It would probably be messy, with black jeans and T-shirts strewn everywhere.

"Well, your place is—more organized. And somewhat cleaner," he said.

"Well, I am a chick. And I thought you liked a *clean* environment."

"I do, but my hoarding problem isn't as contained as yours."

I scratched my forehead, slightly annoyed. "I have a younger brother. And I've smelled and seen worse things in his room. Matter of fact, he once left a pile of clothes on the floor so high I wonder to this day if someone hid Jimmy Hoffa's body inside it." My nose twitched from the memory. "Actually, come to think of it, it *did* smell like he hid a body in there. Anyway, just let me in. I need to use the ladies room."

"Are you sure? This place is *messy.*"

I wanted to choke the guy. "Yes, I'm sure. You're mysterious all the time, and it would be nice to see that you're a normal human being like everyone else."

"I wouldn't say I'm *normal.*"

"Oh, c'mon. Have you ever had guests? Female guests?"

He didn't answer my question as he opened the door and led me into the hallway. Something was up with Nick. The veil that prevented me from smelling his emotions withered away, leaving him exposed. His normally sweet scent of cinnamon had turned bitter, almost as if someone had burned popcorn. Was he anxious? Underneath that, something else lingered—his true scent, a subtle aftershave.

One of the other tenants opened the door to his unit, an elderly gentleman with his German shepherd. The dog tried to lick my hand, but I stuffed it into my pocket. Nick said, "Afternoon, Mr. Blacklowski."

"Hey, Nicky." He glanced my way with suspicion. "You have plans for Thanksgiving?" he asked.

"No, Sir." As Nick tried to push me down the hall, I heard him say, "But I do plan to head out of town to visit family. Tell the missus I send my regrets."

The elderly gentleman left with a gruff, "Suit yourself."

I laughed. "What was that all about?"

"Ever since I moved in, the Blacklowskis have tried to hook me up with their daughter."

"What, she's not your type?"

"Well, I have nothing against witches, but this one is old enough to have seen the Pilgrims land on Plymouth Rock."

At the doorway, he hesitated again.

"Oh, come on. I have to use the bathroom." I reached for his keys. "Are you going to make me go find a public restroom?"

He shook his head and put the key in the lock. "This is the first time I've had company at my new place. It isn't in the best shape today. Well, for the past couple of years, none of my apartments have been in the best shape."

My bladder protested at the ongoing delay, so I jabbed him in the arm. "Enough of the small talk. I know this bothers you. I can sense your stress. But I promise I won't say anything critical." I made the gesture to zip my lips. "I promise like a good Russian Catholic girl."

"You're Catholic?"

"Not really, but I thought it would help you open the door faster."

Reluctantly, he turned the key and opened the door slightly. When I peered into the apartment behind him, I thought I'd drop where I stood. My mouth gaped and I tried to keep words from spilling forth.

Beyond the doorway lay an apartment filled to the hilt with stuff. There was so much, I couldn't fathom how he managed to store it all inside the small space. From one side of the room to the other, there was only a narrow path to walk through the junk. Broomsticks, wands, a tire inflator, and a pile of books lay in one pile. In another, I spied mounds of teapots, boxes of teabags, and a large serving tray.

Nothing smelled dirty. Even with the precarious heap of watches on an antique old dresser, the desk covered in papers, and an overwhelmed coat rack. I peered at an ornate mahogany coffee table, barely visible under the folds of a few dark blue quilts. Engravings, in some language I didn't know, had been carved into the sides. How beautiful. Too bad he covered it up. Out of all the things he had, what I didn't see were old containers with food or dust. Matter of fact, it was clean chaos, if one could call something that.

I didn't speak as Nick led me inside. What could I say without hurting his feelings? He seemed ready to blurt out apologies, but he busied himself by heading to the back of the apartment. I followed him until I spotted the door to the bathroom.

How can he possibly live like this? But I knew the answer to my question. This was exactly like my own existence—but in a more extreme form.

With my foot, I shoved a box of worn leather hats to the side and pushed the door open. I prayed the room was free of junk and clean. Hopefully I'd only find the items one usually sees in a man's bathroom. To my relief, the only clutter in his bathroom was a T-shirt on the floor. On the sink sat the usual manly stuff: shaving cream, cologne, and an aftershave bottle. The pleasant scent of his aftershave drew my nose. So that's what I smelled. Nick must wear it every day. Definitely an enjoyable scent.

I didn't linger at the sink due to the incessant cries of my bladder. I raised the lid of the toilet and leapt back as the water gurgled.

"Oh, shit!" I squealed. A growl emerged from my throat when the water stirred again. There was something living inside Nick's toilet.

I heard footsteps coming to the door. "You okay, Nat?"

"The water in your toilet is moving."

"Oh, you found my pet. I was looking for her and she wasn't in her aquarium."

I used my heel to lower the lid and I sat on it to hold it closed. "So she hangs out in here? You *let* her do this? What is she?"

"She's a water sprite. I used to have a familiar, but keeping a regular animal isn't easy with all this stuff in my apartment."

So why couldn't he lock the lid or something? "You do realize toilet water isn't the most sanitary thing, don't you?"

"Look, I left a ward on the door to keep her out, but she got through it again. If you need to use the bathroom, let me in so I can take her out."

I opened the door. "Remind me not to shake your hand in the future."

Nick entered the small bathroom and lifted the lid. I tried to hold back my horror as I heard him whistle to call the water sprite. The water stirred and a misty cloud formed over the bowl. Then the sprite settled into Nick's hand. As the room filled with the scent of raspberries I cracked a smile. "Is that from your pet?"

"Yeah. She's the cleanest thing in this entire apartment, believe me."

I examined the creature, but its essence kept forming and then collapsing into mist. One minute it was a delicate fairy—wings and all—and the next it swirled into vapor. It radiated affection toward us that filled me with peace. In Nick's hand, the water sprite's solid form appeared humanlike with abnormally wide eyes and an unruly mop of white hair. It fidgeted with endless energy.

Nick looked up at me and smiled. I couldn't resist returning a toothy grin. It wasn't often that I encountered such things. Even for a werewolf who wasn't totally unaware of the supernatural, these past couple of weeks had revealed wisps of a magical world I hadn't seen before.

"Nat, I . . ."

From the way he gazed at my lips, I couldn't help it: My heart beat faster. His own quickened. All the signs I'd seen were true—he saw me as much more than a friend. Yet why did I hesitate when it came to Nick? I'd gone out on a date with Quinton. Would affection from Nick be so bad when I craved it? Thoughts of kissing Nick swirled through my mind. Those lips. His large hands on me. Especially the idea of feeling that calming spell on my girlie bits. But instead of giving in, I scratched my arm and took a half step back. I needed more time to sort things out. Time to end this intimate moment between us.

"Other than the fact that it breaks into the bathroom, it's beautiful. Okay, out you two. I need to powder my nose."

Five minutes later, I came out to find Nick and his sprite in the living room. Perched on a pile of clothes, Nick was browsing through a tome as I entered. The sprite played on his arms and climbed up to his head to play with his curls. The whole scene was comical yet endearing; it was like watching a puppy play with its owner. "You got what you needed?" I asked.

"Yeah. I got it. We need to drop it off real quick before we eat."

Nick's errand was to take a leather jacket to Tyler's place. He lived just a few streets away from Nick, and needed much more than a pep talk before a big date. For the next twenty minutes we lived through a saga of epic proportions as we tried to convince one dwarf that he could socialize like everyone else. The only thing he seemed excited about was her photo, which he showed us on his cell phone. She wasn't the most attractive gal, but, hey, a few extra nose hairs shouldn't get in the way of love. At first, I didn't think we'd be able to get him to go, but after a private conversation with Nick, Tyler was ready.

Once we shoved Tyler out the door and on his way, we walked to Nick's car. Quite curious, I asked Nick how he'd convinced Tyler to go on his date. "Did you use magic on him?"

Nick chuckled. "Everyone needs a push in the right direction once in a while. When I can't make him man up with words, I have to try a more direct approach."

"So you charmed him faster than a cobra escaping a snakeskin outlet store?"

"Pretty much."

Soon enough, we reached Ralph's Traveling Cart. When I'd first encountered his ancient metal cart, Old Ralph had told me that humans thought he had a hot dog stand. The warlock did actually sell hot dogs, since they were so popular with his human customers, but the majority of his profit came from supernaturals. Fairies wanted his pumpkin cupcakes, while the wizards kept materializing in line for magical five-hour energy drinks. And of course the werewolves who were lucky enough to find him craved his meat sticks. They were so tasty and reminded me of the *shashlik* kebabs I've eaten at home.

Nick offered to pay for the seven meat sticks I gobbled down, but I declined. This wasn't a date, and I didn't want him to feel obligated, especially since I bought the rest of Ralph's meat sticks to take home in a box. Aggie would be proud.

Spending the day with Nick had put me in the best mood I'd been in for a while. Maybe it was the city—or the meat sticks. The only thing that mattered was that for a few hours I didn't have the weight of the pending attack on my shoulders.

Once Nick dropped me off, I found Aggie on the covered porch. She sat in a lawn chair staring at the sunset through the forest. My guards had long since left. Her red hair fell to her shoulders from under a colorful stocking cap. Her eyes, usually a light blue, shone a vivid violet. The beginning of her change. Just like her, I could sense sundown in my bones. The sky was overcast, and rain kept falling, but the pull of the moon still tugged at us like a mother drawing her child into an embrace. She would call us tonight to hunt in her forest.

"Come inside for a bit to warm up. We'll head out to the fields soon."

The pouring rain made the hunt miserable, but Aggie and I enjoyed our night out anyway. Since I didn't run with the pack, we hunted together on my land. There were always meager pickings among the puddles in the thickets and brush, but it was better than nothing. Aggie had only chased down a cottontail or two before we gave up and settled down back at the cottage.

Ever the thoughtful friend, Aggie shook off the dampness of the rain before she entered through the partially opened back door. We curled up next to the dying embers of the fireplace and waited for the dawn.

A few hours later, a strange noise stirred me from sleep. At first I thought it was the rain against the house. All week the pitter-patter of raindrops across the roof had lulled me to sleep. But tonight felt different. In my body, panic stirred. *Something was wrong.* Aggie stood as well. An overwhelming urge to flee gripped my body. I couldn't sense why, but the wolf within smelled a change in the air and urged me to leave the house. Aggie circled a few times and whimpered.

The noise—a rumble in the earth—increased tenfold and a deafening roar hammered the side of the cottage. The glass from the windows exploded, and Aggie and I fled into the kitchen. We scampered along the tile floor, with our claws clicking against the surface. I watched in horror as a torrent of floodwater swept into the kitchen. I thought my heart would explode out of my chest. The water rose higher and higher.

Aggie left my side and headed for the back door. She came back to nip at my heels when I didn't move. The water had reached my chest, yet I couldn't budge. The wolf within wanted to flee from this unsafe place. At the same time, I was paralyzed by the thought of my precious ornaments being destroyed. But the compulsion to follow the wolf's bidding was too strong. During this time of the month, the human couldn't win, would never win. The human in me reeled. This couldn't be happening. I had no control over myself, couldn't make myself move my things up to the attic.

My heavy heart sank as the water rose. I took one step through the water and then two. The frigid water soaked my downy coat, chilling my skin. By the time I followed Aggie outside, the water had surrounded my home.

We tried to swim across the flowing river, but once we'd gone just a few feet, the deluge carried us away into the glen.

Chapter 21

When I woke, I thought my memories of the night before were just a bad dream. A dream of my death and resurrection. But instead only death remained. I was naked and lying alongside a creek bank a few miles from my home. Most of the time, the creek held just enough water for the birds to play. But today the water roared down the crack in the earth and headed east toward the sea.

With cold, numb fingers, I touched my face. Bruises and cuts covered my body. Somehow I'd survived—but Aggie. Where was Aggie? I stood and ambled away from the embankment. With my nose in the air, I tried to catch her scent. Nothing. The water left the air damp with death but none of them carried a wolf's scent. Flashes of the flood crossed my eyes and I winced. *The rising water. The boxes drifting around the house. Oh, God, no.*

My breath came out in a mad rush and I collapsed on the ground. The chill in the air and my naked body didn't exist. Only the emptiness I felt knowing that Aggie was missing and that my ornaments—my children—were destroyed.

Get up, find Aggie. I stumbled back toward my home and tried to search along the ground. About a mile closer, I spotted Aggie curled in a ball next to thick bushes. I limped to her side and checked her. She was breathing and, thank goodness, I detected a strong heartbeat.

A chill passed over my body and I tried to rub my hands over my arms. Where was the sun when I needed it? With a grunt, I picked Aggie up and headed toward the house. I stumbled two steps and fell. My knees took the brunt of the blow and I grimaced as Aggie rolled a few feet away.

A shadow passed over us. When I glanced up, I saw Thorn reaching for me just as I collapsed unconscious to the ground.

The warmth of my childhood blankets enveloped me in a cocoon of safety and a disguise of normalcy. But things weren't normal. This bed wasn't mine—not anymore anyway. I tried to sit up, but the bruises and cuts all over my body kept me prone. The old mattress creaked as I shifted to a position that would allow me to comfortably peek outside.

Through a slit in the curtains, I peered at the overcast sky. Splotches of gray covered the stars. Without the light of the moon, darkness prevailed in the room.

I lay inside the blankets and tried to rest. But sleep wouldn't return. When I closed my eyes, all I could see was the rising water again, the ornaments floating around, and the dirty leaves soiling my belongings. I touched the shell around my neck. Listened for Heidi's words, hoping they'd anchor me before I got carried away.

My breath quickened. I gripped the blankets, trying to reach for anything. My things . . . My little children . . . I had to get up. I had to see if maybe some of them were okay. Tears flowed down my cheeks, and my body jerked while uncontrollable sobs shook my chest. This wasn't fair. I'd endured so much already. When would my bad luck end?

I froze as I heard footsteps shuffling just outside my room. I lay still as the door opened. I detected my grandmother's scent first. And then came the touch of her hands on my forehead, and with them, a wave of comfort. Her fingertips traced circles along my cheek, wiping away my tears before they could wet the blankets.

I croaked, "Where's Aggie? Is she here?" There were more questions I had to ask, but first I needed to know if Aggie was well.

She whispered, "She's at your aunt Vera's, resting. Don't worry about her."

My hands clenched into fists. I had to ask. I had to know. "Please tell me everything is okay, *babushka*. Please tell me all my things aren't gone." My words emerged sounding like a child's. I tried to gather the strength to raise my voice but I couldn't.

Instead of answering me, she asked, "Do you remember this blanket?"

I managed a nod.

"It belonged to my mother, Ludmilla Gordeyeva. Bless her heart. She made a terrible werewolf." She gazed out the window for a moment before she faced me again. In the darkness I could make out her light brown eyes glowing like shiny bits of topaz.

"Before she brought my brothers and me to America, she toiled all day with my father in the fields. While she was out, I took care of the house and minded my younger brother."

"Mikhail," I whispered. She'd spoken his name before.

She nodded and smoothed back my hair. "He was a miserable brat who grew up to be a selfish bastard, but that's another story." She laughed softly. "I'd make breakfast for them and clean the house. Mama hated coming home to filth. In many ways, you remind me of her."

"Mom says I look like Great-grandma."

"You take after her, yes. She also had your collecting habit."

My grandmother spoke often and fondly of her mother. But she never spoke about her eccentricities. Maybe she couldn't shame her in front of our family. The only stories I knew were good ones, like the one about the time she managed to harvest an entire crop of potatoes single-handedly, after my great-grandfather fell over a sack of beets and knocked himself unconscious.

During my childhood I recalled Grandma saying, "My mother told me, 'Your papa is sleeping near the beets. Now, mind the lunch, 'cause I'll be hungry by the time that ingrate wakes up from his nap.'"

I blinked twice before asking, "What did she . . . hoard?"

"I'd found her hiding spot in the cellar. At first, I thought she was buying things for me for when I got married: a garment chest, cooking utensils, fabric for a wedding dress . . . She often told me while we were at the market that she'd found some beautiful things she thought I'd like when I had my own household. I felt grateful to her for all the gifts."

She sighed and patted my hand before she continued. "Instead, I caught her in the middle of the night lining them up and cleaning them like a dutiful mother. Mikhail had awakened from a dream crying for Mama and she hadn't answered. That's when she told me to mind my own business and go back to bed."

I nodded during this exchange and wondered how my grandmother had survived living in a household with a hoarder.

"How bad did it get?" I didn't want to ask. For people who hoarded, the path was always the same, whether they collected for friends or for themselves. In the end they never wanted to let it go.

"Bad enough that everyone noticed and my father had to speak with her. She filled the cellar, and it became a problem when we needed to store food. She begged him to let her keep her things."

I nodded and tried to picture my grandmother with her mother and father as they had been back then, along with her toddler brother, Mikhail.

"After my father spoke to my mother, she promised not to collect anything anymore. But even afterward I knew she'd brought things home. Then it became all about the thrill of stealing when she couldn't afford what she wanted. She hid stuff all over the house." From her frown, I knew she didn't like recounting her mother's thefts. "Natalya, I knew eventually someone in the family would be like my mother. I thought perhaps Olga or your mother, but never you."

I bit my lower lip. Grandma rarely mentioned my mental illness to me. She always spoke of positive things, like memories of the past, to make everyone laugh. But evidently today was meant for harsh realities.

"I heard from your papa that a levee on the creek leading to your farm broke. The water flooded your land and your home."

I couldn't form words or thoughts. The roof of my mouth went dry as tears spilled down my cheeks. I thought I'd cried so much lately that they'd dried up—but apparently I still had plenty left.

"How much . . . how much is left?" I managed.

"Shhhh . . . Don't worry about that right now, my child."

With a strained voice, I said urgently, "Grandma, don't hold my hand right now. I need to know."

She looked away and wiped her face. My grief had carried over to her. "Your papa told me we won't know for a few days yet. The water hasn't receded."

I gripped her waist as I shed more tears and gave in to the despair that overwhelmed me. Old Farley had wanted me to leave my hometown, but I didn't think I'd be starting my new life with a completely clean slate.

The next morning, life in the Stravinsky household carried on just as if my tragedy hadn't occurred. No one spoke of it or my upcoming banishment. Instead, they treated me exactly as if I'd never left five years ago. When I descended the stairs, Grandma and Aunt Olga greeted me.

"Morning, Natalya," Grandma said.

Aunt Olga smiled and waved before returning to the soap opera she was watching with Grandma. They kept up their banter on the activities of the floozy heroine as the music droned on.

The scent of breakfast drew me to the kitchen. When my grandmother stayed at my parents' house, my mother would make food in the morning and leave it warm on the stove for Aunt Olga and Grandma. And boy, did she lay it all out. Not only had she warmed up the dumplings from last night's meal, but she'd also left out the fixings for breakfast sandwiches and baked some cherry-filled *rogaliki*. Off to the side I found a personal favorite. Lovely *kasha,* or porridge, the way my mother fixed it, made my mouth water. It was a simple dish, but she gave it her own personal touch by adding just the right amount of seasonings.

I got out a plate, but was surprised to see Aunt Olga take it from my hands. With a gentle touch, she pushed my disheveled hair behind my ears, then proceeded to fill my plate.

"Sit down next to your grandmama," she said.

At first, I just couldn't make myself move. The kindness behind her gesture shone in her eyes, and I wasn't sure how to react. When I didn't say anything, she kissed my forehead and pushed me gently toward the living room.

For the next three hours, I ate my food and watched soap operas with my aunt and grandmother. At first, I squirmed in my seat with the plate in my hands. Everything around me was so familiar, and yet, at the same time, so uncomfortable.

Then my grandmother and aunt laughed and I couldn't help glancing at the screen. An old episode of *Santa Barbara* with voice-overs in Russian absorbed their rapt attention. I barely remembered the show myself, but I did recall how, when I was a teenager, my mother used to watch it in the evenings. Those were the good ol' days, when Cruz Castillo and Eden Capwell had enough mishaps in their relationship to qualify them for a front-row seat in Dr. Frank's group. Why was I even watching this? Cruz had a hairstyle that resembled a black wool carpet.

Oh, yes, the misty memories of childhood. My brother would play in the corner with his G.I. Joes and his current prisoners of war, the My Little Ponies from my room. Meanwhile, I'd sit in my mom's lap while she braided my hair and watched soap operas.

As I watched the show, I tried hard to borrow their calm energy to clamp down on my persistent anxiety. I cracked a weak smile as Eden returned to town, and to the saddened Cruz, who'd thought she was dead. I'd completely forgotten that the chick had a multiple-personality disorder and had returned to town many times, even after everyone thought she'd plunged to her death from a cliff. (*Where do the writers get this stuff?*)

Grandma said, "I always thought Cruz deserved better. With Eden's illness, he should forget about her."

Aunt Olga nodded seriously as if they were speaking about important legislation in Congress that would feed orphans in Atlantic City.

We also had a gentleman caller that afternoon. But not in the way you'd think. How cousin Yuri could afford to call Grandma internationally every other day, I didn't know. They chatted for about twenty minutes. I know Grandma has endless kindness for all her grandchildren, but when he started asking for money I'd had enough. If Nick could give a "man-up" pep talk, I could sure as hell try one on for size.

"Grandma, say goodbye to Yuri." I reached for the phone and she reluctantly turned it over after a few parting words.

I put the phone to my ear. "Yuri, please hold. We need to have a little chitchat."

With a curt smile, I excused myself to the dining room. My conversation began crisply. "Our family might be too kind to do this on any other day, but today is your lucky day."

We watched TV for two hours before it was time to eat lunch, which came with a tea service. How these two women sat around all day watching these shows I just couldn't fathom. My fingers twitched and my stomach churned uncomfortably from waiting. How I wished I could leave here and venture out to see my own home. To hell with Bill and The Bends. I had damage to survey!

My aunt detected my rising anxiety and made me drink herbal tea by the gallon-full. By mid-afternoon, I'd used the bathroom more times than I could remember. As soon as I emptied one cup, she filled it again.

"By the time you finish this next pot, you'll be Mellow Mindy," she said, with a conspiratorial smile.

"She doesn't need tea," said my grandmother. "A few hours and some shots of vodka will have her calm and collected."

I chuckled, imagining my grandmother slipping me

some liquor to help me forget my sorrows. I gazed out the window at the overcast sky. The rain had ended long ago, but puddles still covered the streets. The whole scene drew me deeper into sadness. Across the street, a set of small urns lay overturned and broken on a porch. Sunflowers in another neighbor's yard no longer stood tall, reaching toward the sun; their green stalks were bent and frayed. The flood hadn't ravaged this neighborhood, but its passing had left its mark.

By the time my parents came home from work, the whole scene felt surreal. Here I was, in my parents' home again, and I had to wonder if the welcoming embrace they offered would last.

A hand slid down my back, drawing me from slumber. Fingertips caressed my shoulders before they rested on my hips. My nostrils flared. *Thorn.* He pressed his body against my back, enveloping me in the warmth generated from his hard torso.

"How did you sneak inside?"

"I have my ways," he whispered into my hair.

"You're not supposed to be here." I tried to whisper but my voice came out strained. How long had it been since we'd last made love?

Maybe back in my apartment in NYC, when all I had to worry about was my job. Both of us had been hungry for success in the new world as college-educated professionals. We'd both wandered off the edge and now we were trying to climb back up.

"I . . . hadn't expected you to come find me. I woke up alone after the flood."

He shushed me as he hugged me close. I couldn't prevent the sorrow from clutching my chest and leaving me breathless for a moment. All my things. They couldn't be gone. This had to be a dream. Hell, I had Thorn with me in my childhood bedroom touching me like a horny teenager. His hand shifted and I decided that if this was indeed a dream, I wanted it to end on a positive note. A *very* positive note.

The heat from his breath against my ear stirred my blood. I stifled a growl when he gripped my waist. The gesture seemed so subtle, yet his palm burned my skin. Before I could chastise him for his roaming hands, they slipped up my T-shirt and played with the heated skin under my breasts. What kind of game was he playing tonight? Had he just swatted away Erica's warning like an incessantly buzzing horsefly? It's amazing how the slightest touch from him could turn into a heated caress. So warm. So perfect. When his hand ventured upward to caress the underside of my left breast I turned around.

"How I've needed you," I whispered into his mouth before I captured it with mine.

"I've wanted you too." He didn't need to say anything more. We pressed against each other as if we were in danger of losing this moment and never getting it back. It just felt so right to be here with him, holding him close. Why couldn't everything that had gone wrong right itself again so we could be together? All those times when we passed each other on the street, and I couldn't deny the shiver that passed over me when he glanced my way. It was almost as if, every time we met, we exchanged a secret, a secret that spanned the years, without breaking even when miles separated us. And even when he'd left for San Diego, I'd wondered if he still thought of me.

Our lips parted for a moment. With tenderness, he wiped a single tear from my cheek. "No more tears. You're stronger than you think."

"I'd feel stronger if I knew whether this thing between us could last—"

He covered my mouth with a finger as he stretched himself on top of me. Another stolen moment perhaps ruined.

But the truth was the truth. Outside this room was reality: the rest of the pack, who depended on him to stand as their leader. I could beg and plead with him, but that would mean he'd have to make a choice. The ultimate choice: between me and his pack. I couldn't help feeling resentment toward him. The bitterness stirred deep within my soul and dug at me until I felt guilty for such thoughts. God help me, was I strong enough to move on from this? To turn him away when he felt so good? I doubted it.

I ran my hands down his back and under his shirt, tracing my fingers along his hard muscles. The weight of his body pressing into mine left me urgent with need—the need for him to take me into the forest again. To rip my clothes away and claim me as his mate. He kissed me again and I couldn't hold back a moan. One eager hand rubbed against a nipple. We would've kept going—but a noise came from the hallway. Thorn's head rose.

By the time my grandmother knocked on my door, Thorn had opened the window and left. A chilly breeze flowed into the room and blew over my china doll on my dressing table. The wind fanned my face, then went back outside. My heart escaped with it into the night.

By morning, I woke with resolve to finalize my last days at work, check on Aggie, and finally see the carnage that awaited me at my home. My aunts didn't think visiting the site was such a wise move in my condition, but I had to know. I had to *see* it. Waiting was making me anxious and jittery.

"Stop pacing, Nat," Aunt Vera complained. "You're driving me into the nuthouse with all this walking." She'd brought Aggie over from her place so we could see each other.

"I don't see why you try to keep me here," I said.

"Because they know you'll crack like a barely boiled egg," cackled Aggie. She joked from the comfort of the armchair. I'd learned earlier that she'd bruised her knee and had a minor concussion. When she'd arrived, I hugged her close until she said, "Hey, careful there. I hit my head on a rock. My dad said I was hardheaded but I guess he didn't mean I really *was*."

"What the hell happened to you?" I'd asked her.

"I went over the river and through the woods before I hit my bucket on Plymouth Rock."

I didn't find her story humorous at all. She spoke as if New Jersey got flooded often.

"Sit your butt down before I kick you with my good leg." She started to stand but I took the hint and plopped down next to Aunt Vera.

My grandmother sat to the side, sewing a quilt for the baby. I marveled at how hard she worked and gushed about the newest arrival. Even if the baby didn't turn out to be a werewolf, the women in my family would still go loco for a lotion-scented infant in a bassinet. A half-nymph and half-werewolf baby qualified just fine for Grandma's love.

Aunt Vera picked up her car keys. "I'll take you to spend a few hours at work. Then later this afternoon you can see your home."

My jaw dropped. "You're tormenting me on purpose."

"No, we're not. We've seen your place. We want you to be calm and ready for it."

Oh, yeah, a few hours with Bill would really make me calm. I grabbed my coat from the closet and said a silent prayer that harpies and other irate customers would stay away from South Toms River for the day.

We rode in silence from my parents' home into town. Aunt Vera was a no-nonsense woman; even though she was usually soft-spoken, she didn't hesitate to push hard when necessary. Every family needed a bulldog like her in their corner. She filled the position quite well, while, by contrast, Aunt Olga was the European pageant princess. I wondered where that left my mother. I guess she represented all the cooking-obssessed fifth-grade teachers.

We pulled up to The Bends. Before I could shut the door, Aunt Vera said, "Have a good afternoon, Nat. I'll be back later to pick you up." Her stern face cracked into a smile. "Take it easy and relax. We'll get through tonight together."

I hadn't expected her to say such words. With great respect for my aunt, I nodded and tried to share in her optimism. The time I'd spent with my family this weekend hadn't been what I'd expected either. It was a damn shame I wouldn't be around to enjoy their company much longer.

Inside, I found that The Bends was still functioning, but not at the level I preferred. The clerks were doing their jobs well enough, but they'd left bits of paper and garbage around the registers.

The back room also left more than a little to be desired. Bill hadn't thrown away the boxes from the incoming merchandise. A pile of antiques waited on a table to be entered into the cataloging system. That goblin hadn't done a damn thing since I'd left. Had he simply unlocked the door, herded the employees in to work, and then collected his money and headed home? From the state of the single bathroom and the dock, I suspected that was exactly what had occurred. I had only a few hours until Aunt Vera picked me up. Time to get to work.

When Aunt Vera's car pulled up at The Bends later that day, I couldn't dam the anxiety that was pouring out of me in waves. My palms were damp with sweat, and I thought I'd start to pant like the mutt that was always hanging around outside the store.

I had to see my home, yet part of me didn't want to. I didn't want to think about the debris I'd have to clean up or the repairs I'd have to make. Or the tons of money it would all take. I had a bit of money saved for emergency repairs, but a flooded home would have wood damage and the potential for rot. And mold. I couldn't even think of it without increasing my tension.

During the drive, Vera could smell my anxiety. "Roll down the window, Nat."

Locked in place, I slowly moved toward the switch. Instead of waiting, she used the window control on the driver's side. The breeze chilled my face and forced me to close my eyes.

My imagination was too active. Way too active. I could only see ruins. Maybe a tree had fallen across my lawn into my house. Broken ornaments covered with mud and dead leaves. I had to unclench my fists, they'd lost circulation from my squeezing them too long. But somehow, after all my waiting, the drive went by too fast. I needed more time to prepare. More time to relax before I saw my house.

As we turned down the driveway, I saw less carnage right away than I'd expected. The lawn was cleared. A large pile of brush, with branches and dead leaves, stood off to the side. One of my uncles continued to add to the pile. He nodded my way. Once we reached the house, however, I saw that all my landscaping was ruined. The water had washed away my flowers and knocked over the gnomes who guarded them. I choked back a cry when I saw the boarded-up windows on the bottom floor. The garage door was open, revealing a monstrous pile of black garbage bags. Had they *thrown away* my Christmas boxes?

Vera didn't have time to stop before I opened my car door. "Hey!"

I had to know. Did they really have the *audacity* to throw my ornaments away?

I ran up the driveway panting with a rising fury. They wouldn't *dare*. I was just in time to catch my father coming out the door from the kitchen to the garage. He peered at me as I tore open one of the bags. With my claws exposed, I ripped into the plastic. I'd tear them all to pieces if they'd thrown them away. All these days of treating me like a daughter again . . . it was all just so they could come here and toss out all my belongings behind my back.

Within the folds of the bag I found nothing but soiled newspapers from the recycling bin behind my house.

"Nat?" my father called. But his voice sounded far away as I cut into another bag.

"Where are my ornaments?" I hissed. "Where did you put them?"

"No one threw them away." He touched my shoulder. "Come into the house."

I snatched my shoulder away. "You kept me at your house this whole time so you could throw them away."

"Get in the house now, Natalya." He growled under his breath and I snapped to attention like a well-trained soldier. When my father commanded, the wolf obeyed. I clutched the garbage bag's remnants in one hand while part of me fought to be allowed to check the contents of the others. I had to see. The garage was a mess, with all my gardening supplies in one corner. A stain on the wall indicated that the water had risen as high as my hips. High enough to enter my first floor and ruin the pristine condition of my home. I didn't want to enter the house— yet I had to see.

I followed my father inside. The kitchen wasn't as bad.

Dirt littered the floor, and a line from the floodwater stained the walls.

"How much damage is there?" I asked.

"Not as bad as I thought. Your mother called the insurance company and filed a claim. One of their people toured the house. Most of the appliances aren't salvageable, but your home has good bones and should hold up just fine."

My father actually thought I was referring to the contents of the kitchen and the major structural components of the house.

"I meant the boxes. The white boxes all over the house." I paused for a moment as my throat caught. "Are they gone?"

He continued into the living room. I sighed in relief to see the Precious Moments figurines still on the fireplace mantel, but everything else was gone. My family had pushed my discolored furniture against the wall. The stench from the fields lingered in the house and was sour in my nostrils. This couldn't be happening to me. All this had to be some sort of punishment. For trying to straighten my life out. As I reached to touch one of my figurines I felt numb inside. Empty and void.

"We tried to save as many as we could." He took my hand and guided me into the dining room. This was where they'd stored what remained of all my treasures. The worst of the lot sat on the kitchen table, where Aunt Olga was wiping them off and wrapping them in newspaper. Helping her was a conveyor belt of three family members drying and wrapping them before carefully depositing them in a box. I covered my mouth with my hand. Even my brat of a cousin had come here after school and stood quietly drying ornaments. I could hug the little guy for coming.

What could I say to my family now? My hoarded items

were exposed for them to see. Yet here they were, trying to help me pick up the pieces. My world now consisted of nothing but a soiled home with floors smelling of earth and rot. Yet here I stood united with my family—a member of the Stravinsky pack.

Chapter 22

Even though my home still lacked power and heat, I wanted to sleep in my own bed. My aunt protested, but my father grumbled, "Some wolves need to guard their territory. Leave her be, Vera."

"What about the Long Island werewolves?" she whispered.

"Pretty soon whether she wants to stay here won't matter. I sense them coming soon, no matter what."

I knew my father's words were true. He'd told me once that he could sense upcoming battles in his bones. The itch to fight would come over him, and he'd tell his employer he needed several days off.

This had happened often when I was a toddler. All the while my mother would just stay at home, cooking large meals and keeping the house clean, with a child balanced on her hip. It was as if every family that had a stay-at-home mother also had a dad who battled other werewolves on occasion.

When I became a teen, I began to notice that life played out just the way Old Farley had described it to me. Werewolves had become much bolder when they tried to take over one another's territory. Especially valuable territory like South Toms River. In hindsight, Old Farley should have seen a takeover attempt coming sooner or later.

That Wednesday morning, I spent my time surveying the damage in my backyard. Even though my family had done a fine job of tossing out most of the debris, they'd still left me with a bit of work to do. I had contractors going in and out, making assessments on repairs. In the meantime, I cleaned up. I tried to concentrate on my own task, raking the leaves, but my head just wasn't in the right place. My gaze kept drifting over to the car. I felt an itch to pick up the keys, rush out to the nearest store, and . . . A loud snap brought my attention back to the rake. I'd broken the poor thing in two. I stared at the pieces for a minute before my resolve broke as well.

Oh, screw this! I marched into the house and grabbed my keys. I was tired of feeling morose, dejected, and withdrawn. With my purse in hand, I drove south down the Garden State Parkway with the wild glee of a happy holiday junkie who didn't care what she got. I stopped at a McDonald's for breakfast, where they had holiday mugs for sale. I bought five mugs and two Happy Meals with Cheerful Christmas Cathy Dolls inside to boot. I didn't give a damn if they could clearly see that I didn't have any kids with me.

Next stop, Kmart. Most of the clerks had seen me there before. But not like this. I had on a pair of dirty jeans I used for yard work. My hair looked crazy. But that sure as hell didn't stop me from grabbing a shopping cart and striding purposefully down to the Christmas aisle. I tossed stuff into the cart without looking at prices. Boxes of tinsel. A supersaver pack of Rudolph the Red-Nosed Reindeer mittens. I didn't care what I was picking up—just as long as I could take it home with me. Just as long as this wonderful feeling could last . . .

"Natalya? It's time to go home."

I slowly turned around to see Aunt Vera waiting patiently behind me.

My heart stopped. My family had never caught me in the act before. I wasn't sure how long she'd been trailing me, but it didn't matter. As soon as I saw the soft expression on her face, I wanted to break down and cry right then and there. I just couldn't look at her. I couldn't see the disappointment on her face. All I could do was stare at the tiny cracks in the floor as my cheeks grew warm.

But then I felt a pair of hands pry mine from the shopping cart. And then she wrapped her arms around me.

"How about we go back to the house and I make you some *kasha* just like your mama makes it?" Even though I stood several inches taller than she, it still comforted me to lean against her.

She was just like the loving aunt I remembered from my childhood. I managed a nod. "That sounds delicious."

An hour later, with a full belly, I stood outside my home again using electrical tape to salvage my rake. After twisting the tape around the handle for the fourth time, I wished I'd just bought another rake during my little shopping spree.

Aunt Vera came outside and, after taking one look at my poor yard, said, "You need some help before I go home?"

"No need. I'm fine." I looked around the shed. I had enough leaves and dirt to keep me busy for days, but I still felt like I had to turn her down.

She snatched the broken rake from me, snorting at its sorry appearance. "You have company. Go take care of him while I get to work."

Company? I turned to see Thorn coming around the house. When our gazes locked, he gestured to the house. Even after the time we'd spent apart, I'd hoped to not have to face him again so soon. Not with me broken down like this.

I followed him up the steps. He let me head inside first before he greeted me.

"Hey, you."

"Are you here to escort me to the border?" Why not get to the point?

His expression didn't change. "You know I'd never do that to you." He assessed my kitchen. "How's the work going?"

"Barely. If you saw the estimates for the repairs, you'd have passed out already."

He ran his hand along a wall in dire need of replacement. "I can only imagine."

"What brings you here?" I wasn't about to ask him directly about that night when he'd kissed me. But from the way his gaze lingered on my lips, I could tell his memory of that night remained vivid.

He paused for a moment, taking in the view through the window over the sink. And then he said, "You need to leave. I've pushed my father as far as I can. I've distracted him to the point of aggravation. But . . ." His Adam's apple bobbed. "I can't keep him from sending out his enforcers to come for you when I'm out defending our territory."

I opened my mouth to speak but nothing came out. *Thorn was ordering me to leave?* "I thought I had a few days left?"

He shook his head. "The Long Island werewolves are coming for my father. Any day now. And in great numbers. They've even joined up with the Burlington pack. I can't protect you if you're still nearby." He gripped the sink and sighed deeply. "Right now, you're vulnerable and I don't want this kind of distraction, not while I'm facing my enemies."

My throat dry, I gulped. I tried to pretend that Thorn hadn't just told me to leave. "Maybe I should hide somewhere so I can stay to help? Have you spoken with my father?"

"Yes, I have—and he agrees with me. The Long Island werewolves have marked you for extermination, and your father believes you're not ready for battle." He ran his hand through his hair. "I thought I'd have a little more time before they came. But I can't ignore all the attacks—all the disappearances. They're coming, and they'll kill everyone who gets in their way."

A throbbing pain swelled deep in my chest—the pain of a broken heart. He couldn't turn me away. Not right now, when I needed him the most. With every fiber of my being, I wanted him to pull me close, so he could make all my fears go away. A mere foot of space separated us.

But I knew that if I took a step forward, he'd take one back. For his sake and mine. The ties had to be cut now.

He drew his keys from his pocket. Our time together was already over.

"Will I see you again?"

He gently touched my shoulder. "I have to lead an army into battle. My trial by fire begins now. I need time I don't have. Hell, time I never had in the first place."

He hadn't answered my question or told me he wanted me to return.

I watched him leave the house, wishing we hadn't crossed that line into becoming more than friends. Wishing we hadn't kissed. Wishing we hadn't made love. If we hadn't met in that registration line back in college, the view of my ruined yard from my kitchen wouldn't feel so disheartening.

* * *

Of all the visitors to my home that afternoon, the last one I'd expected to show up was Nick. He always seemed to know when I needed a friend.

He found me working with the damp, dirty soil in the front yard. I could hear the *slosh, slosh* sound of his black boots in the puddles as he tromped up the driveway.

"No car, huh?" I picked up my winter lilies. The poor plants had survived the onslaught of the water, but they needed replanting so they could survive the winter. In the spring, they'd burst forth with color. Renewed.

"I took the jump point. What happened here?"

I tried to avoid his question. "That's brave of you. I thought the jump point was full of gruesome ghouls." I stood and took off my gardening gloves.

He assessed my yard with a frown. "You didn't come to group therapy yesterday. I got worried."

"A flood—my home was flooded." I didn't need to say much more. He'd know from the look on my face. After a panic attack an hour ago, I'd managed to come back outside to clean again in an attempt to feel normal.

Nick also had things he coveted. Only someone like me could truly understand. He looked at my hands and noticed my tight grip on my gloves. "Nat . . ." With a soft tug, he pulled me into his arms and held me close.

As waves of calm energy flowed from his body into mine, I sighed deeply in relief, and released my anxiety. His shoulder was the perfect height for me to rest my head. I sank into the embrace, resting in arms that wouldn't let me go unless I asked. With my next intake of breath, the scent of his aftershave drifted to my nose and I thought bitterly, *Why hadn't Thorn comforted me like this? Why had the world twisted Thorn and me so far apart?*

I wanted to enjoy the comfort, but I pulled back gently and murmured, "Thanks."

"Dr. Frank told me you never showed up for your private session either. How are you doing?"

I nodded with appreciation. "A lot of my ornaments are gone, but at least I'm still here and alive." Alive—but without the nutcracker I loved or the beautiful set of Kwanzaa candles.

"So you need anything?" He watched as a contractor took his ladder into the backyard.

"I need time to realize that things like this happen that I can't control. But I took this a lot better than I thought I would." My voice began to shake. I wasn't fooling myself. I wasn't okay. This disguise of surviving was a facade. Nick reached for my hand and gripped it.

"And now I have to leave."

"Leave?" He rubbed my wrists, absorbing my pain.

"Yes, the Long Island werewolves are planning an all-out attack in great numbers." I finally looked at his face. His midnight eyes peered down at me with sincere concern. I refused to tell him about the pack banishing me, since I couldn't bear his pity.

"Well, with your home like this, you should find a safe place to stay."

Leaving home would be the safest thing for me to do, but it wasn't the option I wanted. Poor Aggie was at my aunt Olga's while I stayed behind, protecting a shattered home. But I didn't want to go. I didn't want to leave my home or family behind.

"You could stay at my place until you find something," he offered.

I snorted and managed a smile. "Yeah, maybe the water sprite wouldn't mind."

"I'd figure out a way to hide a lot of the stuff. I could clear away some space in one of the rooms."

I tilted my head to the side. "Yeah, you *are* a wizard, after all. But there's no need. One of my uncles owns some furnished rooms in the city where I can stay if necessary."

He nodded. Another wave of reassurance flowed from him. "You know I've always wanted to be there for you."

It took me a moment to realize I stood at a crossroads. I had a man standing here who wanted to take care of me. The easy route would be for me to turn him away and wait for Thorn. Hell, I'd waited for five years without a word from him. But why should I wait more if he was meant to be with Erica?

Instead of turning Nick away, I whispered, "Thanks. It'll be nice to have someone in New York." I squeezed his hand gently. "I have to pack my things this afternoon before it gets dark. This time tomorrow I'll be in the big city."

How do you pack for a trip out of town from which you may never return? I rubbed the tense spot on my forehead at the thought as I rummaged through the few ornament boxes that hadn't gotten wet. I guess you pack thoroughly and make sure no treasures are left behind. In the middle of my packing, Aggie called to see how I was doing.

"I heard from your aunt that you're just planning to skip town without a fight."

"Yeah, my dad called me earlier to make arrangements for an apartment, after Thorn told me I shouldn't stay."

"Well, you're not leaving by yourself."

I laughed. Aggie was the ever-present sidekick. But she shouldn't be traveling. "You need to rest. My mother was really worried about how tired you looked this morning."

Aggie groaned into the phone. "Seriously, Nat. I'm not heading to Vegas anymore. I have to stay here to watch your back. I think I can survive a trip back to New York to keep you company."

"Yes, and you'll pass out while we're driving into the city. When you fall unconscious in the front seat, I'll have to perform mouth-to-mouth."

"I hope you won't be driving while you're giving me some on-the-road action."

"You're not my type. Due to this double X chromosome problem you've got going."

We fell silent for a moment, unable to find words to express the feelings that exist between friends.

I sighed. "Aggie, my aunts will keep an eye on you while you recover. When things cool down, you can stay with me until you're finally ready to head west."

"I thought you'd say as much. Even I know I'm messed up. No matter how many pills or heated blankets they pass my way, I still feel like horseshit."

We ended the conversation, and I finished packing my car. By the end of thirty minutes, I'd filled it to the hilt— with the ornaments. I shrugged. *Clothes are overrated.* Who needed them anyway? I could always buy more in the East Village.

A single box remained in the driver's seat. With a forceful shove, I crammed it into a spot in the back. My father had dropped off the keys earlier for my sublet. It was time to depart. After one last glance back at my old home, I headed out, although part of me wanted to stay. After all, this was my *home*. Why should I let Old Farley turn me away from it?

I tried to hold on to my grandmother's words. This was a temporary setback. Werewolves live for hundreds of years. I'd return someday. I still owned this house and the property.

With resolve and silent tears, I pulled out of the drive-way. But the sadness during the drive north to New York City turned into anxiousness. The buds of doubt bit at my fingers, begging me to turn around.

Many hours later, I found someone waiting for me by the curb in front of my new apartment in New York. Nick.

"How did you find out where I live?"

He grabbed a box and stuffed it under his coat. "I spoke with your father and told him I was part of your therapy group." I watched in amazement as three more boxes disappeared into the folds of his coat. Where could I get one of those?

"That was sweet of you, but right now I'm not feeling social."

He continued taking my boxes. "I completely under-stand. But you still shouldn't leave a car crammed full of boxes out here on the street." He paused to add a sixth box to his coat. "And, werewolf or not, you can't carry all these upstairs by yourself quickly."

I gingerly touched the outside of his coat. "How do you do that?"

He laughed. "I enchanted the coat. Standard wizard spell from the good ol' days. Back then most folks had to cart their belongings around."

Ten minutes later, true to his word, all my things were stacked in the corner of my matchbox living room. I wanted to plop down on the couch but instead I paced. A quick peek outside revealed the night sky and the bright lights of the Upper East Side. But in the darkness I couldn't forget that I had left everyone behind. And I had no idea if Thorn or my family was hurt—or even worse, dead.

Everything I'd been through had culminated in this moment. The attack from the Long Island werewolves,

Alex's kidnapping, my grandmother's transformation—all of it had led to the moment when my pack would strike back.

Nick reached out to touch me, but I backed away. "I can't stay here. I have to go to my family." Panic rose in my gut and my words came out in a growl. How dare this *wizard* try to placate me?

"Nat, you need to calm down. Your father told me it was best you stay here tonight."

"Best for whom? I know I'm not pack. But I do have my honor. I love my family, and even if the pack turned me away, I can't sit here and wait for a *phone call* from them to tell me who didn't make it." I bit my lower lip, and my hands trembled. The air in my lungs felt strained, as if I were breathing through a straw. "I refuse to believe that I can't make a difference. I am not the weakest link."

With a soft voice he said, "You're not. Matter of fact, I see strength in you that even the werewolves can't see. A fire in your essence sits here." He used only his fingertips to touch my heart but a wave of calm drenched me.

I emitted a deep sigh that turned into a grateful hum.

"In the old days, wizards prepared the soldiers for battle. My great-grandfather worked in such a manner. He taught me a great spell that I've never used before—until now." He touched my eyelids with his fingers. "Close your eyes. Imagine that you're heading into battle and your enemies will soon be under your feet—"

Chapter 23

In wolf form, I burst through a jump point and sprinted through the forest to the main country road.

Lindell Park was ten miles outside South Toms River. When I was younger my father would often take Alex and me there to fish in the creeks for young catfish. After we'd caught a few my father would remove the skins and cook them over a fire. The succulent scent of fish made my mouth water in remembrance. Those were the good ol' days. The pleasant memories lightened my feet and propelled me forward.

As I raced up to the parking lot, I noticed rows and rows of vehicles. Trucks, SUVs, and even campers lined the space. In the darkness, I could make out my brother's and father's trucks.

Nick had told me the battle would take place here. But was I too late to help them? The branches didn't bother me as I sprinted toward the battlefield. I could taste violence in the air, the sweat on the werewolves' backs.

When I entered the clearing, I was met with an awesome sight: the pack defending its territory from a swarm of Long Island werewolves running toward them in the distance. For every wolf in my pack—we were fifty strong—many more adversaries raced to meet them.

I swallowed my fear even though the numbers seemed too great for us.

I thought my beating heart would break through my rib cage, but Nick's spell held true. I had no fear—or doubts—when I jumped into the fray. These wolves would fear me, and I would end them with a single bite—or two.

The first wolf didn't know what hit him when I rammed him in the chest. The Long Island wolf tumbled a few feet after I pounced on him.

The bloodlust sank into my flesh and I welcomed it. No one, whether they moved as a beast or a man, would stand in my way tonight. I tore at them—at anyone who came my way. Their fear flooded the air, and the wolf within relished the glow of battle. I could see myself in the reflection of their eyes. Teeth snapping. Eyes dark yellow with rage. I'd been in this state before, but the dark thoughts of the past flew away with the wind. In the heat of the battle I could ignore the needs of the human—of the fragile woman who cowered from blood, from death and dying.

With fire flowing through my veins, I jumped into a fight between Erica's best friend, Becky, and one of the Long Island werewolves. The moonlight cast a glow against her attacker's burnt-orange coat, making him an easy target. I pounced on his back, and, after a vicious bite to his neck, I expected him to flee. But when he instead lunged for Becky again, I surged forward, ready to just end it. I didn't retreat even when he yipped in pain. Nor did I show mercy when Becky joined me at his neck.

Tonight death would prevail for those who wanted to take out the South Toms River pack.

My victories were small and insignificant. As the bodies began to pile up for the Long Island pack, I had

a constant reminder that our pack was outnumbered.
Dark forms continued to fill the fields. The shadows
surrounded and overwhelmed us. Our luck had run
out.

A wolf rushed in to bite one of my legs while another
tried to claw at my snout. Hot pain, slick and startling,
sliced up my leg. Another wolf chomped down on
my paw and pulled backward. I hoped for a moment
that perhaps my father or brother would come to my
rescue—but no one came. I had to get out of this fight
on my own.

I twisted around and nipped at the wolf on my leg,
freeing it so I could attack the other wolf, but he pounced
on my back and bit through the fur. Everything around
me turned into a blur. All that mattered was this moment, this chance to prove myself worthy to take down
another enemy. But yet another attacker joined the wolf
on my back. I held strong, not even crying out from the
impact.

My attackers' crushing weight pushed me to the
ground. I didn't want to give up. I still had the fire from
Nick's spell. But even magic had its limits, and I could
feel my life leaking away as the wolves snapped at me,
growling and hissing.

I surrendered to the feeling, and prepared myself to
join my grandfather, who roamed in the great forests
with God.

But then the stench of death blanketed the field.
Grubby hands reached across my body, yanking and
pulling at the wolves on my back.

"Get off!" a gravelly voice grunted.

One of my attackers left me to strike at this new
presence, while the other one, far more stubborn, still
clung to me. Until one moaning voice turned into
many. One pair of hands turned into several. They

clawed at the wolf, ripping and shredding without abandon.

I stumbled away and watched in horror as Quinton's zombie horde descended on the invading pack. Just like before, a strange mist slithered through the trees after the zombies, enough to cover the battlefield like a tattered death shroud.

The zombies, with their limbs haphazardly stapled, clipped, or however the hell Quinton had stitched them back together, flopped about trying to catch the invaders. Surprisingly, Quinton's minions were able to tell which wolves didn't run with our pack. Their slow, staggering gait made them easy targets to overwhelm, but when a group of them managed to surrounded one of the enemy werewolves, it wasn't pretty.

From my perspective on the ground, chaos continued to swirl around me. While the South Toms River pack scrambled with the Long Island pack at one end of the field, the Burlington werewolves regrouped to outwit the zombies. This pack had speed as its advantage, and now the swarm of dark-brown wolves used it to herd the zombies into a vulnerable position. They were about to be slaughtered.

But Quinton hadn't allowed his children to march into battle alone. Among the surrounded zombies stood their master, wielding a massive club, and wearing a suit that wouldn't be out of place at a funeral. The Bends' janitor swung his weapon at any enemy who ventured too close into the inner circle of zombies. He had impossible odds, but he continued to fight.

The battlefield swam in and out of focus. My wounds continued to bleed. But it was no time to pass out yet. I had work to do. I shook my dizziness away and reentered the fray.

One werewolf wrenched the club from Quinton's hands, so he whipped out a shotgun from his back holster. Gunshots filled the air as I leapt on a werewolf on the outer ring of the zombies' attackers. My move was foolhardy to say the least, but by this point I was already bleeding from too many places to count, and every invader was on my shit list.

The wolf I pounced on yelped when my claws pierced its coat. I could almost sense its pain, since I had plenty of my own to deal with. By the time I snapped its neck, with one vicious bite, its cohorts surrounded me. Ten of them. Ten sets of yellow eyes. Ten sets of bared teeth.

The first one crept forward. And then the next.

I said a silent prayer, thanking Nick for his spell. At any other time I would've given up or frozen on the spot with fear. Right now, I wanted all of them to come for me so I could take even one of them out before I died.

They didn't bother circling. They all rushed in my direction and pounced in a wave of sharp claws and fangs. Death rode not far behind them. They left me no chance to defend myself. The mass of bodies pressed my snout into the dirt. I tried to resist. To fight.

Suddenly a bright light enveloped the forest floor. I had to close my eyes from the painful flash. The wolves on my back flew off. Everything around me was lifted from the ground and then violently slammed back down.

The air rushed out of my lungs, and my body sagged to the cold ground. What the hell was that? Within the fog of my jolted brain, I spotted a man in white. His form faded in and out, like a menacing wraith. But it was Nick wielding a grand white staff. Like an artilleryman with his machine gun, he blasted the Burlington werewolves with bolts of white lightning. The air sizzled and cracked as burnt flesh met his spells.

From the edge of the forest, others emerged and jumped into the fray. Abby the Muse, dressed in full Roman centurion's regalia complete with sword and shield, jumped on a wolf. She brought the edge of her shield down, slamming his head into the ground.

Our saviors just kept coming as I lay quietly, trying to heal. Raj came to Quinton's rescue. He used his bare hands to grasp two werewolves and throw them across the field. They landed with heavy thumps, their bodies twitching from the impact. Heidi's weapon of choice appeared to be the trident. And though the werewolves came at her in droves, they also had to reckon with Lilith, who took up the rear with a scimitar to slice them to ribbons. I must have been only partially awake at this point. Had I really seen a *succubus with a scimitar*? But wield it she did. I tried to rise but my body needed more time.

Tyler, dressed in armor with a battle-axe, came behind Heidi and Lilith to watch their backs. To my surprise, the dwarf wore an angry snarl as his sharp axe sliced into the midsection of an attacker.

The dwarf wasn't the only person who acted out of character. Abby cackled and stabbed a wolf with her sword. I'd never seen her look so animated. The quiet woman had vanished, leaving behind only a fierce intensity.

Meanwhile, Nick culled the Burlington pack, allowing the South Toms River pack to continue forward. All the while, the earth shook every time the Long Island pack drew close enough to fall under his levitation spell.

I tried to keep my head up to watch the battle, but I

quickly weakened. The soft pine needles offered a comfortable pillow while I rested. Even with a battle raging around me, my body begged for oblivion.

The shadows behind me shifted, alerting me to danger. Before I could react, a set of clawed hands snaked out to grab my legs. I scrambled to hold on to something, but couldn't. The claws gripped tighter, yanking and pulling me farther away from the pack. I raked the ground in a panic, watching as the field turned into dense forest.

Not long after, my captor flipped me over. The rough jerking motion slammed my head into a tree. Dizziness swept over me again, and I couldn't focus my vision long enough to make out the dark form that hovered over me.

"You made this far too easy for me," the hoarse voice whispered. Not the voice of a man or a wolf, but deeper. A man who had already initiated the change, but still had enough self-control to halt the process in the middle. Only a very powerful werewolf could do such things.

The man pressed his face against my snout. A blanket of hair touched my face. I'd smelled this person before. "It was so simple to capture you, like plucking fruit off a tree," he said. "And now I'm going to pluck your little heart out for what you did."

The sound of a knife leaving a sheath caught my breath. In response, I changed back into human form. My human eyes squinted to view my attacker, but I didn't need to see him to know it was Luther, the leader of the Long Island werewolves.

The tip of the blade slid up my thigh and nicked one of my wounds. My body jerked in response. Luther released a choked laugh.

"You think I'll let you live after what you did to my boy?" he sneered.

Oh, God.

Up close I caught the scent of death on his breath. In werewolf form he'd killed many tonight. I tried to think of anything other than his face. Yes, I'd seen a face similar to his before. In the same state, with death in his eyes. Blood everywhere. A death at my hands though. Everything had come full circle after what I'd done to his son.

The flash of memories came in a blinding rush—memories of blood that flew before my eyes like vicious spears. Blood that I'd spilled for Deirdre.

When the cold blade pierced my side, I didn't cry out. He raised the blade again, but a werewolf with a tawny coat burst through the trees and crashed into us.

Thorn managed to land on top of Luther, but Luther drew his legs up to toss Thorn off. They snapped and swiped at each other, fangs bared in a battle for dominance. The knife lay not far from me. I wanted to get up and help, but I'd lost too much blood.

The two alphas continued to attack each other, sharp teeth bared in their primal struggle to tear each other's throats out. Then their fight brought them closer to me. I tried to crawl out of the way, but couldn't. Thorn landed on me with a heavy thump. He quickly realized his error and tried to roll off, but then Luther found the knife and lost no time exploiting his advantage.

With a rough yank, he grabbed me by the hair and dragged me a few feet away. "Step back or I'll slit her throat."

Thorn changed back into his human form, his dark eyes focused on Luther.

"I have every right to take her, boy," Luther hissed.

"You hide behind a female," Thorn said. "Your business is with me."

Luther laughed. "I'm not the one who's hiding something. Perhaps your little lover hasn't revealed all her secrets." He jabbed my neck with the tip of his knife. "How about you tell him about the blood debt you *owe* me, Natalya?"

When I didn't speak, he jabbed me again. Needles of pain cascaded down my neck into my back.

My legs wobbled before I spoke. "It happened in New York . . . I met his son during an editorial meeting. He was one of our authors." I kept my gaze trained on Thorn. "During the meeting, I sensed something was wrong with him. Something I couldn't place . . ."

"Get to the point!" Luther snapped.

"I saw him again not long after. The night Deirdre disappeared." My voice turned bitter, and I didn't care about the knife at my neck. Let the bastard hear it all. "And when I found that piece of shit with that girl, I lost it. He'd hurt her, so I took pleasure in hurting him."

The stab wound in my side ached and gave me pause, but I continued through panted breaths. "I killed Luther's son five years ago. And I'd damn well do it again."

Luther's hand twitched. Debt or not, he planned to end my life now.

Thorn rushed at us, slamming Luther's hand to knock the blade away from my neck. We collapsed on the ground again, bodies rolling and arms grasping to control the knife. I'd grown far too weak to help, but I fought for it nonetheless.

Suddenly I saw Luther plunge the blade into Thorn, who roared as the knife pierced his belly.

The second time the blade went down, I cried out. I wanted to take Thorn's place. To give up my life and accept the consequences of my actions.

I twisted and clawed at Luther, only to have him viciously kick me away. I managed to crawl toward them again as he stabbed Thorn a third time. I squeezed my eyes shut when the knife met flesh. I gathered everything I had to try again.

Suddenly, a violent wind blew through the trees. Was it Nick? The stench of rot and ozone came from where Luther attacked Thorn. Along with the smell, the wind swirled up leaves and pine needles into a whirlwind around us. The forest's stiff trunks appeared to shift and bend. To warp as what little heat in the air disappeared.

Luther, positioned over a chanting Thorn, stared with wide eyes as the blade in Thorn's chest began to move. To slowly rise from it.

Luther stumbled backward, spewing curses as he tried to run. Then Thorn's hands snaked out—one to snatch Luther and the other to grab the blade. In one swift second, Luther sputtered and fell, the knife embedded in his heart.

The Long Island pack leader crashed to the ground, and the leaves drifted to the ground after him.

When I could find my voice, I asked Thorn, "What did you do?"

Thorn didn't answer, merely taking the blade from Luther's body and tossing it aside. The wounds on Thorn's chest continued to close, leaving me wondering what old magic he knew. All the signs were there. The chanting. The telltale ozone from the magic. But I'd seen what had happened to my grandmother. What price would Thorn pay?

"Will you be all right?" I murmured. "Are you hurt?"

"Not anymore." He brushed his fingertips over my mouth. Then he checked the knife wound on my side.

I winced and slapped his hand away. "No need to check. I got the memo that I've been stabbed."

He chuckled. "Still the same Nat."

I had revealed so many things. How could I be the same Natalya he'd known? I'd killed the pack leader's son. "What I said about Luther's son—"

"It's over and done with." His firm voice silenced me as he picked me up. I wanted to say more, but now wasn't the time. I suspected that a talk would come later. My demons always came back to haunt me—in one form or another.

Thorn returned me to the spot where I'd been resting before Luther's attack. We'd both been stabbed, and yet Thorn managed to walk back to the pack with just a few scratches to show for it. My grandmother had some explaining to do about this old magic. *Big-time.*

I shut my eyes for a bit. Every so often I felt people prodding me to check my condition. With his wet snout, Alex poked my belly and I twitched for good measure. My father also came by, pushing me until I moved.

By now the battle was over. The scent of blood and death littered the forest floor. The werewolves who'd survived now had to clean up the carnage and dispose of the bodies, for soon these dead wolves would resume their human forms—not the best thing for the authorities to find the next day.

Before I could bask in the pit of my pain, I spied the ragtag bunch who'd come to our rescue. Nick stood off to the side healing Lilith. She had a heavenly smile on her face as the glow of his power bathed her body. I was sure the succubus would be grateful for his attentions for days to come—even if he didn't especially want the favor returned. Tyler waited next to Abby. He cradled his bloodied battle-axe in his hands and smiled with glee, even through the pain of his wounds.

I remained in my safe spot, under the branches of a tree. I didn't want attention. I just wanted to sleep. And after I'd slumbered, with time, I'd awaken renewed.

Chapter 24

You look like a cat beat your ass as comeuppance for everything dogs have done to them." Aggie plopped down on the bed beside me.

In return for Aggie's kind words, I gave her the middle finger. Two would have been even more appropriate, but I was too tired. I was so tired I didn't want to move.

She poked me in the side. "It's been a few days now. I've completely healed and I've come to kick you out of bed."

I groaned against my pillows. "Leave me alone. I mean, you don't have to stay here anymore. If you need money for the bus trip, I'll pay for it so you can head west."

Her anger burned so hot it practically seared me. I shouldn't have said that, and I immediately wished I could take the words back.

"Is that what you think? That I came here to say goodbye? After all this time we've spent together? I thought you knew me better than that."

"I'm sorry, Aggie. I didn't mean it."

"In all seriousness, the pack is safe now. That piece of shit Farley even said you could stay here." She chewed her lower lip. "You may not be part of the pack, but at least it's still here if you want to join." She shoved me toward the edge of the bed. "Now get off your ass. The Long Island werewolves are gone, and I told your aunt

Olga we'd come downstairs and watch an episode of
Santa Barbara with her in ten minutes."

I fought to keep my perch on the bed. The comfort of
the covers would hide me until I could face the world
again. "I have werewolf hearing. I can hear that damn
show from up here. Matter of fact, I've seen each episode often enough to repeat all the words."

"Be that as it may," she yanked on my leg, "you're starting to stink. So get your ass into the shower, wash your
nasty hair, and come downstairs to dwell with the living."

I sat on the bed fuming while Aggie grinned, her hands
on her hips.

"My hair doesn't smell that bad."

"Well, it sure as hell don't smell like sunshine. Get your
butt in there. Do I have to tempt you with the pie your
grandma promised me?"

"Promised *you*?" I wrenched myself from the bed.
"I thought your name was Aggie McClure, not Aggie
Stravinsky."

"Well, if Alex wasn't married to that nymph, I'd have
a ring on my finger, the way your aunts operate. I could've
sworn while I slept I heard Vera talking about how I'd
make a fine match for your cousin Leonard."

I put on a robe and slippers. "Cousin Lenny? That guy
is fresh out of high school."

As she left the room, she snorted. "Well, at least I know
that, if he can't get a job, we can move back in with his
parents."

At Aggie's insistence, I survived the day in zombie mode.
I sat diligently with the others watching TV but I was seriously distracted.

What the hell was I going to do? My home didn't have
power yet. The contractors needed more time for repairs.
I didn't want to venture into town yet, even though I
knew work would help me feel better. Already every

werewolf I encountered looked at me with new respect. My grandmother had beamed at me as I came downstairs to join them, and Aunt Olga chatted me up during the show.

But it was more than that. I'd survived the battle and the flood, yet my place in the pack remained out of reach. All I had was my family. Was that all I deserved?

When the episode ended, I decided I couldn't take it anymore. I had to head into town and release the nervous energy at The Bends. After he'd heard about the battle, Bill was more than grateful to have me back. He'd grumbled into the phone, "About time you guys took out the trash. If it isn't werewolves, it's those damn leprechauns trying to hold a goblin back." I didn't ask him to elaborate—the last thing I wanted to hear was one of Bill's tales about the extortion activities of leprechaun gangs.

I didn't have any of my usual work clothes at my parents' house, but a few of my mother's things would work. The entire process of dressing in different clothes should have sent shock waves through my body. And indeed, when I stood in front of the mirror in my mother's clothes, it was hard not to cry. It wasn't as if I saw my mother in my own reflection in the mirror—no, I take after my chestnut-haired father. What I saw instead was a broken woman who'd only wanted to be a part of a family.

A relationship wouldn't hurt either.

As I prepared to leave the house, Aggie limped to my side. "I could ride with you there and pick you up later if you like."

"Sure, that sounds good. Just like we did a few weeks ago."

She patted my arm. "I think this will be good for you. A few hours anally cataloging old junk should have you patched together in no time."

"Is that all you think I do at work?"

She opened the door. "Oh, you mean besides running the register and cussing out customers? Yeah, pretty much."

The rest of the ride was silent. Aggie let me out and headed off into the sunset. I gazed at The Bends. The streets weren't that busy.

A few people trickled through the store. Not much to stress over. The cashiers waved in my direction.

"Good to see you up and about, Nat. Bill said you had an accident in the family," one of the older cashiers said. The sixty-year-old woman, a human, often filled in when someone couldn't make it.

"Thanks, Ida. I just needed a few days to sort things out."

I turned to look for Bill, but he was nowhere in sight. I ventured a look out the window, only to see Thorn standing on the curb across the street. He nodded my way before he stuffed his hands in his pockets and walked away.

You may not see me, but I'll always be around.

When I turned from the window, for the first time in a long time, I was at peace. With the way things are right now, we can't be more than friends. And honestly, part of me still doesn't want to be just friends. But I have to make peace with that and live in the gray area that remains. I couldn't help but smile.

That smile didn't last long when I saw the madness in the back office. Piles and piles of boxes, and I had no idea where they'd come from or what was inside. Just another day cataloguing the backlog of merchandise and picking up the boxes Bill had cast aside. I set about my work with a sigh.

This was where I belonged. Aggie was right. The Bends was the perfect place for a hoarding werewolf.

* * *

Therapy day came not long after. As I prepared to head into the city, I still suffered from a few aches and pains. But while I drove into New York, I went over all the good things I knew I had. The contractors had completed the work on my property, and I'd be back in my own home soon. My uncle had even found another tenant for the apartment I'd be abandoning.

And as the holiday season approached, I found myself less tempted to buy things. Key word *less*. As a matter of fact, I'd been working with Aggie on plans to create a lawn showcase using the gaudy plastic ornaments that had survived the flood.

"Why keep those things in boxes? They survived the flood. Why not put them out in front so everyone can see how good they look?" she'd said.

I arrived in Manhattan at Dr. Frank's office. The old wizard greeted me warmly outside the meeting room. "Great to see you, Nat." When he led me in, I saw the others waiting with coffee.

I hadn't asked them to help me—but still they'd come to help the pack. What could I say? Other than "I brought you some muffins. Prepackaged."

A grinning Tyler was the first to step forward. "You look great, Nat. Oh, blueberry and strawberry." He plucked two muffins from the basket and found a seat.

I breathed a sigh of relief as Raj came next, along with Abby. I offered my heartfelt thanks as they helped themselves.

"Okay, everyone. Let's get started." Lilith and Nick entered the room as Dr. Frank finished his introductions.

Lilith took a seat between Heidi and Abby. Nick sat in the open seat between Dr. Frank and the Muse. He nodded in my direction and snagged a muffin with a smile.

His fingers brushed against mine and I welcomed the warmth.

"Glad to see you came," he whispered.

Dr. Frank began with, "Well, after speaking with most of you this week, I learned that you've been busy." A few eyes flashed in my direction. "I hope in between frolicking in the forest you had time to do your exercises."

Raj and Abby nodded while Lilith frowned and inspected her nails.

I opened my mouth to speak, but Tyler beat me to it. "I didn't complete my exercises, but I have some new developments to report." He grinned from ear to ear with rosy cheeks. For a brief moment, his face actually resembled that of a cheery dwarf. "I met someone new. And we've seen each other a few times."

A round of congratulations went around. I laughed with delight. Good news always lightened everyone's mood.

"When did this happen?" I asked.

"Last week. After the batt—I mean, that stuff that happened, I went to my family's healer. She saw my wounds and afterward she introduced me to her daughter." He smiled sheepishly. Who would've thought he'd get a hookup from the local dwarf doctor's office?

"That sounds great, Tyler," said Dr. Frank. "From our talk yesterday, I can see an improvement in your attitude. How about you share with everyone how you plan to stay on track?"

Tyler took a monstrous bite of his muffin. Hardly your average dwarf-sized bite. "Well, I think this week will be about staying positive for once. Last week I felt alive." His eyes met mine for a moment with a grin. "I never thought in a million years that crashing a battle would lead me to new places."

"Well, this is a topic we don't have to tiptoe around anymore. I know that *all* of you foolishly jumped into a skirmish between werewolf packs." Nick and Raj turned away from Dr. Frank. Everyone had done this for me, so I spoke up.

"Don't fuss at them about it. I—"

Nick interrupted me. "I was the one who asked them to follow me down the rabbit hole into danger, Sir." He wrung his hands. "But Nat was brave enough to head out there alone. Once I told Tyler what was happening, he spread the word, and everyone showed up to help."

"We all really wanted to help," Heidi added. "Sometimes our friends get cast adrift in rough waters. But in the end, all they need is an anchor or two."

Abby nodded while I touched the seashell on my necklace. I couldn't resist smiling at the memory of her Roman regalia. The Muse sure knew how to use a sword. "At first I didn't think it was such as good idea, though, but sometimes," Abby paused to look in my direction, "you have to stand up for people who believe in you. The ones who can see you for who you are."

Lilith filed her nails—well-manicured for once. "To be honest, I did it 'cause you hooked me up the other day." She grinned, revealing a red line where her lipstick had smeared her teeth. "I'm getting married in a few months. My fiancé is coming in from Russia."

Wow, my cousin Yuri sure worked the international phone lines fast. I guess my little chitchat about settling down paid off. At first I feared for his safety, but then Aunt Vera told me that Yuri could suck the life out of any woman, so I suspected they'd be perfect for each other.

After all the kind words, I left the meeting a half hour later in tears. I'd known these people for less than two months and yet they'd offered their lives to protect me and my family. They didn't live in my town. Or live by the Code. They knew only that my home was in danger— and that they could help me by making a stand. The whole thing left me beaming with happiness as I headed to my car. Even if I didn't have Thorn in my life, I had people who truly believed in me.

My phone buzzed from a new message. It was from my mother. The family planned a fine feast tonight. She'd prepared braised pheasant with sauerkraut for dinner, and since Aggie had invited herself over already, my mom thought I might want to tag along. I grinned and flipped on some jazz to prepare for the drive home.

I'd be plenty hungry in an hour or two. And, after all, a werewolf like me could never turn down a perfectly good meal with the Stravinsky pack.

Read on for an excerpt from
KEPT
by Shawntelle Madison

Published by Ballantine Books

I hadn't expected a man—other than my brother—to call me the next day at five A.M. to begin my training. I recognized the number right away, and it wasn't Alex's; caller ID really made it hard to be surprised these days.

I let the phone ring three times before I picked it up and blurted, "Thorn Grantham, unless you're calling to give me a free pass to avoid the trials, there's no reason for you to call me at this hour."

"Meet me at the high school track in thirty minutes." Then the phone went dead.

I hadn't heard his voice in a while, so I wouldn't have minded a "Hey, you" or perhaps a "Sorry to wake you at five in the morning." But all I got was an order to start my training.

If my foggy memory served me correctly, wasn't it *Alex* who was supposed to have called me for a training session? And if so, why had my sneaky brother asked this particular person to help me out—the one man I wanted to avoid at all costs? Alex knew my ex-boyfriend was engaged to another woman. His blatant attempt to hook us up was just useless.

I heard Aggie snoring in her room as I plodded into my bathroom to get ready. I was tempted to bang on her door and wake her up so she could offer moral support at the track.

Ten minutes later, after a cold shower and half a pot

of rich Colombian coffee, I hurried out of my house and drove out to the local high school track.

While I drove, I mentally went over the three individual elements of the trials. Werewolves, like humans, had special initiation ceremonies. In order to be accepted as a productive member of the pack, a candidate had to prove she could defend herself and protect her clan mates—in essence, show herself to be of sound mind, body, and spirit.

The first challenge I'd have to face was the ten-mile run. If I survived the second part, a grueling obstacle course, I'd then have to show I could dominate my enemies. The ten-mile run and the obstacle course were intended to wear me down down before the final hardship—a fight with one of my fellow candidates. I saw this stage as a pissing match in which the combat-ready candidates could shine and achieve a higher rank within the pack. In terms of self-confidence, I didn't have much for the last part, as I wasn't a fighter. But what I did have was an undying drive to join the pack—no matter how insurmountable the odds.

When I pulled into the lot, the track was empty; it was early morning after all. Just a few lights illuminated the stands, but even in the darkness I had keen vision and could see no one was waiting for me. It was not until I left my car and entered the stadium that I found a blond-haired man in jeans and a T-shirt waiting for me on the bleachers, gazing at the woods surrounding the high school grounds.

Despite his brusque offer to help me train for the trials, I knew that avoiding Thorn was my best course of action. For the sake of my heart, anyway. Letting go of the past was a lot easier when the past kept out of your way. Yet I still came here to see him.

Thorn was only a few feet away when I caught his scent. A chilled breeze brought it to me: a mix of denim, leather, and mild soap. To my nose it was a perfect combination. "How did Alex convince you to do this?"

He stared at me in a way that made me uncomfortable. "Alex said something about you needing help and how he couldn't do it since he's busy preparing for the baby's arrival. So he asked me to help you and I said yes."

I sighed. "He never planned to help me at all."

"Why would you say something like that?" Thorn indicated I should follow him to the track.

"You don't see what he's trying to do? Get us together here alone?"

He shrugged. "We're both adults. It's not like we don't both know what we can and can't do."

Then he glanced briefly at my shoes: a pair of running shoes that had never left their shoe box until today. "Have you ever run in those things before?" he asked.

I rolled my eyes. "I have to dress up for work every day. That means heels, not sneakers."

"Do you do everything in heels? Never mind, don't answer that. My mind went to the wrong place real fast."

I suppressed a smile and tried not to follow his mind into the gutter. It wasn't easy though, with the way his T-shirt clung to his body. My fingers itched to trace a line along the rock-hard abs under his shirt.

"Are you really ready to face the trials?" He took in my appearance and I wondered if he was thinking that the battle with the Long Island werewolves had damaged me permanently in some way. It had, but not in the way he might have thought. I mean, let's keep it real here: Who could get through a fight to the death in which you watched the man you loved get stabbed through the heart, and not walk away just a little a bit frazzled? Especially someone in my fragile condition.

"I'm hanging in there. I'll do just fine." I waved my hand as if I wouldn't bat an eye at what he had in mind today.

He paused. Maybe he didn't believe me. But instead of brushing me off, he began his spiel. "Let's get you started with the endurance stage. You need to show you're capable of a ten-mile run."

"Sounds easy enough. I've run that far many times during the full moon."

His hazel eyes went to slits. "In human form."

My mouth snapped shut. *Oh.* I tried to remember the last time I ran *anywhere* when not in wolf form. As a werewolf I had honed senses and a powerful physique, but I knew that in my human form I wasn't in the best physical shape. I was a size six, but that was mostly due to my skinny Russian-girl genes. (Which my mother loved to remind me would disappear after I had kids.)

"I'll do fine." I left him behind and jogged down the track. Would he follow me? I turned briefly to see him sitting down on the bleachers to watch my progress.

"You're not coming?" I asked.

"You have the pace of a were-sloth participating in the Olympics. You'd slow me down to the point of aggravation."

After a few minutes and a few laps (I wasn't keeping count), I became winded. As I passed him I asked, "How am I doing?"

"You need another lap to complete one mile. At the rate you're running, I could go pick up a breakfast sandwich and still make it back before you're done with your ten miles."

"A mile?" I glanced at my watch. It had taken me eight minutes to do less than a mile. I had to be in better shape than this if I was going to survive the trials. But my chest burned and my shins ached. As a werewolf, I sucked: Like all werewolves, I had natural agility and speed, but evidently, endurance wasn't an automatically included ability.

By the time I completed three miles, I was reduced to

walking. I avoided Thorn's eyes each time I passed him. Why stir up his animosity?

Thirty minutes later, I plopped down on the other side of the track and lay down between the lanes. All this torture and I still had a long work day ahead of me.

A shadow passed over my head. It was Thorn. "This'll be a long week for you. Expect to be here at four A.M. tomorrow."

"Don't athletes get a day of rest between events?"

He snorted. "A day of rest is for people who exert themselves. See you bright and early tomorrow, Nat." With that he walked off the track and disappeared into the woods.

A part of me warned myself not to watch him walk away. But I couldn't help it. Between training for the trials and wanting Thorn, the trials would be far easier for me to deal with.